The Stolen Valley

By

R J Turner

Best Wishes
R Turn

Published by Leaf by Leaf Press 2023
www.leafbyleafpress.com

Copyright 2023 © R. J. Turner

The Author asserts his rights to be identified as the author of this work in accordance with the Copyright, Design and Patents Act 1988.

ISBN 978-1-9993122-8-2

All rights reserved. No part of this publication may be reproduced, stored in or introduced into a retrieval system, or transmitted in any form by any means without the prior written permission of the publisher. Any person who does an unauthorised act in relation to this publication may be liable to criminal prosecution and civil claim for damages.

Acknowledgements

My thanks go to Liverpool Reference Library; the Powys Archives at Llandrindod Wells; Dr. Gladys Mary Coles, poet, biographer and lecturer (for her encouraging response to the early chapters); Meirion Edwards, Lecturer in Welsh (for checking my use of Welsh and making useful suggestions); John Heap for his help with preparing the manuscript for publication.

I would also like to thank Peter Aughton for his wonderful book, 'Liverpool, A people's history', published by Carnegie Publishing; 'The Policeman's Story' by Special Constable David Jones, published by St.Wddyn's Parochial Church Council; and innumerable websites for details about clothing, photography etc. of the late Victorian period.

Author's Note.

Most of the details about the building of the dam and the flooding of the valley are accurate, but sometimes the sequence of events has been altered for narrative purposes.

R J Turner

R.J.Turner was born in Bridgnorth, Shropshire. He moved to London, Wiltshire and Northamptonshire as teacher and headteacher. After retirement he returned to Shropshire. He now lives in Oswestry with his wife, son and their French bulldog.

Since retirement he has written two contemporary crime novels, 'A Perfect Alibi' and 'Murder on the Moss' published by Leaf by Leaf, and an historical crime novel 'Wicked Harvest' published by Pegasus.

'The Stolen Valley' was intended to be the second novel in a trilogy but reads perfectly well on its own. It is not a crime novel.

The Stolen Valley

By

R J Turner

Part One

1889

'Your engineer, indeed, lives and moves and has his being in a constant attitude of regarding nature from this strictly professional point of view. "Hello! Here's a river running through a wide vale, with a narrow neck at its lower end" he says to himself joyfully. "Hooray! I see a chance for a dam. Let's immediately dam it." And he proceeds forthwith to find somebody who will stand the expense of damming, and pay him by the way for his arduous labour of superintendence.'

From 'A Submerged Village' by Mr Allen, originally published in The English Illustrated Magazine, March 1890

The Stolen Valley

1

The Letter

Tom Parker hefted the postbag onto his other shoulder and strode down the hill towards Hope Underhill. When he reached the village it seemed to be deserted. In the square, which was not a square at all but an elongated triangle where three roads met, nothing moved. Even the air was still. No breeze disturbed the leaves of the old oak in the centre of the square. Any birds in its branches were silent, deep in the cool of the thickest foliage; dogs lay in its shadow, tongues lolling from their slimy jaws; only cats were happy to brave the afternoon sun, lying curled on doorsteps and window sills, deep in guiltless sleep.

No traffic passed by at this hour, because the village was not on the road to anywhere of importance. The village shop was shut. There were no mewling toddlers sprawled in the dust and no mothers gossiping in the square. No hammering came from the blacksmith's anvil; no clash of the sexton's spade in the stony soil of the graveyard. So where had everyone gone?

For the answer to that question, you would have to go into the surrounding fields on the side of Long Hill, above the water meadows but below the higher slopes, where bracken, heather and gorse ruled. Between, in those small, tilting, misshapen fields the harvest had just begun. The horses stamped, snorting, up and down along the edge of the crop, pulling the old reaping machine, whose spinning paddles and clattering blades felled the next swathe and flung it out onto the stubble.

As usual the beginning of harvest had drawn many onlookers. The women had come out to join their husbands and bring their midday snack. Now they sat in the shade of the hedgerows to suckle their babies or let their toddlers romp around in the stubble for a while. The men would be working late today so there was no need to rush home and prepare a meal. The blacksmith, the shopkeeper and the sexton had all come to share this thrilling annual event, thankful like everyone that the weather was good, after all those dreadful summers of the last decade, when the crops had been blown into a tangled mess, soaked by the endless rain, and sometimes simply been left to rot in the fields.

But the village was not in fact deserted. As Tom walked past the church and approached the Schoolmaster's house he could hear the singing of a familiar hymn from the school next door. He pulled a letter from his bag and peered at it. It was just an ordinary envelope, addressed in a neat hand, postmarked Llanfyllin, which he guessed from the peculiar spelling was somewhere in Wales. 'Don't get many letters from there,' thought Tom, but as he pushed it under the master's door, he had no idea how that letter would change so many lives.

> 'All things bright and beautiful
> All creatures great and small
> All things wise and wonderful
> The Lord God made them all'

The children stood to sing the last hymn of the whole school year. The Master had let them choose. He was a tall, thin, bearded man in his forties, with a gaunt, rather fierce face and touches of grey at the edges of his thick dark hair. He thought Mrs Alexander's hymn very trite but he knew the children liked it. As country children they recognised the world it described and they loved its easy lilting tune.

> 'Each little flower that opens
> Each little bird that sings
> He made their glowing colours
> He made their tiny wings'

The Letter

The Master, John Noble, always brought the whole school together for this last assembly of the year. His plump young assistant had led the infants to sit in front of the older children in the big room, where they wriggled impatiently through the prayers and tried to keep up with the hymn. In spite of his own lost faith he enjoyed hearing the children sing, even the growlers among the older boys who would not be returning next term. Some of these had been restless for ages and some had already escaped to help in the fields, but those who remained were filled now with a mixture of joy and sadness. Soon they would not have to suffer the drudgery and discipline of the classroom, but they would miss the companionship of their classmates, especially some of the older girls, whom they often tormented as a way of expressing their adolescent yearnings.

John glanced quickly through the next verse, which he always made sure was omitted.

> 'The rich man in his castle
> The poor man at his gate
> He made them high or lowly
> And ordered their estate.'

It made him angry to think there were many who still adhered to the view that people should know their place and stay in it. He knew that even in this little school there were children with intelligence and talent who, if given the chance, might accomplish great things. But he also knew that most of those who were leaving today were destined to spend their lives labouring in the fields if they were boys or toiling from early morning till late at night in domestic service if they were girls.

> 'The cold winds in the winter
> The pleasant summer sun

> The ripe fruits in the garden
> He made them every one.'

The piano, old and of doubtful intonation, rang out loudly under the singing. The Master's second wife, Ella, had taught herself to play so that she could help out her husband on these occasions, and this was a tune she could now play with vigorous confidence. She also helped with the sewing classes, which H.M.I had commented on as 'much improved' in their last report.

> 'He gave us eyes to see them
> And lips that we might tell
> How great is God almighty
> Who has made all things well.'

John still paid lip service to the religious rituals because this was a church school and the church was his employer but he had long ago ceased to believe in God the creator and knew for certain that all things were not made well. The hard years of the agricultural depression that had marred his first years as Master of the school in the early 1880's may have eased a little but poverty, disease and injustice still stalked these hills and valleys. And it was the wicked murder of a beautiful young woman that had caused the vacancy at the school which he had been asked to fill.

> 'All things bright and beautiful...'

Now as the children threw themselves wholeheartedly into the final chorus the Master forgot his own discontent for a moment and gave a slight smile of pleasure, not something he had done much of late. Some of the children noticed and smiled back in appreciation. Those smiles continued during the Lord's Prayer after which they expected to be dismissed, then faded as the master bored them with a familiar homily about being proud representatives of the

The Letter

school (this for the leavers) and keeping safe during the holidays (for the rest) but at last the children were able to rush noisily out of the schoolroom and for once the Master did not call them to order. Instead, when the last pupil had left, he turned to his wife, who was putting away the music and closing the piano lid, and said sourly,

'Well, thank goodness that's over.'

Ella came over to her husband and took his hands in hers.

'What is it John? What's wrong?'

He snatched away his hands, saying, 'Nothing!' then added, 'I'm going for a walk.'

Ella felt tears pricking as she watched her husband grab his hat and cane and walk away. But lately she had found that tears came easily and she thought she knew why. She and John had been married now for almost nine years, but it was only lately that he had begun to behave like this. Perhaps it was her own fault; she knew that the changes happening inside her made her moody and sometimes she found herself nagging him without real cause. But she did not think she deserved his recent coldness. If only he would tell her what was wrong she might be able to help, but he did not seem to want to confide in her any more. So, sighing, she locked the school room and entered the school house, picking up that letter from the floor and putting it on the table for her husband to read when he came back from his walk.

Ella's mood lightened as she saw her son, named after her husband, waiting for his tea. Little John loved his food and hated exercise so he was becoming plump. He had been a sickly baby, and perhaps over cosseted because of that, though he was still not really healthy. Perhaps that was why his father always seemed impatient with him. But it was not just that. At six little John showed no interest in learning and in fact could barely read, throwing his father into rage, when he tried to teach him. 'What will people think?' he asked the boy, 'When they find that the schoolmaster's son cannot even read properly'.

Meanwhile that Master strode along the village street, past the ancient church, across the bridge, where the Hope Brook had dried to a mere trickle, and on up the steep winding road towards the 'purple headed mountains' which were in fact many feet short of the required height for that nomenclature but when the heather bloomed they were definitely purple.

John had taken this walk many, many times since he had returned to his home village. It usually cleared his mind as it loosened his limbs, but not today. The more he walked the more despondent he became. He had not noticed how quickly he had been walking until he reached the top. He was sweating and out of breath, so he took off his coat, flung it on the springy turf, sat down on it and peered into the valley below. His heart was thumping under his waistcoat and a slight ache pulsed across his temples. This trickle of pain in the head was occurring more regularly but when Ella had suggested that it might be failing sight — she had noticed that he held his books at arm's length now — he had retorted angrily, 'There's nothing wrong with my eyes!' However, when he consulted Dr McKenzie the old ditherer had told him, 'Aye, lad, tha's needing spectacles. 'Tis natural. We canna stay wee boys for ever.' Well then, was that the cause of his present ennui? 'Perhaps that's it,' he muttered to himself. 'Perhaps I'm just getting old.'

He had been twenty nine when he returned to the village of his birth after eight years away. Those had been difficult but exciting years spent partly in Africa, where he and his first wife, Elizabeth, had gone out as missionaries and where he had lost both her and his faith. When he returned to England he stayed with his wife's parents for a while. His father-in-law was a schoolteacher. One day John accompanied him to his school and discovered that he too had a talent for teaching so he completed a brief training and took up a post at an elementary school in Bedford. Two years later he received a letter from his father's sister in Shrewsbury telling him that his father was now too ill for her to cope with alone, so he resigned his post and returned to Shropshire. His father died within a few weeks and it was at his funeral in Hope Underhill that John had been offered the post of master at the village school, vacated by the disappearance of Harriet Owen, his young predecessor.

Now as he looked down into the valley- his distance vision seemed as good as ever- he saw that small field where the schoolmistress's corpse had been discovered during that harvest of 1879 and where his investigations into her murder had begun and continued long after the police had given up or pretended they knew who was responsible.

Even now he shuddered as he remembered that woman's decomposing body lying among the barley in her blue dress. But he also remembered the satisfaction of trapping her murderer into a confession and attending the trial in Shrewsbury where the evil Whiting, late Rector of the parish of Hope Underhill, had been found guilty and hanged. In that same terrible few months he had met Ella and in the following spring they were married.

'Ella! My poor Ella,' he mused. Of course she was not the pretty young widow she had been at that time. She had put on weight when she was pregnant with little John and had not been able to lose it again. Her skin, which had always been pale, had lost its glow. Her golden hair had thinned and darkened a little so that sometimes now it reminded him of brittle straw. And those large blue eyes, which had once glittered with sexual desire, had lost their lustre and become slightly hooded. Most importantly she had lost her taste for lovemaking. This happened very rarely now, always at his instigation and left him unsatisfied and Ella melancholy.

'But it's not your fault, my dear,' he murmured, in an imaginary conversation, that would never actually take place.' It is I who has changed. I have grown weary of it all.'

The trouble was that he had become restless. He knew from his weekly Chronicle that things were changing rapidly in the wider world. Railways criss-crossed the land and trains travelled at ever faster speeds. Steamships traversed the oceans in days rather than the weeks taken by the old sailing ships. And it was not even necessary to travel to speak to someone when you could use the telegraph, or sometimes even the new-fangled telephone to communicate. Queen Victoria's Empire stretched ever further year by year, though John's experience in Africa made him wonder about the value of this. There were daily advances in medicine; Jenner had beaten smallpox, the cause of cholera had been identified, a patient could be anaesthetised when undergoing an operation and disinfectant could be used to fight germs.

Great social change was happening too. Women were no longer to be considered mere chattels in law. Most adult males now had the vote. More and more workers were prepared to fight for better conditions, though they were still obstructed by those who held the power. Only last month, he had read of the Matchgirls in East London, who worked in terrible conditions, involving dangerous chemicals and some of them developed phosphorus necrosis, sometimes called 'phossy jaw', a very painful and disfiguring disease. They had gone on strike and managed to gain some improvements. Yes, it seemed that change was happening everywhere, except here in Hope Underhill, where the only things that changed were the seasons.

He felt stifled by the village and by the school routine. The school now ran like clockwork. The annual report was always fairly favourable. Attendance was good. His teaching and that of his assistant, was deemed satisfactory. But the curriculum was almost as narrow as it had been when he started. Most of the children learned to read and write and do some simple arithmetic. They learned about history, but it was always British history and taught as a series of great events in the formation of the British Empire; Clive in India, Wolfe at Quebec, etc. Science was, at its best, a study of plants and animals. Geography consisted of learning which bits of the world, and there were many of them, which belonged to Britain, coloured red on the map. Of course he must never mention that great man, Darwin, whose 'Origin of Species' had so excited John in his youth, and been the main cause of his loss of faith. Instead he must go on telling the old Bible stories and allow the present rector to come in and tell his pupils how God had made the world in seven days and that they must always try to be good and know their place.

In Hope Underhill that place was usually clearly defined. There was the Squire, who lived in the Manor House, and owned most of the land. There was the Rector who helped the Squire to maintain the status quo. There were the tenant farmers who were just recovering from the worst of the Agricultural Depression and slightly below them in status, though often much better off financially, were those who by luck or canny dealings made good livings as millers, tanners, hauliers and the like. Next there were the shopkeeper and the blacksmith and the local constable – Hope Underhill had recently acquired its own. Almost at the bottom there were the farm labourers, and that was by far the largest group, who struggled to keep their families on a barely living wage. Lastly there were those could not even do that, so they roamed the land as tramps or entered the workhouse.

Perhaps it was those years in Africa that had given John his wanderlust. He longed to get away from the village, even if just for the school holiday and only as far as the coast, but Ella was not interested. Her improved status from labourer's widow to headmaster's wife seemed to satisfy her completely. She had never left Hope Underhill and had no desire to do so. She had friends and family around her, although there were some in the village who resented her promotion to the school house and thought she had got a little above herself. She dearly loved her husband and her son, and of course her daughter Amy, from her previous marriage.

'Amy. Ah Amy,' thought John, 'The one positive in it all.' A couple of years ago she had been a gawky girl but in the last twelve months she had blossomed into a lovely young woman. She was clever, learnt quickly and would surely achieve great things in the future. He was proud of her, for he had helped to make her what she was. But there were times when he worried about what his feelings for her really were.

At that very moment Amy Williams, she had kept her father's name, was sitting next to the carrier, Arnold Gosling, on the front seat of his cart as it lumbered along the road from Acton Bishop. Arnold had been very taken with the young girl beside him. He decided from his surreptitious glances that she was a rare beauty. He used the bounce of the wagon over ruts in the road to move closer to her. Then his free hand, the other held the reins, seemed to accidentally fall onto Amy's thigh. She did not scream or even move away. Instead she said quite straightforwardly,

'Now then, Arnold! You know that's not right. What would Jane say?'

Jane was Mrs Gosling, and she would have said a great deal, and as Arnold was very frightened of her he slid his fat buttocks back across the seat, muttered mild oaths under his breath, and told his ageing horse to 'Giddy-up!'.

However it was easy to understand Arnold's feelings. Amy was indeed a beauty. At seventeen, almost eighteen, she was tall and slim, though her simple dress revealed a burgeoning figure. She was one of those naturally graceful girls who did not need deportment lessons to keep her head erect. Her face was striking rather than merely pretty, with a firm jaw, high cheekbones, a straight nose and well-shaped lips that were always slightly curled in an enigmatic smile. Her long hair, pinned up under a small straw hat, but gradually slipping down as the cart bumped and shook, was a rich gold, with a touch of red in certain lights. But it was the eyes that were her most attractive feature – deep green like her father's- and glinting with the excitement of simply being young.

'Home for the holidays, eh?' asked Arnold.

'Yes, but I won't be going back to Acton Bishop.'

'Shame about that,' thought Arnold, 'I 'uddent 'ave minded another ride alongside this'n.'

'I shall be going to college after the holiday so that I can become a properly qualified teacher.'

'I see. Following in your father's footsteps?'

'Yes. Well, my stepfather's anyway.'

'Oh, ah... I remember your real dad well. I was at school with poor Alec, see. He were a bit younger than me, mind.'

Amy could barely conjure up an image of her father now. She was only six years old when he had been killed in a farm accident. All she could remember was a tall man with red hair who was always smiling. Then when she was nine another man came into her life, or strictly speaking into her mother's life, but she never once resented the new man's arrival. She knew how much happier he made her mother. This new man smiled less, but was full of knowledge and ideas. He had recognised *her* intelligence at once. They were soul mates from the start. She had worried that the arrival of little John, six years ago, might have caused her stepfather to give her less attention, but not at all. In fact John was often glad to get away from his sickly son and continue their long walks and intellectual intercourse.

Her mother on the other hand became entirely engrossed in her son, partly because he was very ill for the first year of his life and she had to give him her undivided attention. Now she seemed unable to lose the habit. It was little John this and little John that; she seemed almost to forget that she had a daughter, and when they did relate they seemed to be in constant conflict.

At first it was her refusal to go to church every Sunday. Through discussion with her stepfather she had soon shared his atheism. He had explained Darwin's theory of evolution to her and she saw at once how it demolished the whole idea of God making the world in seven days. She had read about the fossils of those creatures that had lived in the warm seas or crawled upon the earth millions of years ago. She read the Chronicle avidly once her stepfather relinquished it and was interested in everything. She was particularly excited by scientific discoveries of every kind and much concerned about social problems.

At first she thought that her stepfather was being hypocritical by continuing to attend church when he did not believe, but he explained to her that for the sake of his post he must continue to pay lip-service. He also asked her not to discuss Darwin's ideas with anyone else. She understood.

Her mother was unable to accept her daughter's attitude. Ella had never lost her faith, in spite of her dealings with that evil clergyman, who had murdered her husband's predecessor, and in fact little John's gradual improvement in health seemed an answer to her constant prayers. She made sure that her son was baptised within days of his birth and she took him to church with her as soon as he was well enough, though he often fell asleep in her arms as soon as the service began.

Of course Amy loved her little brother, but she soon tired of his company. She could not imagine ever wanting a child of her own, knowing that such an occurrence would put a stop to all her plans for the future. She thought her mother's life was incredibly boring. And lately her mother seemed especially irritated by her daughter's company. She was always complaining that her daughter was too much concerned with her appearance, and even implied that she flaunted herself in front of men. This was not true at all and Amy had snapped back angrily that at least she would never let herself go as her mother had. Later she regretted her rudeness and apologised and for a while they got on rather better than before. It was almost as if Ella had seen some truth in what her daughter had said.

Amy also thought about her mother's comments. She knew that men were attracted to her, but she did not react to their admiration. In fact she thought most of the young men she knew were either dull or stupid or both. Sometimes she thought that her stepfather was the only man she really admired.

At thirteen Amy had become a pupil-teacher at her stepfather's school. At sixteen she was appointed as an assistant in the larger school at Acton Bishop. She had lodged there, with the schoolmistress, by the term. At first she had been rather homesick,

The Letter

but also excited by the prospect of moving on, if only for a few miles, and Miss Watson had a wonderful library of novels and poetry which she had devoured completely during her stay. Her stepfather's reminiscences about his time in Africa had filled her with a longing to travel, and she saw her move to Acton Bishop as the first step in learning how to cope away from home. Now she was making that journey for the last time. And in a few weeks' time she would be moving on to that college in another county altogether.

Once he had been put in his place Arnold chatted amiably enough, for the rest of the journey, telling Amy about her father as a young man, between deep sucks on his clay pipe.

'He were right 'andsome, even as a lad. Girls was always arter him. But he 'ated school. He wanted to be up and doing. Larking about, like; takin' risks. By God, he did some daft things. I remember him once climbing this tree, for a bet. One of the tallest trees you ever seen. And he did it and all. But coming down a branch give way and he fell and broke 'is arm. But 'e didn't mind much, 'cause it were 'is right arm so he couldn't do no writin' for a while.'

Arnold laughed at the memory. But his laughter stirred up something in his chest and ended as raucous coughing and violent expectoration. Soon as the worst was over the pipe was back between his teeth and rumbling away in its bowl as he inhaled again.

Amy knew that she shared a little of her father's recklessness, but she had loved school and soaked up learning like wet muslin over a milk jug sucks up water in hot weather. She wondered what her life would have been like if her father had not been killed. Would they have got on? Would he have helped to develop her mind as John had done? No, she thought, we would have been quite poor, and I would probably have been sent into service as soon as I was old enough. She shuddered at the thought.

At last they reached the school house. Arnold helped her down from the cart, perhaps more attentively than necessary, then unloaded her heavy trunk as easily as if it were hat box and took it to the door. Amy thanked him and put the coins in his broad hand. Then she tidied her hair and moved towards the school house door, pausing as she heard raised voices inside, which happened quite frequently of late. She purposely rattled the latch before pushing the door open and the altercation ceased.

John smiled as she walked in, Ella quickly wiped away a tear and whispered, 'Welcome home' and little John ran as fast as his fat legs would allow, took hold of her skirts and asked, 'Did you bring it?'

She had promised to bring him a present when she came home.

'Yes, but it's in my trunk. Perhaps you could help your father to carry it in?' Little John was not enthusiastic about anything which required physical effort but when his gift was the reward he was glad to obey. While father and son went out to fetch the trunk, Amy crossed to her mother, kissed her cheek and asked, 'So what was the quarrel about, this time?' Ella did not reply but pointed to the letter lying open on the table.

Her stepfather came back into the room, saying, 'It's good to have you home, my dear.' Little John was kneeling in front of the trunk trying to lift the catches. 'You'll need this,' said Amy, taking a key from her purse and showing him how to turn it in the lock. When the lid was lifted she took out a small packet from the top and handed it to her brother. There was a brief flurry of pretty paper, then little John cried with delight, 'Oh! Oh! Look, Mamma!' In his hand he held up a perfect model of a soldier, with a bright red coat and a musket in his hand.

'Take it up to your room, Johnnie,' said his father, 'and put it with the rest. Then you can play battles for a while.' It seemed strange that a boy who was so placid and sedentary should have such an interest in military things, but John saw that it might be a way of stirring an interest in history as time went by, so he was prepared to encourage it.

The little boy gave his big sister a quick kiss and ran up the stairs. Ella meanwhile had gone into the kitchen to make a pot of

The Letter

tea. Amy asked her stepfather, 'Why should a letter cause you to quarrel?'

'Sit down, my dear, and read it. It's addressed to all of us.'

Her mother returned and placed cup of tea beside her as Amy read.

My dear Friends,

It is many years since we were all together and I know it is remiss of me to seek your help again but you were so kind to me and George at that dreadful time and I have no one else to ask, so please forgive me.

As you know my grandson and I returned to Wales three years ago, to look after my brother when he became ill. When he died he left me his house and a small legacy so I was able to send George to school in Oswestry, where he is doing very well indeed.

When we came back to Llanwddyn and this lovely house I had no idea that I would be forced to move on again so soon. But they are building a huge dam and will soon be flooding this whole valley, so everyone has to move to a new village nearby.

I did not want to move, but all the rest of the villagers have gone and they are destroying the houses. Now I have had a letter demanding that I leave in one week's time or, as they put it, I shall be 'forcefully evicted'. Well, I am now an old woman and I do not know what to do. I know that there is a little house waiting for me in the new village, but this is a big house with lots of furniture and don't know how I shall get it all to the new house and where I shall put it.

Please, please would you come and help me. The furniture is so heavy. My brother liked good things. We shall need a wagon. There is plenty of room for you all in this house and my neighbour in the new village, a Mrs Evans, says that she has room for anyone we cannot fit into my new house when the move has been made.

When they flood the valley there is to be an enormous lake, the water of which, George tells me, will be sent by a big pipe – he calls it an aqua something- to Liverpool, which does not have enough good water of its own. George has been fascinated by the whole thing and now wants to become an engineer.

Please come. It will be wonderful to see you all again. George has never stopped talking of Amy in all these years. And I would be delighted to see your little boy, Ella dear, of whom you have told me so much in your letters.

Affectionately yours,

Megan Owen

Amy put the letter back on the table and sipped her tea, 'Well we must go, of course. We must help her.'

'But your mother refuses,' said John. 'She doesn't want to travel all that way. And does not think it would be good for little John.'

'Is it that far away?'

'No. I have looked at my maps and checked my timetables. It's not much more than forty miles as the crow flies. We would catch the morning coach to Shrewsbury, then go by train to Llanfyllin, with just two changes, and from there we can hire a carriage for the last few miles.'

'That sounds fun, doesn't it mother.'

'Not to me. Coaches, trains and carriages. All that way. I would hate it. And I'm sure that little John would get ill again.'

'Oh, mother, you never want to go anywhere!'

'I know. I like it here.'

'But surely you would be pleased to see Mrs Owen again and George. He must be, what, fifteen now. I can hardly believe it.'

'Yes, I would like to see them, but I cannot make such a journey. I am not up to it, and neither is little John.'

'It's no use, Amy. Your mother and I have been through all that.'

Amy looked at her mother and wondered if perhaps she was ill. She went to her, knelt down and took her hands, as if she was a little girl again.

'Are you unwell, Mother?'

Ella patted her daughter's head, pleased that she was showing concern. 'Oh, it's nothing much. Just something a woman suffers with when she reaches a certain age. There is so much suffering in a woman's life. One day you'll know.'

Actually, Amy already knew. She had read about it in some book that was she was not supposed to have read. Now a lot of things made sense. But that was far, far away for her. She had a whole life to live. She stood up and turned to her stepfather.

'Well then, John, you and I must go alone. That is, if mother doesn't mind.'

Ella nodded her approval. When Amy looked at her stepfather she saw a fire come alight in his eyes. A fire she had not seen for a good while. He asked, 'When would you be ready to go?'

'Why, tomorrow of course! Everything in my trunk is clean. I shall simply fill a small suitcase and we can be on our way.'

The Stolen Valley

2

Joseph's Story

As John Noble and his stepdaughter set out next morning for the Vyrnwy Valley another couple were beginning the last stage of their journey to the same place. Yesterday, they had travelled by train from Liverpool to the place the English called Bala, in North Wales, and had stayed overnight at the White Lion Hotel. Now they were on the road taking them across the mountains between Bala and the Vyrnwy valley. A carriage had been sent to convey them to Vyrnwy Hall, built above the valley that was soon to become a lake, where they were to stay for a while at the invitation of some of Joseph's old friends.

Inside the carriage sat a portly man in his late fifties. He had a large head with a pair of spectacles perched on his long curved nose. His curly hair was grey but his bushy beard and thick eyebrows were still quite black. The face, where it was not hidden by hair, was pleasant enough. He was immaculately dressed, in morning clothes, with no concession to the rural environment. He lowered the newspaper he was reading and spoke to his son. Even though he had lived in England for most of his life there was still something about his accent which suggested that it was not the country of his birth.

'Philip, my boy, you cannot imagine how excited I am. I have waited nearly twenty years for this day. At last the dam is nearly complete and soon the lake will begin to fill. Now I am to see it with mine own eyes. It was such a struggle at first to persuade the Corporation to go ahead, but soon our city will have good clean water for all to drink'

The young man put down his copy of Borrow's 'Wild Wales', which he had purchased when he knew that he would be accompanying his father on this first visit to that country, and asked with some vehemence, 'But what of the people who lived in this valley? They have been turned out of their homes.'

'But it is for the greater good. The landowners have been generously compensated and the villagers have been provided with new houses. Much better houses. And a new church and a chapel. I have seen the plans.'

'It still doesn't seem right to me. Those people are Welsh. The valley belongs to them. What right have we English to come and take away their land just so we can have clean water? It seems to me that we are stealing their valley from them.'

'That's rubbish!'

'I'm told that the valley is very beautiful. Soon it will be just a large lake and an artificial one at that. Well at least I've brought my camera and equipment so that I can make a record of what will be lost.'

The younger man looked nothing like his father. He was tall, thin, slightly stooping and very pale. His yellowish hair fell in curtains round his long face. It might be a handsome face one day, but was as yet unformed and a permanent look of disdain rather spoiled it. The young man's clothes were more suited to an artist's studio than the wild landscape they were crossing. Suddenly he pointed out of the carriage window.

'Oh, Father, look at that!'

Their journey had begun through a wooded valley, where the road twisted and turned, crossing and re-crossing a frothing stream, so that the sound of tumbling water was always with them and that water flashed where sunlight pierced the closely clustered trees. Gradually the road had narrowed and climbed steadily until they were on top of a range of bleak hills. Now the older man peered over the top of his spectacles at the view.

'What is it? I can't see anything.'

'Exactly! Nothing but miles and miles of bare mountain as far as the eye can see. Thank goodness such wilderness remains. That is how Wales should be. Stop the carriage! I must capture that.'

'Don't be stupid, Philip! It will take ages to unload your camera and all the rest. The driver could hardly find room for it as it was. And we cannot afford the time. The Bradshaw's are expecting us for lunch.'

'Very well, Father! But the only reason I was prepared to share this little holiday with you was so that I could take photographs. I intend to have a special exhibition at the Liverpool Photographic Society. I shall call it 'The Stolen Valley!'

'I don't like that title though I'm sure it will be a splendid show. But remember, Philip, that photography is only a hobby. You are training to be a doctor. When you are fully qualified you can take over my practice and I can retire at last.'

'I'm still not sure…'

'Look, my boy, I'm prepared to indulge your hobby. And at least photography has a scientific basis. But forget all that art business. You can't live on art. The world doesn't need any more painters. Let those Frenchies do the painting. I suppose you get that leaning from your mother, God rest her soul.'

'Was mother artistic?'

'Well she dabbled in watercolours. And sketched from life.'

'Why have I never seen any of her work?'

'I destroyed it all when she died. I couldn't bear to look at it.'

The older man returned to his newspaper but the young man did not pick up his book, instead he frowned as he studied his father for a while, then asked suddenly, 'Tell me, Father, this water business…Why does it mean so much to you?'

'Oh, that's a long, long story.'

'Well, now's the time to tell it. You've rarely told me anything about your past. And we have nothing else to do.'

'Well, I suppose…But I don't know where to begin.'

'At the beginning, as they say.'

'But where is that?' He reluctantly folded his newspaper and put it on the seat beside him. 'Very well, I'll try. You know that my parents brought me to this country when I was a boy. That was in the thirties. I was born in Germany. We Jews had been settled in that part of Germany for centuries. But things began to change. Suddenly we were not so welcome. Of course it was nothing like the problems the Jews are suffering now in Russia and Poland. Those poor people...'

'Yes, I've read about them in the Echo. Thousands waiting for ships to America. Swindlers promising them tickets then disappearing with the money. Several families living in one room.'

'But at least they have us to help. We have our charitable organisations. We were the lucky ones so we must do what we can for our less fortunate fellows. You see, it was different for us. For a start there were not many of us, just a few dozen arriving at a time. And because we were able to be independent –most of us were well educated and some of us were quite well off- our arrival was hardly noticed. I'm not sure why we came to Liverpool. Perhaps my father had originally intended for us to go on to America, but we settled in quickly and soon learned to speak English, rather better than some of the natives. Of course we continued to practise our religion but not in an ostentatious way. The people of Liverpool welcomed us for the skills we had... Some of those arriving now were just poor peasants where they came from. They have nothing but the clothes on their backs and speak only Yiddish.

'We early arrivals soon became respected citizens. We did business with the English. Some of us became their business partners. And we mixed with them socially. There was a joke that we had become more English than the English. My father changed his name from Levy to Lever, and I became Joseph, with the English spelling, instead of J-O-Z-E-F. He did well in his business and bought the house on Brownlow Hill. He wanted me to join him in the business. But I had always dreamed of becoming a doctor. I don't really know why, but I never wanted to be anything else. I studied hard and achieved my ambition. My father helped me to start a practice among the better off families who lived around us in that part of Liverpool. I was a good doctor and soon got a reputation, particularly among the women, for being a good listener. My wealthy patients paid me well.

'Before I knew it I was in my thirties: a respected doctor: plenty of money; plenty of friends; lots of pretty girls around me. Yes, life was very good. Then I met Eleanor.'

'My mother?' asked Philip. He had no memory of her. She had died so long ago that her existence seemed no more than a familiar fairy tale. His father continued.

'She was the most beautiful woman I had ever seen. I say, woman, but in fact she was only eighteen. What on earth she saw in me I cannot imagine. This English rose- and she was English of course- with her golden hair and such blue eyes you never saw. And there was I, in my thirties, my hair already thinning and my belly spreading fast. But it was love at first sight for us both. We were married within a year and a year later you were born. I was so incredibly happy. My cup was full.'

Philip glanced out of the carriage window. They were still crossing that bleak plateau, where sheep munched among the heather or lay in the shade of the few stunted trees on this warm morning. Perhaps soon the old man and his son would get their first glimpse of the Vyrnwy Valley. Meanwhile Joseph continued his tale.

'I suppose I should have known it was too good to last. When you were about four years old your mother became pregnant again. You should have had a little sister but she was stillborn and your mother died in giving birth.'

The old man did not speak for a while, but his son saw a glint in his father's dark eyes.

'My whole world collapsed. I cared about nothing. I neglected you completely. If it had not been for Eleanor's family I don't know what would have happened. My own parents had both passed on by that time. Eleanor's mother and father took you into their own home and looked after you as their son.'

'Yes,' Philip said, 'When I was little I thought William and Elizabeth were my parents, I hardly ever saw you.'

'I know now that my behaviour was inexcusable, but I couldn't help it. I think I must have been slightly deranged for a while. I know that I certainly considered suicide.'

Philip was shocked. He had never heard this before. And his father had always seemed such an optimistic avuncular sort of person that, for him to think of killing himself, seemed completely out of character.

'I couldn't bear to be in the house, except in the day, for most of which I was asleep. I had never been a particularly zealous attendant at synagogue. Now I gave up altogether. I blamed God for taking away my Eleanor. I did not want to see any of my old friends. As soon as night came I would go out, just walking about the city, down by the docks or through the poorest districts where I could wander anonymously under the dim street lamps. And I began to drink. Whenever I saw a public house I went in and drank until I was nearly insensible. Often I didn't manage to make it back home. Sometimes William would drive around the streets until he found me, collapsed on the pavement. He would throw me into the brougham and bring me home, where I would sleep through the following day. Looking back I can't believe how kind they both were.'

Joseph was so full of painful memories that he could not go on for a while. Philip glanced out of the window and saw that the landscape had changed again. The carriage was rattling down a steep hill into a narrow cleft between the hills in company with another stream; one of the many which would soon be pouring their waters in to the valley to form that lake once the dam was complete.

'Look, Father. We're going down into the valley.'

But his father was miles away and in a different time. He simply nodded and went on.

'Of course I neglected my patients and my practice folded. My father had left me the house and a small legacy but I was rapidly drinking this away. Even now William and Elizabeth didn't desert me. I continued my nightly wanderings, especially in that area between Scotland Road and the docks. I saw sights in those streets that would have horrified me if I had been sober, but I never was sober.

Joseph's Story

How I managed for so long not to be robbed or murdered I don't know.'

Again the older man paused and sighed.

'I had begun my wanderings after Eleanor had died in the spring. Now winter was approaching. One late November evening I went out as usual about eight o'clock. Mist from the river had combined with smoke from the ship's funnels and the factory chimneys to make a dense, foul-smelling, sulphurous murk. Soon I had no idea where I was and when I saw a light in the window of some dingy public house I immediately went in out of the cold. The place was full of evil looking men, even more disreputable than usual. I noticed that a couple of particularly vicious looking characters were studying me. Perhaps even at that stage of my disintegration they were able to discern that my clothes had once been good, and they guessed I might have some money in my pockets. I tried to slip away. The streets were very empty on that chilly night and my stumbling footsteps echoed through the fog. I knew soon enough that I was being followed and I tried to run. But I had no idea where to run for safety. Then I saw this alley and thought that if I could slip into it my pursuers might not notice and go on down the street. But the alley simply led into a small court surrounded by hideous looking houses and there was no other way out. I lay low in the shadows cast by the dismal light of one poor street lamp, my heart thumping, hoping that I had escaped but I soon saw two dark shapes enter the court and move towards me. I cried out but no one came to my aid, so they attacked me, knocked me out, stole my overcoat with a few coins in its pockets, and left me sprawled on the filthy cobbles.

When I woke again, shivering with cold and with a terrible ache in my head, I lay still for a while, to make sure that those men had gone. In the silence I heard the steady drip of water from a pump. A savage thirst welled in me and I was about to take a drink when I heard another sound, a moan of pain, and I saw this child, a girl of four or five, lying barefoot on the cobbles in her soiled clothes. I lifted her head and even in that dim light I could see that she was very ill. Something about that little waif's face sobered me up immediately. I knew at once what was wrong. I asked her, "Did you drink from the pump?"

She nodded, moaned again as another wave of pain swept through her. I managed to stand, struggled to the nearest door and knocked. No-one answered. When I pushed at the door it swung open. The stench was unbelievable. There were two people lying on the floor. Both dead!

I tried another door. More dead! The other houses were deserted. I wrapped the little girl in my jacket- she was shivering violently- laid her on one of the doorsteps and stumbled to the nearest police station. I explained that there had been an outbreak of cholera -for that is what it was: one of the last outbreaks in the city- and that the pump must be put out of use at once. I did not think anyone from outside this miserable court would use this pump, so at least the outbreak might be limited to these few houses.

At first, when they saw the state of my clothes, and smelt my breath, they were about to kick me out, but when I mentioned William's name their attitude changed.

It was too late to save the little girl or anyone else in that horrid court, but I seemed to come alive again. When the water supply was investigated it was discovered that the water had become contaminated from the drains of the nearby sailors' hospital. From that day I vowed that I would do everything to find a better source of water for everyone in our city.'

At that moment the driver called out something in Welsh, which neither of his passengers understood, but looking out of the window Philip saw they were passing between the stone pillars of a rather grand gateway and entering a drive which climbed steeply up the valley wall into the trees. Obviously they were nearing their destination, but he wanted to hear the rest of Joseph's story.

'Go on, Father.'

'Well, I reopened my practice and my patients soon flocked back. No. it wasn't loyalty. They had simply discovered that most of the other doctors were not as sympathetic to their little ailments. I began to charge even more for my services, but now the money wasn't spent on luxuries or my social life. Instead I opened a second practice near that place where the little girl had died. And any free time I had, I spent badgering anyone I knew who had any influence with the Corporation and at last, after several years, they decided to investigate the water problem and look for a solution.

'Two sources were found. Of course the Members of the Corporation tried to go for the less expensive option, but it was obvious that this source would soon be insufficient. Then some expert suggested the Vyrnwy Valley and as soon as I looked at his plans I knew that he had found the answer. It took several more years to persuade the Corporation that this was the right plan. It is now eight years since the work started and it might take another year or two to get the water flowing down to Liverpool but...'

Suddenly the carriage wheels ground over gravel and the driver shouted something to the horses that was unmistakable in English or Welsh and they came to an abrupt halt, leaving the carriage rocking on its springs. They had arrived at Vyrnwy Hall.

The Stolen Valley

3

Meetings

As the carriage carrying the Levers ground to a halt in front of Vyrnwy Hall and the Bradshaws came out to greet their guests, two men were hard at work in the valley below, demolishing what was left of old Llanwddyn village. It was hot work in the August sun so both men paused for a moment, sat on a pile of stones which had been a cottage until yesterday and each took a drink from his bottle of cold tea, though the older man had surreptitiously slipped in something stronger. Now only a few buildings remained standing. One was the cottage next door and two more in a short terrace, another the shell of the old church- the fittings had already been removed- and the last was a pleasantly proportioned house, built more than a hundred years ago, standing alone above the village on the banks of the river which wound through this once lively and populous village.

One of the men was about fifty. He was short in stature but sturdy. His thick curls, where they showed under a dusty cap, were silvery now and his face deeply lined. Both men's faces were tanned from working mainly out-of-doors. The younger man, in his early twenties one might guess, was taller than his father, though still only of medium height, but with broad shoulders above a slim, athletic frame. When he lifted his cap and shook away the dust the curls on his head were thick and black. His handsome face might have been hewn from the rock in the quarries where he and his father usually worked.

The men looked up, smiling, when they saw a woman walking towards them from the large house above the village. She was a tiny woman in her late seventies, her back rather bent, but still lively in her movements and intelligent in her gaze. She was carrying a large basket. She addressed the men in Welsh and their conversation continued in that language for the sake of the older man who spoke very little English.

'Bore da'

'Bore da. Mae hi'n braf on'd ydy hi.'

'Rydych hi'n boeth oddi ar eich gwaith, rwyf yn siwr.'

(In English: 'Good Morning'

'A fine day it is today.'

'Very warm for your work, I am sure.')

Where's the boy today?'

'Oh, he went out early. He's gone down to Llanfyllin. We had a telegram. My friends from England are arriving today.'

'He's a fine boy. You must be proud. Your grandson you say?'

'Yes, his mother died when he was very small, just six years old'

'Well, lucky to have such a grandmother, he is.'

Mrs Owen was embarrassed by any praise so she turned away. She had lived in this village as a girl and her family had been Welsh speakers, but when she married Thomas Owen, he took her to live in Lancashire, where there was plenty of work in the cotton mills, and where she rapidly learned English. In fact she had lived so long in Lancashire that she had even picked up the accent of the place. Now she slipped easily from one language to the other.

The young man spoke again. 'We must be getting back to our work. But don't worry. We won't be knocking your house down just yet. We're in no hurry to go back to the quarry.'

'I must be on my way as well, Huw bach. The shop is open now in the new village, so no more long trips to Llanfyllin. My guests will be hungry when they get here. Da boch. Goodbye to you both.'

The old woman trotted away, in her neat black clothes and shawl, along the road down the valley, which would soon be disappearing under the great lake

Huw and his father returned to the last stones of the cottage wall, which they were demolishing with sledge hammer and pickaxe.

Huw Morris, that was the older man's name, and Gwyn, his son, were skilled rockmen from slate quarries further west. It was their task in those quarries to drill into the rocky hillside and fill those holes with explosive to bring down great chunks of slate for the other men to work on. When they saw the advertisement asking for skilled men to help demolish the village of Llanwddyn they were happy to apply. Work in the quarries was hard, dangerous and poorly paid. Here, in the Vyrnwy Valley, they could work at their own pace, without a foreman watching their every move and for better wages than they had ever had in their lives. They had come here in their cart, pulled over the mountains by their nimble pony, had taken over a disused shepherd's hut and set up camp beside the village. They had 'borrowed' some explosive from the quarry store and hidden it in a disused sheep-fold some distance away.

At first they had been rather daunted by the task. After all this was no small hamlet they had been asked to destroy. There were thirty seven houses, three public houses, two chapels and the church. And the village made a pretty picture in this verdant valley surrounded by steep sided hills. But if they didn't do the job it would still be done. They had been given other labourers to help at first, though they alone were trusted with the explosives, but these men had gradually been employed elsewhere as the number of buildings diminished.

Of course there had been protests when plans for the dam and lake were first mooted. Many of the families had lived here for generations. And it was worst for the farmers who would lose not only their houses but their fields as well. The local people knew little of the scheme until the first trial holes were dug, then a petition with more than three hundred names expressing opposition to the scheme was sent to the local Member of Parliament, but having been sent. this petition was never heard of again. What could a few hundred people in a Welsh village do when a vast English city with thousands of inhabitants stood to benefit.

The Stolen Valley

Most of the villagers had already moved out of their houses before Gwyn and Huw arrived, and the others soon left when they saw the demolition taking place, except Mrs Owen. At first she was very aloof, even aggressive towards the two men. She blamed them for what was happening to the village where she was born and to which she had so recently returned. As each house tumbled it seemed to release its store of memories: the whistling of the shepherds as they crossed the valley to meet at the pub and the landlady's echoing whistle to draw them in; the dancing and ball games on fine summer afternoons; the sports days held at Christmas, on Good Friday and St John's Day; the cock fighting and the football matches played by moonlight with a hundred men or more on the field at one time. She remembered the people who lived in the village. There was that family of ten who lived in the smallest cottage; the ugly old woman called Meg who lived alone with her black cat and was thought to be a witch; and all the boys and girls with whom she had shared games and mischief in those distant, mostly happy days.

Of course it was George who changed his grandmother's attitude to these strangers who were destroying her village. He had come home from school for the holidays and seen the men going about their work and with his natural friendliness and curiosity had soon made friends with Huw and his father. He made his grandmother see that it was not their fault; they were simply doing a job. From then on her attitude changed and she began to take them a drink, now and again, or stop for a chat, asking them where they came from and discovering a little about their home and family. So when the letter came to tell her that she must leave the house by a certain date it was to Huw and Gwyn she turned to for advice. How could she and George make such a move? They agreed at once to let her use their cart but they did not dare to be seen helping her on a working day and nothing could be done in Wales on a Sunday. Mrs Owen explained that she had written to some friends in England for help as well, so when the telegram arrived to say that they were coming, it was then agreed that the move would happen on the next Saturday afternoon and Mrs Owen was greatly relieved.

George Owen sat in his favourite place, a rocky outcrop above the eastern end of the dam, where the last huge stones had just been set in place. The dam was like a giant wall, wide at the base and gradually narrowing towards the crest, where a row of arches would allow the water to flow through when the lake was full, and above these arches ran a roadway between stone walls, with turrets at each end.

Once it had been like looking into a disturbed anthill. There had been more than a thousand workers living in large terraces of huts, with even their own hospital, which had been busy because there were many accidents and even several deaths as the dam had risen. Smoke, steam and dust had filled the air above the site. Men moved everywhere: operating the little railway bringing the huge stones, the smallest of which weighed two tons and the largest as much as ten, from a specially opened quarry about a mile away; driving the steam cranes which lifted the heavy pieces of masonry into place; laying the mortar which would hold them firm; unloading pieces of steel, cement, tools and all the other equipment which had to be brought by horse and cart from the railhead at Llanfyllin about ten miles away; making the new road that would encircle the lake when it was filled, and building that strange tower at the side of the valley, a few hundred yards north of the dam. This tower, with its conical roof and fairy tale turrets shimmering in the August heat, would stand in the water when the lake was full.

When George and his grandmother had returned to live in the valley the dam was only half as high as now, but even then it was a remarkable sight, and in his holidays George would be up early to watch with fascination as the dam rose stone by stone. Or he would try to build his own dam across the little stream that joined the river just above the village. He tried to copy the design of the real dam and became frustrated when his models were always undermined and his little lakes shrank quickly away. But he was delighted when at last he managed to make one secure enough to hold back the flow and form a decent miniature lake. From that moment he decided that when he grew up he would become an engineer. When he told this to the well-dressed men who stood proudly studying plans and giving orders near the proper dam they recognised his enthusiasm and were glad to answer his intelligent questions.

He had learned from them that the road around the lake would be eleven miles long, that when filled the lake would hold 13,000 million gallons, that the water would be drawn into that strange tower by hydraulic machinery and strained through wire gauze before making its 68 mile journey along an aqueduct to Liverpool. And eavesdropping the other day, on a conversation between two top-hatted men who had arrived in a carriage and stood surveying the scene, he had discovered that in the next few days one set of valves at the base of the dam was to be closed and the water allowed to rise a few feet as a trial.

But it was not only workmen who bustled about the scene below. Those men had to eat and drink and farmer's wives walked miles from their farms and small-holdings to sell eggs and butter for at least a penny a dozen or twopence a pound more than they could hope for in the nearest market. And there were those women who preferred the lively company of these men who had come from distant parts to the dreary stick-in-the-muds of their lonely hill farms. Many a marriage was made or destroyed and many a child was born in or out of wedlock while the great dam grew across the lower end of the valley.

Now the dam was completed, the rails leading to the quarry had been lifted, the unused or broken stones taken away and the steam cranes had moved on to the next project. Only a few men remained, making last minute touches to the dam, working on the tower or the tunnel that would take the water though the hills, completing the roadway or bringing up the last few supplies from Llanfyllin. One of these men had agreed to give George a lift on his empty cart to meet the midday train when the unloading was complete. Meanwhile he sat on his splendid vantage point and ate a breakfast of bread and cheese.

George, at fifteen, was a good looking lad, with his mother's fine features, her dark brown hair and lively brown eyes. He had not been too keen to go away from the valley while all this activity took place but he knew that he was lucky to have a good education and that without it he could never achieve his ambition of becoming an engineer. He knew too that his grandmother was growing older, perhaps even becoming rather frail, and that soon he would need to care for her, as she had cared for him for as long as he could remember.

He did not really remember his mother, because even before she was killed she had spent a year in Hope Underhill and had only come back to Lancashire for one visit when he had been ill. But he remembered very clearly the visit he and his grandmother had made to that village, after her death, when they had stayed at Ella's cottage for several weeks. It had been his first taste of country life. And above all he remembered Amy, with her long, lovely fair hair and enchanting smile. He had followed her everywhere. She had taught him how to climb trees, where the best blackberries were to be found, how to make a bow and arrows from hazel wands and twine. He was only six years old and she was nearly nine but he had fallen hopelessly in love. He had never seen her since that time, but Amy had written to him once or twice and he kept her letters in his treasure box, along with a locket his mother had worn and a children's version of the Odyssey which she had given him on that last visit she had made to Lancashire.

Just then George heard a shout from below him and saw a man standing beside an empty wagon, waving urgently, so he scrambled down from his rocky lookout and jumped aboard.

Philip left his father snoozing on the terrace of Vyrnwy Hall and set out to explore. He had not yet unpacked his photographic equipment and anyway he wanted to reconnoitre the scene before he began to take photographs. It was very pleasant walking down the driveway, in the shadow of moss-covered trees, with the scent of thriving vegetation which was rarely caught even in the largest and most magnificent city park, and the delicate trickling of some hidden stream. When he reached the pillared gateway he crossed the road which had brought them from Bala and took a narrow path beside a widening stream, by now almost a river, which he could see meandering across the valley below.

Abruptly the trees ended and Philip was shocked by what he saw. The trees had been felled and cleared along what he guessed would soon be a roadway, pieces of rock had been tipped out from wagons to make the foundations and groups of men were spreading finer pieces of crushed rock over this and tamping it down to make a smooth surface. Below him on the valley floor was a scene of dreadful devastation.

Piles of stone and tumbled slate and dusty timbers showed where houses had once stood. Only one large building remained in the middle of the ruins – a church surrounded by a small graveyard- and one other house some distance away. For a moment it reminded him of photographs he had seen of an archaeological excavation –was it Schliemann's Troy? -but then he remembered another photograph, in a recent newspaper, of a city raised to the ground by a terrible earthquake. As he approached this place of destruction he almost expected to see corpses lying among the debris. Instead he saw two men, one young and one old, hacking at the stones of a half demolished wall. He approached them angrily, calling out,

'How can you do this? How can you destroy these homes?'

The older man looked at him, with a frown, but the younger one answered, 'Because that's our job. And the people who lived here are long gone.'

When Huw had first seen the man approaching he had nudged his father and both began to attack the wall with more vigour, thinking that it must be some kind of overseer sent to check on their progress. But as he came closer they could see that the young man's clothes were too casual, though obviously expensive, and his light coloured hair too long for him to be connected with the demolition business. When he spoke it was obvious to Huw that he was just one of those English toffs, come to see what real work looked like.

'Would you not come any closer, Sir. This is not a safe place for sight-seers. You could study the church. We've not started on that yet. But don't go inside it.'

'You are Welsh?' asked Philip.

'That I am. And my father too. He speaks very little of the English.'

'Then I do not understand. How can you as Welshmen destroy the beauty of this place.'

'Better for us to do it, than some English men, with half the skill and for twice the pay.' Huw was becoming irritated by this young man and took a few steps towards him as he asked, 'But may I ask what business it is of yours?'

'I am a photographer. I intend to use my camera to record what is happening here. I shall begin tomorrow.'

'You'll take no photographs or me and my father without our permission.' 'Very well. But it would be a shame not to show you working so hard. The nobility of labour, you know.'

'The nobility of labour, my ass! Bet you've never lifted a shovel in your whole lifetime.'

'Well, you would certainly win that wager. But each to his own as they say. Perhaps I should explain that I have almost completed my training as a doctor.'

Huw's attitude softened slightly. He had considerable respect for the medical profession, for the care they had given his mother, even though they could not save her in the end. He turned to his father and spoke in Welsh. The older man nodded and lifted his cap to Philip.

'Look,' said the Englishman, 'I'm sorry we seem to have got off on the wrong foot. I really meant no harm. I know it's not your fault. I just don't happen to agree with this whole lake business. Let me introduce myself. My name is Philip Lever. Yours?'

'I am called Huw Morris. My father's name is Gwyn.'

Huw came over to Philip and shook his hand. The older man raised his cap again.

'Is there anyone still living here?' asked Philip.

'Just two people. D'you see that house above the village? Mrs Owen lives there, with her grandson. But they are soon to move to the new village. Then the house will be demolished.'

'I would like to meet her.'

'Very well. But I will take you there. She might be worried by the arrival of a stranger.'

As the time for the train to arrive drew near George became quite nervous. Would he recognise them? After all it was nearly nine years since he had last seen them. But he reasoned that there would not be that many passengers. After all it was only a branch line and this was the terminus. The train would be mixed with one or, at the most, two passenger carriages at the front and a row of goods wagons behind, bringing materials and equipment for the dam, supplies for the workmen who remained, and a few animals from the nearest market. Surely there would not be more than one middle aged man with his daughter and though he guessed that Amy would have changed a great deal, her father would be more or less the same. He had been rather in awe of John when they had stayed in Hope Underhill, partly because he was a schoolmaster, but also because he was so tall and stern looking. At that time George still associated grown men with the beatings he and his mother had received from his father, before that poor man had fallen into a canal lock in a drunken stupor and been drowned. But he had soon learned that Mr Noble was not like that at all.

The shriek of the engine's whistle and a pillar of steam rising above the trees below the town told him that the train was nearly here so George found a good vantage point on the platform and watched. At last the engine thumped up the incline into the station until it almost reached the buffers, then stopped with a screech of brakes and great sigh of steam. Doors were pushed open and passengers began to step down onto the platform from the single carriage. There were a couple of farmers returning from market, scarlet faced from standing in the sun beside the pens, followed by a hearty lunch. Next came a small man in a dark suit and bowler hat, carrying a black leather case, then two middle aged ladies laden with shopping, followed by a bored looking boy with perhaps his mother, then all at once a sudden crowd so that it was difficult to distinguish between the passengers.

At last the platform was almost empty, but there was no sign of Mr Noble or Amy. George panicked. Had he missed them? Had they gone by in the crowd? Had they missed the train? But just as he was about to rush out of the station, in case they were waiting in the forecourt, this beautiful young woman approached him, smiled and asked, 'George? Is it really George?'

He would not have recognised her as this tall, slender young woman, in a smart green dress, with her hair piled up under a little green hat with a small bird nesting on it, but he knew that smile. He managed to blurt out 'Amy!' in a funny voice that went up and down an octave, but could say no more. Her stepfather joined them and shook his hand. He had been speaking to a porter, who was now wheeling their luggage along on a trolley.

'He's going to find us a carriage,' said John Noble. 'I believe we have a few miles to go yet. So on the way, George, you can tell us all about yourself.'

Sitting in Mrs Owen's garden in the late afternoon, sipping the home made cordial she had brought out to them, it was easy to imagine what this valley had been like before work on the dam had begun. Several damson trees, heavy with fruit, hid the ruined village from sight, and looking northwards there was no sign that anything had changed. The hay had been gathered in the surrounding fields for the last time and a few cattle were gathered at the river's edge slaking their thirst.

Work on the dam and roadway had ceased for the day and the valley was quiet again. The antagonism between Huw and Philip had faded. Huw had been keen to learn about the great city of Liverpool, which he had never visited and could hardly imagine, while the young Englishman was entranced by Huw's description of his home among the 'real' mountains to the west. Meanwhile Gwyn and Mrs Owen were talking quietly in Welsh and Philip liked what he heard of that lilting tongue.

Suddenly there was the tapping of hooves in the distance and soon a carriage stopped in front of the house. Mrs Owen rose, twisting her hands in her apron, and hurried out to greet her guests. She brought them back into the garden where introductions were made all round.

John followed Mrs Owen into the house to make the arrangements for their stay. George was chattering away to Amy, almost as if the years since their last meeting had vanished. He was explaining some aspect of the construction of the dam and she listened with unfeigned interest, but he soon noticed the effect she was having on the two young men. They stood, almost gawping, as she removed that rather silly hat and shook out her beautiful hair.

'You must take me to see the dam in the morning,' she told George. 'I didn't really get a chance to see it as we hurried past.'

Philip was the first to come out of his trance.

'I wonder Miss Williams...' - John had already explained that Amy was his stepdaughter, with another surname- 'Do you ride?'

'Oh yes,' Amy said, slightly puzzled by the question.

'You see, my father and I are staying with friends at Vyrnwy Hall up there, in those woods.' He pointed vaguely in the direction of the Hall which could not be seen from this point in the valley because of the tall trees surrounding it. 'They have a splendid stable with many mounts. I could bring one each for us and a pony for George and he could show us both his beloved dam.'

'That's very kind, Mr...'

'Lever...'

'But I really came to help Mrs Owen prepare for her move. I'm not sure...'

Her father and Mrs Owen had come back into the garden just in time to hear Philip's invitation.

'Oh don't worry about that, Amy dear,' Mrs Owen said. 'There'll be time enough to get everything ready before Saturday afternoon. Gwyn and Huw are going to help me with the move when they finish work at midday. They have a cart...'

She turned to Gwyn and spoke a few words in Welsh. He nodded and smiled.

'But you'd like to see the dam as well, wouldn't you, John?' asked Amy.

'No hurry, my dear. I am sure you would prefer younger company. I may walk over to the see the dam later in the day.'

Huw had stepped forward when Mrs Owen had mentioned the move, glad to be the centre of attention again. He had been filled with resentment with the thought that Philip would enjoy the company of this lovely girl next day while he had to go on working and he could not escape sounding rather sarcastic when he asked the young man, 'What about your photographs, Mr Lever?'

'Oh, they can wait.'

'Are you a photographer?' asked Amy.

'It is just a hobby of mine. I am to be a doctor.'

John looked at Philip with increased respect. He had liked this pleasant, well dressed young man at once.

'Yes,' continued Philip, 'I want to capture the beauty of this valley before it is destroyed for ever. I shall have an exhibition of my photographs in Liverpool. The people of that city must be shown what has been lost so that they can have clean water.'

George was excited by the thought of riding a pony tomorrow, something he had only done only once or twice before, and showing his friend the wonderful dam, but when he glanced at Amy he noticed that while the others were looking at Philip as he spoke in his sophisticated drawl it was not his face that she was studying but that of Huw. George wondered why he felt so jealous of that gaze.

4

The Move

Joseph lay in bed next morning thinking about his son. Philip had shown little interest in women in his life so far. Perhaps if he met a suitable young woman and married her he might settle down and think less about art and poetry. He remembered himself at his son's age. He had been passionate about medicine but that had not stopped him admiring several of the young women he met. He had thought himself in love quite often before he met Eleanor and knew real love. And in the meantime he had learned about sex from occasional visits to the kind of woman he would never fall in love with. But he could not imagine Philip doing the same. The boy was too romantic and idealistic for that. So it was quite a shock when at breakfast he saw a blush on Philip's cheeks as he announced.

'Father, I'm going riding this morning, with someone I met yesterday and her young friend. I have asked Cyril if I may borrow a couple of ponies for them and he has agreed. Would you care to join us?'

'Not on your life! You know I hate horses. And they hate me.'

Joseph paused to take a mouthful of kedgeree, then suddenly realised what Philip had said.

'You said *her* friend...' he murmured, 'So who is *she*?'

'Miss Williams.' The blush deepened. 'She is the stepdaughter of someone I met yesterday. Mr John Noble. They are staying with a friend in the last house left in the old village.'

'I thought everyone had moved to the new village long ago.'

'Well, Mrs Owen and her grandson are the last to leave. And they will be moving on Saturday. It is the grandson George who will be riding with me and Miss Williams, as our guide.'

Joseph had a sudden devilish notion to tease his son. He watched the blush deepen even further on his son's pale cheeks as he asked, 'May I ask the first name of this Miss Williams?'

'Amy'

'A pretty name. Is she pretty too?'

'I suppose…yes'

Joseph smiled at his son's discomfiture. Philip was glad to change the subject.

'What about you, Father? How will you spend your morning?'

'I am going to inspect the dam. Cyril showed me the path last night. Apparently it soon joins the new road where that has been completed. He and Gwendoline are meeting their gamekeeper this morning to prepare for the coming season. I was not keen to spend a morning discussing the massacre of wild birds.'

Cyril Bradshaw had been a business partner of his father-in-law and Joseph had been their doctor for many years. Personally he had little in common with them, but when they learned of his involvement with the Vyrnwy water scheme they had invited him to come and stay at the Hall where they spent most of their time since Cyril's retirement.

'Perhaps I may see you and your friends when I reach the dam. By the way, what occupation does this Mr Noble have?'

'I believe he is a village schoolmaster, Father. Somewhere in England.'

'I see…Well eat up, lad. You've hardly touched your breakfast.'

'I'm not hungry.'

Joseph turned away to hide a mischievous smile. Then he excused himself and went to prepare for his walk.

The Move

Phew! It was hot! By the time Joseph reached the new road he almost wished he *was* on horseback. He had not walked this far for ages and the extra weight he had put on in recent years caused him to sweat ferociously under his heavy clothes. His heartbeat was stumbling in that disconcerting, uncomfortable way again. Of course, as a doctor, he knew what was wrong, and if he had been treating someone else he would have known what to recommend; less food, less alcohol, less tobacco and much more exercise. But for himself he knew that it was too late to change. He paused to wipe the sweat from his brow and to inspect the straining tower. He knew the purpose of this tower, from the plans he had seen in Liverpool and he delighted in its appearance. Several years ago he had taken a brief holiday in Germany, partly to rediscover his heritage, and this tower reminded him so much of those castles which stood on rocky hilltops above the Rhine.

The tower, which was not quite completed, rose from the valley floor, like a wide stone pillar, and was joined to the valley wall by a small stone bridge with several arches. There were a few gaps in the lower stonework where eventually pipework might be inserted and joined to the machinery inside which he knew had not yet been installed. Perhaps it was the heat which helped him to imagine the filled lake lapping about a third of the way up the tower and swirling through those arches. As he stared the lake became almost tangible and he longed to plunge into its cool, clear water. He remembered the little girl lying beside the dripping pump in that filthy court. 'My God,' he murmured, 'Let the water flow soon...!'

He walked on towards the dam, knowing that the water would not actually reach Liverpool for a couple more years. It was intended that the water should flow the whole way by gravity, so the aqueduct began as a tunnel – more than two miles long -which at this moment was being cut through the solid rock of the surrounding hills.

When he reached the dam he walked down into the valley and got as close as he could to the gigantic stone wall, which rose high above him, far higher he guessed than even the tallest warehouses on the waterfront of his adopted city. And he knew that the foundations of this incredible construction went down into the solid rock many tens of feet below the bottom of the valley.

Feeling rather dizzy he sat down on the tumbled remains of a dry stone wall. He seemed very aware of things immediately around him, as if his spectacles had magically increased their strength: the stone he sat on with its veins of quartz, the frizzled grass and thistles, a pile of sheep droppings like brown musket balls and the white bone of a rabbit's skull. Soon all these things would be at the bottom of the lake, probably eighty feet below the surface. He shuddered at the thought and reached for the hip flask in his coat pocket. He knew that he still drank too much but since that fateful day when he found a new purpose in life he had kept his drinking more or less under control. Now he took just a nip from the flask, which always helped to steady him for a while, and was about to put it back in his pocket when he saw another man sitting on a similar stone a few yards away, staring at the dam. He called out.

'Astonishing, isn't it.'

The man turned and replied, 'In all my travels I never saw anything like it.'

Joseph lifted the flask.

'Would you care for a sip?'

'Thank you, but I won't.'

The man stood up and came over to Joseph, who noticed how tall and thin the man was.

'I find that if I drink in the day it makes me sleepy. A sign of getting old I suppose.'

'Nonsense! You're a good deal younger than me. And what's this about your travels?'

The man sat down again on a nearer stone. It took him a while to fold his tall frame down to Joseph's level.

'When I was much younger I spent a few years in Africa. As a missionary. But my wife died and when I came back to England I became a schoolteacher. Now I have remarried and we have a young son.'

Joseph laughed.

'And do you have a stepdaughter called Amy?'

The man looked astonished.

'I do indeed.'

'Well, what a coincidence. My name is Lever. Joseph Lever. I have a son called Philip. I believe you may have met him.'

'Philip! Yes, indeed. A fine lad. Going to be a doctor.'

'Following in his father's footsteps, but somewhat reluctantly I fear.'

'Well, Amy is to go to teacher training college this autumn. In her stepfather's footsteps I suppose. But there is no reluctance on her part. My name is John Noble by the way. But do call me John.'

He proffered his hand which Joseph shook vigorously.

'Look, John, I'd like you and your stepdaughter to join us for a meal this evening. I'm staying with old friends of my wife's parents. At Vyrnwy Hall. But to be honest I find them rather boring. It's all huntin', shootin' and fishin' with them. I would much prefer to talk to you about Africa and I know that Philip would enjoy some younger company.'

'That's very kind. But won't your friends mind.'

'Not at all. The more the merrier so far as they're concerned. What I suggest is this. We walk back together now to your friend's house in the old village and leave a message for Philip and your stepdaughter. Then this evening we can send a carriage to collect you.'

'But, John, we cannot possibly accept the invitation. I have absolutely nothing suitable to wear. I came prepared to help Harriet with her move and to explore the countryside. The only decent dress I brought was the one I wear at school.'

Amy was not in the best of moods. The day had been disappointing. It was good to be on horseback again, and she liked being with George, but to be frank, she did not enjoy Philip's company. When they reached the dam she wanted to ask George so many questions about its construction but Philip kept interrupting with his contempt for the whole project and his disgust at what was being done to this beautiful valley.

Later when they rode up the valley past the old village she saw Gwyn and Huw working hard among the remains. She wanted to stop and talk to them, but Huw seemed angry about something and Philip held a handkerchief to his face and told her that the dust would get into his lungs, so they followed the river which ran through the village towards its source among the surrounding hills.

Philip kept stopping and holding up his fingers to make a square and telling her what a fine photographic composition the scene would make. He did not allow Amy to see for herself, or let her hear the silence of the place. If he wasn't planning his photographs he was quoting from a favourite poem. They rode beside the river for a while up into the wooded hills. The long dry days had reduced the water level so the river dropped gently over terraces of rock. They dismounted, letting the horse and ponies drink, while they sat for a while on the bank in the shade.

Soon Phillip began,

> 'It was the deep midnoon: one silvery cloud
> Had lost its way between the piney sides
> > Of this long glen...'

For once the words seemed appropriate. Amy asked, 'Who wrote that?'

'Tennyson. Do you know his work?'

'Oh him! He is always so gloomy. And his women are stupid. Mariana in her moated grange, "I am aweary, aweary. I would that I were dead." And that Lady of Shallot falling in love with a man she sees in a mirror and losing her own life. I much prefer Mr Browning.

He is much more lively, though sometimes rather difficult to understand.'

But what annoyed her most about Philip was the way he kept glancing at her. He seemed unable to look her full in the face yet she knew that his eyes were always upon her. So the thought of spending yet more time in his company did not fill her with delight.

'May I make a suggestion,' said Mrs Owen. 'I have a dress that I made for my daughter which she never wore. It was for her to wear when George and I were able to join her in the village. She was much the same size as you, though perhaps not quite so slender. I have kept it wrapped up in her trunk ever since. It will need a touch of the smoothing iron. But I'm sure it will do. Come and try it on.'

Amy was not so sure. Surely the dress would be unsuitable. After all it would be old fashioned by now.

George was gloomy too. He was jealous of Philip who had come between him and his friend. Amy was such fun when he was with her alone. They were interested in the same things and seemed to see them in the same way. And he felt sorry for Huw, whom he liked and admired, for having to work so hard while Philip had such an easy life. But perhaps he was not being fair. Perhaps it was hard in another way studying to be a doctor.

John sat reading in the evening light from a window. It was beginning to grow dull in the room and George was just about to light the lamp when Amy returned wearing the dress. Suddenly the room was filled with light again. The dress was made of pale green satin and Amy's pale shoulders, her slender neck and her lovely face grew out of it like a flower from its foliage. She had lifted her hair and that reddish tint among the gold complemented the green of the dress, which of course matched her emerald eyes.

John sighed, seeing his step daughter simply through a man's eyes and knowing how most men feel when confronted by such female beauty. He remembered for a moment when he had first seen Amy and her mother sitting outside their cottage in the evening light. Ella had been the beautiful young woman then, and

Amy just a pretty child. Now he had helped to make a fascinating woman of that child and he knew how hard it would be to let her go.

There were twelve at table that evening at the lodge, but they soon divided into two parties. At one end the Bradshaws and their guests from the field sports fraternity were deep into coveys, woodcock, twelve bores and such like, while at the other end John thrilled Joseph with his tales of Africa. Then Joseph explained briefly why he was so interested in the dam and the lake that it would form.

When Amy first appeared in the room Joseph had gasped and muttered, 'Elean...' but he had soon learned that this young woman was a very different person to that much loved, short lived, wife. It was obvious that Philip was infatuated with her but Joseph guessed that she was not much interested in him. In fact she seemed more taken with Joseph himself, which was very flattering.

'So you have worked among the poor in Liverpool and will know how terrible a poor woman's life can be.' said Amy.

'Oh, yes, especially among the Irish, who are Catholics and have so many children.'

'Perhaps one day we can make things better for them, but not I doubt until women have the vote.'

Amy's voice had risen with her passion and there was a sudden silence in the room. Their hostess looked down from the other end of the table and said, 'My dear, I am sure you will think us quite old fashioned but we do not allow politics or religion to be discussed at meal times. It is not good for the digestion.'

Amy was about to respond in a combative manner but she saw her stepfather shake his head and so she said meekly, 'I do apologise' and gave the sort of smile she knew would calm the threatened storm.

When Joseph explained the origin of his interest in the water scheme Amy had some difficulty keeping back her tears. But Philip tried to make a joke of it all, saying, 'So you see my father has suffered for many years from water on the brain.'

These were almost the first words Philip had spoken that evening. He had tried not to gaze at Amy but this was the first time in his life he had felt this way about a woman and it was a very disturbing sensation. At last he had the courage to ask, 'Tell me, Miss Williams, are you intending to return to…where was it? …as soon as you have helped Mrs Owen to move to the new village?'

'Well,' Amy explained, 'That's up to my stepfather. Though I think he is glad to be away from our village for a while. It is called Hope Underhill, by the way. And do call me Amy, please.'

'Your mother did not want to come with you?' asked Joseph.

'No. My little brother is not very strong. She felt that the journey would not suit him.' She turned to her step-father. 'Isn't that right, John?'

John felt a pang of guilt. He had hardly thought of Ella or little John since they had left Hope Underhill and he had not found such congenial company as Joseph for a long time. He added as if in excuse, 'She has family and many friends in the village.'

Joseph asked, 'So, Amy, you are going to be a school teacher, like your stepfather.'

'Yes, for a while, but I would also like to travel. Find out about life in other countries. One day I would like to make a difference in the world.'

'And I am sure you will,' thought Joseph, looking into those sparkling green eyes, and noticing the effect this young woman was having on his son, 'but not necessarily in the way you think.'

While the dessert was being served Philip looked at Amy directly for the first time and, with a pink glow spreading across his cheeks, asked, 'Are you interested at all in photography…Amy?'

Of course she was. She had read a little about it and had made a pinhole camera once out of a cardboard box and tried to explain its principles to her pupils. But she guessed what Philip's next words would be and could not stand the thought of spending more time with this patronising man and his quotations from gloomy Tennyson. At last the words came out, almost as she expected.

'I intend to begin my photographic record of the destruction of the valley tomorrow. I wondered whether you and George might like to assist me. There is a good deal of equipment to be set up.'

Yes, thought Amy, and it will be George and I who do the carrying and setting up while you wander about making squares with your fingers and perfecting the composition. But then she realised she had the perfect excuse.

'Naturally I would be delighted to assist you, but I won't have the time. Mrs Owen will be moving in two days' time and we have a good deal to do before then. As for George you must ask him yourself.'

With that rebuff, justified though it may be, Philip shrank back into his shell. After taking a mouthful of a most delicious tart and swallowing it with appreciative murmurs, Joseph turned to his new friend.

'What about you, John. Will you be fully occupied with preparing for this move?'

'Oh, no, I'm not much good at packing. I'll be of more use when we begin to load things onto the cart.'

'Well then, may I suggest that we go together to inspect the new village tomorrow. We can find out which of the houses has been allocated to Mrs Owen, and it will be interesting to see whether the houses match up to the plans.'

Amy saw her stepfather smile and thought that he had not looked so happy for a long time.

The Move

Mrs Owen seemed to have overcome the sadness and worry that had afflicted her of late and was now almost looking forward to the move.

'There's a fine new chapel, with proper heating. I've already been there a few times. And a well-stocked shop. Oh yes, and a Post Office where you can send telegrams.'

She had decided that she could not possibly take all the furniture from her brother's house to the new, much smaller cottage, so she arranged for a dealer to come and take most of the larger pieces away. It was obvious that the dealer was diddling her, paying her only a fraction of the value of a fine dresser, a large oak table and several pine wardrobes, but now she just wanted to be rid of the stuff.

The next two days were fun for George. As he and Amy helped to pack the best crockery in straw filled boxes and wrap the pictures in wads of old newspapers he told her about his school and his ambition to become an engineer. She told him about her teaching post and some of the naughty things her pupils tried before she established her authority. But mostly they just joked and sang while they worked. George preferred to see Amy in her more ordinary clothes, especially with a pinafore over them, which made her look more like the girl he used to know.

Amy had asked Mrs Owen to teach her learn a little Welsh. They had all laughed at first when she tried to sound the double 'LL' with which so many Welsh place names began and the double 'DD' which became something like the English 'th' but soon she managed these sounds quite well.

'Why do you want to learn Welsh, my dear? You won't be here in Wales for more than a week or so.'

'Because it is different and new to me. I always want to know everything.'

But it wasn't work all the time. She and George often took a break and walked among the ruins of the village. They saw Philip in the distance, setting up his camera and plunging under a cloak to take his photographs. He waved to them but Amy just lifted her hand in a desultory fashion and turned quickly away. These walks often seemed to end where Gwyn and Huw were working. The men were delighted when Amy tried out her latest phrase of Welsh on them, but when Gwyn replied with a stream of Welsh she could only nod. George noticed that Huw had lost his anger now and that he seemed to stand taller when Amy was around and that she seemed unusually shy in his presence.

One time Mrs Owen asked Amy to take a can of tea to the men and she and George sat with them on the rubble while they drank. Amy asked Huw, 'What is it like? Where you come from?'

There was passion and pride in Huw's voice as he answered.

'That's real Wales. There's mountains so high it takes all day to get to the top and back. Mind you the tops are often hidden in the clouds. And the valleys have lakes, real lakes, clear and deep, which have been there since time began.'

'I'd like to see such a place.'

'Well, perhaps...'

But the sentence was never completed because Amy had seen Philip approaching. She stood up and said to George, 'Come along. We must not leave your grandmother to do all the work.'

At last the day for moving house arrived. John was pleased that the weather still remained dry, though he had begun to wonder how on earth there would ever be enough rain to swell the river and streams and fill the lake. Just after midday Gwyn and Huw arrived with the pony and cart and while they all shared a lunch they made their plan of campaign.

'It will take several journeys,' said John, in schoolmasterly manner, 'so this is what I suggest. Gwyn, Mrs Owen and I take the first load. She can show us where she wants things to be put.

The Move

Meanwhile George and Huw can get the second load ready for when Gwyn returns.'

'What about me?' asked Amy, determined not to be overlooked.

'You can make sure that everything is properly packed. And keep an eye on these young men.'

'Oh, I think I can manage that,' said Amy brightly, but George noticed that she glanced at Huw as she spoke and that a slight flush suffused her cheeks.

There were still a few pieces of heavy furniture and Amy was astonished by the ease with which Gwyn and Huw lifted them onto the cart, but she could see that it would take several loads to move everything, as the cart was not a large. Soon they had slung ropes round the bedsteads, mattresses, tables, wardrobes and sideboards, to hold them on the cart during the bumpy journey across the valley floor, where the road had not been properly maintained since the dam was planned. She wondered how one pony would ever manage to pull such a load but when she saw how sturdy that pony was and how eager it seemed to be to get started, stamping its hooves on the dusty road and snorting, she realised that it would be fine. After all Huw had told her how this pony had brought them, their tools and provisions over the mountain roads from where they lived, with no trouble at all. She patted the pony's muzzle and admired the gleam of its black coat and laughed when Gwyn spoke to it softly in Welsh and it bared its teeth in a sort of smile.

At last the first load was complete so Gwyn helped Mrs Owen up onto the seat beside him and they set off with John walking behind to see that nothing fell from the cart. When they had gone it was very quiet. Work had finished for the week on the dam and the roadway. Being quite alone among the ruins of the village they could hear the shallow river chuntering over its pebbly bed and the songs of the birds which were recapturing this peaceful spot, not knowing how quickly it would be lost to them for ever.

Huw and George brought down the lighter pieces of furniture from the bedrooms and sitting room and stacked them on the roadway. Amy rolled up the rugs, carried them out and added them to the pile. It took them an hour or so and they guessed that it would still be a while before the empty cart returned so they sat in the shade of a tree and rested. Huw leant his back against the trunk and Amy lay stretched out on the grass. If Huw had put out an arm he might almost have touched her hair. Both had closed their eyes. George could almost feel the tension between them that belied their apparent ease. He felt awkward as he sat watching them both. Suddenly they heard Philip's voice.

'I say, this house moving business looks jolly pleasant.'

Amy sat up and snapped, 'We're resting while we wait for the cart to return.'

She had not spoken to Philip since that evening at the lodge and she resented his appearance now. But there was no point in being unpleasant.

'How's the photography going?'

'Oh, quite well,' He indicated the camera and tripod and the other equipment he was carrying in a canvas bag. 'I shall soon have enough for pictures for my exhibition. I have made a temporary darkroom up at the Hall. Perhaps you and your stepfather – and George of course - would like to come and see them when all this house moving is done.'

'Perhaps,' replied Amy. 'But Mrs Owen will need our help until everything is straight.'

'Oh, I see.'

Philip looked around at the piles of rubble that were once the village of Llanwddyn. 'How long will it take to complete your work here, Huw?'

'A few more days, I reckon. With nobody around we can use more explosive.'

'It seems such a pity,' said Phillip. This is a fine house. Soon it will be a pile of stones, like all the rest.'

'Well, it wouldn't be much use to anyone under the water would it?'

'Will it be completely under the water?'

'Oh yes,' George butted in. 'In a year or so the water here will be very deep.'

Amy watched Philip frowning as he looked around and wondered if he was about to recite more Tennyson. Instead he said,

'It makes you wonder where all that water will come from.'

'Ah well,' said Huw, 'This has been a very dry summer, you see. Normally we get lots of rain in this part of the world. Sometime soon this drought will end and you will see a real Welsh downpour.'

Philip looked up into the cloudless sky and tried to imagine that rain falling on the surrounding hills and swelling the rivers and streams. He muttered,

'tho' the surge
Of some new deluge from a thousand hills
Flung leagues of roaring foam into the gorge...'

Just then they heard the soft thud of hooves in the dust and the clatter of the empty cart. Philip put his wide straw hat on again and stepped out of the shade.

'I'll be on my way.'

'You don't want to give us hand then?' asked Huw, smiling.

'I think not,' said Philip. 'I must get all this stuff back to the Hall.'

He looked at Huw who had risen to his feet and was now standing next to Amy. He was forced to admit, in his heart of hearts, that they made a handsome couple, though Huw was only an inch or two taller than the girl beside him; it was the contrast perhaps, the man's sharp dark physique next to her golden softness. They gave no indication that there was anything between them; how could there be between a mere quarryman and a young woman of education and refinement. Philip was not stupid and he had already accepted that Amy had no feelings for him as yet, but if she would only give herself the chance to get to know him she would recognise his finer qualities. He lifted his hat briefly to them all, saying, with a touch of irony, 'Well, I musn't interfere with all this hard work', and hurried away.

The second load was sent on its way and they began to prepare the third. This time it was the boxes of crockery, the well wrapped pictures, cooking utensils, bedding, clothes and books, mostly belonging to George.

It was late afternoon by now and the air had cooled. Amy suggested a little walk. After all there was no-one about to interfere with the pile of belongings that they had stacked outside the empty house.

'I have never seen your little camp, Huw.'

'Not much to see.'

'Still I would like to see it.'

'Very well.'

So they walked a little way out of the village until they came to a small meadow beside a stream. The shepherd's hut was like a wooden shed on wheels, with a door at the front and a little window at the side. Amy was delighted. She peeped inside and saw how neatly everything was arranged.

'You can't be untidy when there's such a small space,' Huw explained.

The sun had dropped behind the western hills and even in August the light in the valley rapidly began to fade. The three young people sat for a while on the boxes set out as seats around the embers of a fire, in companionable silence. Suddenly Amy asked, 'Do you miss your home, Huw? I mean being away for so long.'

'Dadda and I have been back once or twice to see that Nan was all right.'

'Nan?'

'My younger sister.'

'Is she the only one at home?'

Amy knew that she was being nosey but she could not stop herself.

The Move

'Mam died three years ago,' said Huw, quietly, 'and my older sister has married and gone to live in South Wales.' He paused, then added with a smile, 'And I don't have a wife waiting for me if that's what you mean.'

Even in the fading light George saw Amy's face turn scarlet.

'I'm sorry, Huw, I never meant...'

George broke the awkward silence.

'Shouldn't we be getting back? The cart might have returned.'

But before they moved Huw turned to Amy.

'Look. I wonder if you and your stepfather would like to spend a few days at my home. Our work here will be finished soon. I know John likes to walk. We could climb a mountain called Cadair Idris, which is close to my home, and see the real Wales. And you'd like Nan, in spite...'

'What about me?' asked George.

'There wouldn't be enough room for you as well. It's not a large house. But perhaps another time.'

George got up and strode ahead, so that the others could not see his disappointment.

'How would we get there?' Amy asked.

It was obvious that Huw had already planned this out.

'We can go over the hills to Llanwchllyn in the cart. There's a train from there goes to Dolgellau. Then it's just a few miles so we could hire a carriage.'

Amy had already decided that she would go and she was sure that John would not need much persuading with the promise of a fine mountain to climb.

'When would we go?'

'Next Saturday. We will more or less have finished here by then. We could have a restful day on Sunday, then climb Cadair on Monday – if the weather is good – when all the day trippers have gone.' He almost said 'English trippers' but that seemed rude.

The Stolen Valley

When they had loaded the last cart George and Amy said goodbye to Huw and squeezed onto the seat beside Gwyn. George liked Huw but he was glad to have Amy to himself again.

As they made their way towards the new village in the gathering dusk they met a strange procession of carts and wagons going the other way. The people in these were mainly dressed in black and kept their heads low as they hurried past. Amy longed to know what was going on. George had already gained a fair smattering of Welsh so she asked him to translate her question for Gwyn. When the answer came back it was a strange one.

'I'm not quite sure,' said George, 'but I think Gwyn said, "Better you don't know".

They went on their way in silence. Soon they reached Mrs Owen's new house where they all helped to unload these last light but necessary things. The house still looked rather a shambles but Mrs Owen had prepared a cold supper for them all and made sure that Gwyn had a good portion to take back for Huw. At last Gwyn got up to leave and when Mrs Owen spoke to him it was obvious to Amy that she was thanking him, even though she did not understand the words. He stood there, twisting his old cap in his hands and nodding shyly, and seemed eager to leave.

Outside he lit a hurricane lamp and fixed it onto the cart before setting off into the blackness of the valley for the last time that day.

George and Amy were both very tired, so George went up to the tiny box room – John was to sleep in what would be his bedroom – and Amy went next door to Mrs Evan's house. But although she was tired Amy could not get to sleep. She kept thinking about Huw and all she had learned about him that day. She had already passed on the invitation for them to visit his home and John had said that he would think about it. She remembered her embarrassment when Huw had told her that he had no wife waiting at home and she blushed again at the memory. But why had he thought she meant that? Perhaps he was simply being vain in thinking that she hoped he was single. That would be typical of a man. But there was something about Huw that had caused feelings in her she had not experienced before, and she was not sure how to handle them.

It was almost midnight when Gwyn approached the remains of old Llanwddyn. It was the period of the dark moon so he had only that lamp to guide him along the rutted road from the new village to the old. But as he neared the piles of broken stone he saw a strange sight. Many torches had been lit around the dark mass of the empty church and many men were moving about the surrounding graveyard. Gwyn reined in the pony for a moment, shuddered in the night air and thought of the day of judgement. Then he chuckled and called himself an old fool. These were obviously the very human villagers who had passed them earlier that evening, and he had already guessed what they were doing, which was confirmed when he got closer to the church and was almost choked by the sickly smell in the air. He hurried on to their camp where he found Huw watching the scene in the graveyard. As he took the pony from the shafts and led her towards a pile of hay he heard his son call out angrily in Welsh.

'The bastards! They take our valleys, our water, our slate and our gold. Now even our dead must shift so that they can have their way.'

The Stolen Valley

5

Passing Time

Amy woke late next morning and lay watching motes of dust floating in a shaft of sunlight where she had not completely closed the curtains last night as she had slumped wearily into her bed. It was strange to think that this dust was in the air around you all the time, yet you only noticed it at times like this. She remembered that evil rector Whiting coming to school, when she was a little girl, and telling them that these were the souls of the dead floating in space because they could not get into heaven, having led sinful lives. She was appalled. Was a human soul just a speck of dust? She had asked John about this. He had laughed out loud, but his explanation was no less horrifying when he told her that this dust was partly our old skin mixed with tiny fragments from our clothes and carpets and bedding. The thought of breathing in all that rubbish made her hold a handkerchief in front of her face for a while, but when she went into the garden and breathed the scent from the roses growing on the wall she soon forgot about the other things flying around in the same air.

She knew that she should have been up hours ago, helping Mrs Owen to get the house straight, or going shopping on her behalf, but she could not raise her usual enthusiasm for the coming week. How on earth would she pass the time- a whole week - until they went to Huw's home? And of course she would not be seeing him as often now that they had moved to the new village.

A church bell began tolling some distance away and Amy remembered that it was Sunday. She knew that Mrs Owen usually went to chapel. Surely John would not insist that they attended the new church. After all he did not have to pretend to be a believer in this place where no-one knew him. It occurred to her that the tolling bell was not like the lively tuneful ones that called people to worship at Hope Underhill, but more like the slow sombre clanging of a funeral bell.

When she turned a little in the bed she found that her muscles ached in places where she had hardly known she had muscles. Her body was not used to lifting and carrying as she had done for so many hours yesterday. But what she had done was nothing compared with the way Huw and his father had moved those heavy pieces of furniture. She had seen the way Huw's muscles bunched tightly under his turned up shirt sleeves as the men lifted a large cupboard onto the cart and the way his tanned forearms twisted skilfully as he tied the ropes which secured the load.

John heard that same bell tolling mournfully as he sat in Mrs Owen's kitchen writing to Ella.

My Dearest,

The move is accomplished. Two Welshmen who are demolishing the buildings in the old village lent us their cart and helped us with the move. Now it is a matter of putting things straight. Nothing will happen today because it is Sunday. Amy has been extremely helpful. I am letting her rest this morning...

At that moment Mrs Owen entered the room, dressed in dark clothing. John asked, 'Why is the bell tolling in that strange manner, Megan?'

'We are having a funeral service today for all the dead who were brought from the old village last night and reburied. The service at the new church is for everyone, whether chapel or churchgoers.'

'Did you know that this was going to happen?'

'Oh yes. There were many who still wanted to be able to visit their loved one's graves, when the waters have filled the valley.'

'Was your brother's body moved?'

'No. He was buried near the new chapel anyway because we knew that the lake was coming. And my parents had moved away before they died. But I knew many of those who were moved last night, so I must go and show my respects.'

They became aware that the tolling of the bell had slowed down.

'In fact I must go at once or I shall be late.'

No mirrors had been fixed to the walls yet, so she asked John to check that her black hat was properly fixed, then thanked him and went out. John continued his letter.

We have met some interesting people. One is a respected doctor from Liverpool who was influential in the scheme for building the dam. He is staying nearby with some friends. He has a son called Philip, who is also studying for the medical profession. He is a fine young man and just the sort we would be happy for Amy to meet when she is a little older. They invited us to dine with them and Amy made a great impression.

We have also been invited to stay with Mr Morris and his son Huw, the men who helped with the move. They come from the mountains further west. If the weather is suitable we are going to climb one of those mountains with Huw as our guide. This means that we will not be returning home until at least the middle of next week.

When Amy had first told him about Huw's invitation he had almost refused After all the Morris's were almost peasants who supplemented the income from their little farm by working at a local slate quarry, though Amy had informed him that Huw was trained in some special skill at that quarry. He did not like the idea of Amy getting close to Huw, but he could hardly have refused the visit on those grounds after sharing egalitarian values with his stepdaughter for so many years.

John paused, shaking the ink from the nib and putting down his pen. He was feeling guilty again. He was enjoying so much the change from his usual routine and had hardly thought about Ella or their little son at all. His new friend Joseph, and his son, were so much more interesting than the narrow-minded inhabitants of Hope Underhill and the thought of seeing new places next weekend and climbing that mountain were just what he needed to restore his joie de vivre. Now he added to his letter a sentence that was plainly hypocritical,

It would be splendid if you felt able to join us

He paused again. Should he strike that sentence out and begin again? But he decided that Ella would never agree to come, so he left the sentence in and went on instead.

George has become a splendid fellow. He has grown a good deal since you last saw him and has the dark good looks of his poor mother. His ambition is to become an engineer, like those men who are overseeing the building of this dam.

If only his own son would show more desire to learn, thought John. He seems to go through life in a dream. He is too much tied to his mother's apron strings.

John finished the letter, with the hope that all was well at the school house and the expected expression of love for both mother and son. Tomorrow he would visit the new post office in the village, purchase a stamp and sent the letter on its way. Then his duty would be done.

George woke with a feeling of stickiness between his legs. Oh no, it had happened again. He felt dreadful. The masters at school were always telling the boys how wicked it was to succumb to impure thoughts and how important it was to control one's bodily desires. But how was he to keep such control when he was asleep? His grandmother would surely see the mess. Why had it happened? He remembered dreaming about Amy but surely...

Joseph slept late. He had had a bad night. That sharp pain in his chest woke him several times. When he woke he found that he was covered in sweat. Perhaps it was the summer heat? But when he got out of bed and went to the window he felt that the night air was quite cool. The first time he woke and went to the window – just after midnight- he saw a strange sight in the valley below. There were dozens of lights moving about among the ruins of the old village. What on earth was going on? But at least the pain had eased and feeling exhausted he climbed back into bed. He was asleep in seconds. When he woke again and looked out the lights had gone. It must have been a dream.

The Stolen Valley

Philip had become obsessed with Amy. He saw her lovely face everywhere. When he looked through the lens of his camera he saw her green eyes staring back at him and in his temporary dark room when he placed the photographic plates in the tray of chemicals and swirled it round it was her face that seemed to form before another view of the doomed valley emerged and sharpened.

Perhaps he had always been rather obsessive. There was a doll he had been given when he was a baby. It was just a silly rag doll with a painted face and yellow wool for hair given to him by a servant girl, but it soon became his most important possession. He carried it everywhere. At night time if it could not be found and placed beside him in his bed he would panic and scream until it was discovered. He called the doll Mumby, but could not remember why. He thought he might still have that doll, somewhere.

On his tenth birthday his father had given him a pocket watch; a silver half hunter. It was not a particularly valuable or beautiful watch but for some reason he became obsessive about it. The watch was always in one of his pockets by day and placed on the little cabinet beside his bed at night. If he could hear its solid ticking he would slip easily into sleep but if he had forgotten to wind the watch and the ticking stopped he would wake in panic until he could set it going again. Of course he eventually overwound the watch and it ceased to work, but he had grown up a little by then and was able to put the watch in a drawer and get on with his life.

In his late teens Phillip began his medical studies in Manchester but was soon spending more time at the Manchester City Art Gallery than at his classes. He became obsessed with one particular picture by Dante Gabriel Rossetti called 'The Bower Meadow'. In the foreground of the picture sat two girls playing stringed instruments. Both girls were beautiful, but it was the one on the right that drew him back to the gallery again and again. Her fine oval face and a long straight nose; her shapely red lips half parted; her large eyes staring wide in memory or dream; her gleaming auburn hair drawn back to show a pale, slender neck and perfect ear: Phillip could have knelt there in the gallery and worshipped before her.

He began to look at the women around him in Manchester and at home, but none measured up to his ideal of beauty based on that girl in the picture. Now, in Amy, he felt that he had at last met a living match. But he had not seen her since Saturday and he wondered whether she would still seem quite as beautiful when he saw her again. Well, soon he would know, because this Wednesday, she and her stepfather were coming to dine again at the Hall and to see his photographs of the valley that was soon to be drowned.

John and Amy had decided to walk to the Hall. It was a fine evening and the new road had been completed this far so walking was easy. 'It will be good practice before we climb that mountain,' said John. As they passed the straining tower John suggested that it looked very picturesque but Amy thought there was something rather forbidding about it. They continued along the road until they reached that part of the valley where they were looking down at the ruins of old Llanwddyn. Amy saw that Mrs Owen's old house had now been demolished as well as most of the church, but its tower still stood. She hoped that the rest would be completed by Saturday so that the visit to Huw's home could take place. There was no sign of Gwyn or Huw but when she looked further up the valley she could just make out the shepherd's hut with a blue curl of smoke rising from its chimney pipe.

They dined with just Joseph and his son that evening as the Bradshaws had gone to visit friends in Bala, so it was a more relaxed occasion, where Amy could speak her mind more freely. Again she questioned Joseph about the conditions of the poor in Liverpool. She had a grasp of current affairs that quite staggered him, but it seemed to unnerve his son.

Philip was soon convinced of Amy's beauty. She easily matched the girl in that painting, but there was no dreaminess in this living girl's eyes, only the glitter of intelligence and the fire of ambition. He realised that Amy would never be content just to be a wife, until that fire had been damped down a little.

John told the Levers about their planned visit to the Morris's home and the proposed walk up Cadair Idris. Philip was astonished.

'But surely they have only a cottage. How will they accommodate you?'

'Oh no,' John explained, 'the house is a good size. Gwyn has told Mrs Owen that the place was once a farm. Most of the fields have gone now because they were unprofitable, which is why Gwyn and Huw must work at a nearby quarry, but they still keep a few animals on a small patch of land. Apparently the daughter who remains at home looks after those. Mrs Owen explained to me that this is how many people make a living in that part of Wales.'

Philip felt agitated. It was not fair that Huw should have the company of Amy for several days. What could they possibly have in common? Feeling a warm flush coming to his cheeks he blurted out, 'I have always wanted to climb a mountain. Do you think if I stayed in a nearby hotel I might join you?'

Joseph tried not to laugh. Philip had never shown the slightest interest in climbing mountains, in fact he hardly walked anywhere unless it was to take a photograph, but the reason for his sudden interest in mountaineering was obvious. Amy was puzzled too and not particularly pleased that Philip would be joining them, but she could hardly object.

'I'm sure that would be fine, Philip,' said John, then he turned to Joseph and asked, 'What about you, my friend? Would you like to join our little expedition?'

'Definitely not,' exclaimed Joseph. His heart began to stumble at the very thought.

After the meal Philip took them into another room where he had set out his photographs. He explained to Amy that he used the new 'dry plate' method, which made outdoor photography so much easier. Of course she wanted to know what that meant, so Philip fetched his camera to show her. The camera, a recent model, was beautifully made, measuring perhaps ten inches in length and height and about six inches wide. At the front of the camera was the lens, held in a brass fitting, set into a mahogany base and at the back a there was a ground glass focussing screen, also set in mahogany. Between the front and back pieces of the camera were the bellows, made of leather, which could be expanded or contracted to fix the focus. Philip showed her how the new photographic plates could be slid into the camera between dark slides so that they did not become exposed until the shutter was released. Philip explained that these plates were covered with chemicals that were much more sensitive so that their exposure to the light could be shorter than with the old method. It was no longer possible to simply remove the lens cover and replace it when the exposure was complete. Now a proper shutter, actuated by squeezing a rubber ball at the end of a rubber pipe, allowed the light to enter the camera for less than a second.

Amy asked how much the camera had cost and Philip told her that he had bought a complete photographic outfit for just under £25, which he assured her was a bargain. She tried not to show her shock but she knew that such a sum was more than many people, particularly of the servant class, earned in a whole year.

Now she studied each photograph carefully and saw that they were all beautifully composed and so sharp and clear. But she noticed that none of the photographs showed the ruins of the old village and that there was no sign of life in any of them, except the occasional sheep or cow. It was as if Philip had captured a perfect but uninhabited world.

'By God, this thing were built to last!' said Huw as he thrust his pickaxe into the mortar between the stones of the church tower on Friday morning.

'But we'll have the bugger down today!'

Gwyn watched his son and smiled. Huw had been like this all week, throwing himself into the task of demolishing the remaining structures as if his life depended on it. He knew that it was all to do with the young English girl. Gwyn was not sure how he felt about that. Of course she was a pretty little thing. Even at his age he could appreciate that. But she was English and Huw had spent most of the time since last weekend cursing the English. And he could not see any future in his son's feelings for the girl. Soon she would go back to her English home and her training as a schoolteacher – Huw had told him about that – and they would go back to their home and their work in the quarry.

Soon there was enough of a gap between the stones to insert the explosive. Huw began to pack it in place.

'That's too much,' said Gwyn, 'You'll blow up the whole valley.'

'Doesn't matter now, does it? There's no one around.'

He took out a match with which to light the fuse.

'Well don't light it till I've checked.'

Gwyn climbed over the broken masonry of the nave and went to see if it was all clear. There was no sign of movement anywhere around, except for the swallows, skimming the tumbled stones. Even the cattle had been moved to higher pastures now. He made his way back to the church and started to climb over the demolished wall when he noticed that the fuse had already been lit and the flame was sputtering towards the explosive. He climbed rapidly out again and had got about fifty yards away, when he tripped over a pile of earth left by the recent exhumers and fell into an open grave.

The explosion was tremendous. The whole tower seemed to lift into the air before it came crashing down. Stones were shattered and the pieces scattered everywhere. The pile of soil beside the open grave was pushed by the force of the explosion over the side and half covered Gwyn where he lay. For a while he did not move. Slowly he checked for injuries but the grave had saved his life. However he was still shocked by the power of the explosion, his ears were deafened and his head rang with its sound.

Gradually his hearing recovered and he heard Huw calling out, 'Dada, where are you? Oh my God, what have I done?'

Gwyn decided to make his son suffer for his stupidity. He lay quite still while Huw ran around calling in panic. Then, when he heard his son's voice close by he stood up slowly, with the soil falling from his head and shoulders, like Lazarus rising from his grave.

Huw gasped as the apparition appeared, then laughed with relief when he saw that his father was still alive, but lowered his head in shame when the older man shouted at him.

'You bloody fool! You nearly killed me in your rush to get the job done. I tell you now, come to your senses, or that English girl will be the death of you.'

6

Wild Wales

The road round the valley was almost complete. They crossed a newly built bridge over the feeble trickle of what Huw explained would be a roaring torrent when the rains came. They turned onto a narrow road which clung to the side of the tree-lined valley cut by the stream but soon the trees thinned out and they were on the open mountainside and climbing steeply. They made slow progress in the laden cart. John and Gwyn sat at the front, nodding amiably. Huw had set out boxes in the back as seats for Amy, Philip and himself and had fixed a tarpaulin over the cart to shade them from the sun.

They were crossing the mountains between the Vyrnwy Valley and the western end of Llyn Tegid, called in English, Bala Lake. Even in the strong sunlight the landscape looked bleak. The occasional trees were stunted and permanently tilted by the wind. The few sheep struggling to find patches of rough grass among the gorse and heather were not disturbed by their passage. There was no sign of human habitation at all nor any sign of other travellers. The road soon became no more than a dusty track winding upward and disappearing into the sparse undergrowth.

Philip was not happy seeing Huw and Amy sitting opposite him side by side. Huw had reluctantly agreed to let him share the journey as far as Dolgellau and to join them on their ascent of Cadair Idris but had made it quite clear that there was no room for the young medical student to stay at his home. Philip felt increasingly uncomfortable in the heat, the constant jogging of the cart made him feel slightly nauseous and his nose tickled with the dust kicked up by the pony's hooves. His annoyance and discomfort put scorn into his voice when he looked towards the horizon and asked, 'Does this road actually lead to anywhere?'

'Oh yes' replied Huw. 'It is well used on market days but in winter it is often blocked by snow.'

Amy thought of the hills around her own village when blizzards swept across Long Hill and snowdrifts made the roads impassable. It would be so much worse up here. She was glad the sun was shining now and there was only this gentle cooling breeze.

Just before they reached the top of the mountain the road divided and Huw explained that the branch to the left led down to a place called Dinas Mawddwy and when Amy looked down the valley in that direction she thought she could just make out a tiny group of buildings, shimmering in the heat haze, far below. But their road went on climbing to the very top of the hill.

At last the road levelled out, then began to descend into a wide valley stretching out below her and in the distance Amy saw a forbidding range of cloud capped mountains. Gwyn pointed towards them and said something in Welsh. Huw translated, 'Those are the mountains around Wyddfa – the highest mountain in Wales. The English call it Snowdon.'

Below them there were occasional glimpses of a large lake as they wound down the valley side, where soon full size trees gathered around the road and a few houses began to appear among the tiny stone-walled fields. There were small but sturdy black cattle in some of the fields and in others a rather scant crop was ready to be harvested.

Amy looked across at Philip who smiled back. He seemed altogether happier now that they were among signs of human habitation again and the cart ran more smoothly on a proper metalled road. But that is understandable, she thought, when he is used to living in a large city.

Soon they were entering the village of Llanwchllyn and they heard the distant whistle of train approaching from the east. They crossed the railway line and Gwyn halted the cart at the station, where they unloaded their luggage. As Huw helped her down from the cart Amy thought that he seemed slightly diminished among all these dwellings, but his grip on her waist as she dropped from the cart was reassuringly firm. The train hooted again, a little closer, so Gwyn hurried off to his friend's small-holding where the pony and cart would remain for the next few days. He returned just as the train drew in and soon they were settled together in one compartment as the whistle sounded once more and the train jerked forward, before accelerating slowly up the incline towards the west.

Amy and John had been given window seats, opposite one another. When she glanced across at her stepfather she was startled to see how pale he had become. He had been very quiet on the journey so far and now he looked quite ill. She knew at once that he was starting one of his 'sessions' as he called them: a recurrence of some ailment he had picked up in Africa, and which still afflicted him from time to time. The fever would last a few days, leaving him well again, but totally drained. Doctor McKenzie had given him some tablets to take on these occasions and she saw her stepfather unscrew a little paper packet and swallow one of these. Now she could see the sweat standing on his forehead, though his limbs were shivering. Her first thought was a selfish one. Why now? We will have to return to Llanwddyn, or at least abandon the proposed attempt to climb that mountain Huw had told her so much about.

John seemed to read her thoughts.

'Don't worry my dear. I'll be fine.'

He slumped back in his seat and tried to smile. Next to him Gwyn had fallen asleep. Philip had taken a book from his pocket and begun to read. Amy guessed it was probably more Tennyson but she didn't want to ask. Huw stood and leant out of the opposite window to smoke his pipe. Amy turned to look out of the window on her side and was fascinated by what she saw. The line ran alongside a stream which gradually diminished as they moved towards its source. Sunlight fell through the canopy of leaves and dappled the lichened trunks and mossed boulders that bordered the narrowing stream. Soon that stream withered away entirely but after a short pause another appeared, flowing the other way and the engine ceased to labour as the line began to descend.

Amy looked across at her stepfather, who was now also asleep. The shivering had stopped and his face had regained a little colour but she knew that this would only be a short respite before the fever returned with greater vehemence. What was she to do? Should she insist that they return on the next train? Or should she book a room at a hotel in Dolgellau? Philip would be pleased to help her with that? But then she would never see Huw's home or meet his sister or climb that mountain.

She looked across at Huw. He had extinguished his pipe. He turned slightly and she thought how handsome his profile was, with those high cheek bones, that strong jaw and his mop of dark curls. She was just about to get up to join him and tell him about John when there was a screech of metal applied to metal and the train began to slow down. Huw turned back into the carriage saying, 'We're nearly at Dolgellau.'

Gwyn woke up and stared about him, momentarily disorientated. Philip closed his book and began to take his luggage down from the rack. Then he moved to take Amy's down too, but Huw pushed him aside and brought down her small suitcase. She took her stepfather's hand and rubbed it until he woke, looked at her and smiled.

'I was having such a dream. You were in it, Ella...' Then he saw that it was his stepdaughter, not his wife who stood before him. He shook himself and asked. 'Are we nearly there?'

By now the train had drawn into the station and they were all standing ready to disembark, except John, who remained slumped in his seat. Amy knew that she had to speak. 'My stepfather is not well. It is something that comes upon him from time to time.'

Huw looked as disappointed as Amy had felt when she first noticed that John was ill. He spoke in Welsh to his father who then studied John for a moment before taking his hands and helping him to stand. He spoke again in Welsh and Huw translated. 'My father says we must get him off the train before it goes on to Abermaw. Would you bring his luggage, Philip?'

Huw and Gwyn took an arm each and helped John from the train, just in time, as the last door slammed, a whistle blew and the train moved on again. They sat him on a bench under the platform canopy, where he took another of those tablets, and momentarily revived.

'I'm going to find a hotel,' said Philip, then turning to Amy he asked, 'Shall I book some rooms for you and John.'

'I suppose...'

Huw and Gwyn had a brief exchange in Welsh, then Huw said, 'No. My father says that he will be better looked after with us. He will have peace and quiet and Nan will nurse him.'

Amy's gloom lifted a little with Huw's words. So she was still to see his home and meet his sister, though the ascent of that mountain seemed unlikely.

Philip looked at her, obviously disappointed that his plan had been rejected.

'Very well... But I will hire a horse and ride over tomorrow to see how John is faring. After all I have almost completed my medical studies.'

Huw accepted this and gave him directions to his home. Philip called a porter and asked him to follow with his case. The man was small and dark and did not understand English, but Huw quickly explained and held up a coin. The man smiled and picked up Philip's case. Its owner lifted his hat, turned to Amy, saying, 'Till tomorrow' and strode out of the station with the little man scuttling behind.

Meanwhile Gwyn had disappeared. Now he returned and spoke to his son, who explained that his father had hired a carriage which would be with them directly. John was still feeling the influence of the latest pill so he was able to make his own way out of the station and into the waiting vehicle.

Soon they left the grey stone town behind and were climbing steeply. John fell asleep again, with his head resting on Amy's shoulder. The carriage slowed with the gradient, which had become very great, and the horses were snorting and stamping with the effort of the climb. When Amy next glanced out of the window she saw that they had reached the top of a hill and the driver had pulled off the road to let the horses rest.

Gwyn said something to his son in Welsh and Huw explained. 'My father is going to sit with the driver. They are old friends. So, if you sit here...that is if you don't mind...we can let John lie down on that seat.'

So Amy moved from under the weight of her sleeping stepfather and gently lowered his head onto the seat. He stirred briefly and muttered something unintelligible, but was soon unconscious again. Huw made room for Amy on his seat. A mixture of embarrassment and something else made her blush as she sat down and tried to stop her thighs touching his, but that was impossible. He seemed equally ill at ease, but when he spoke his fine deep voice seemed to calm them both, as well as the motion of the carriage as it set off again.

'You know, Amy, I must tell you how pleased I am that you agreed to come to my home. It is no palace, probably nothing compared with your home in England, but I love it and have missed it very much and am proud to show it to you. I am sorry that your stepfather is ill, but I know that Nan will look after him very well.'

'My English home is not a palace, Huw, merely a school house. A village schoolmaster in England is not a rich man. Our village is quite pretty and set among hills but...' She looked out at a great hump of mountain rising above her on the right, 'nothing like these.'

At that moment they came to the top of the pass. Amy looked out of the window and saw their road snaking down steeply into another valley with almost vertical mountains on both sides and a lake in the middle. It was the most beautiful view she had ever seen and she could not stop herself exclaiming, 'Oh! How lovely.'

Huw smiled and said, 'The lake is called Tal-y-llyn and that mountain,' he pointed to the right, 'is Cadair Idris. We shall be home soon.'

And indeed, just before they reached the bottom of the valley they turned left and bounced along a narrow track. Amy saw a long low house immediately ahead. Huw announced, 'Tynygraig. That means the house near the rock.'

The name was certainly appropriate. The house seemed to be built into a cutting at the foot of a mountain which towered threateningly above it. The walls were made of stone, probably quarried from the mountain itself and the roof was covered in blue-black slate which she knew from Huw's explanation was definitely extracted from the mountains nearby. The grey stone and the dark slate should have made the house forbidding but the afternoon sunlight, the surrounding greenery and the ivy climbing the walls softened the gaunt structure.

As she studied Huw's home Amy saw a young woman, probably about the same age as herself, open the door and run down the lane towards the carriage, smiling and waving.

'That's my dear sister,' said Huw, 'but I must tell you now. Nan was born with a problem in her throat. She cannot speak properly.'

But that problem did not affect Nan's looks. She was slight and dark, quick in her movements as a tiny bird. Her clothes were plain but her face and black hair shone with health and her eyes gleamed like berries after rain.

Gwyn got down from the carriage and was engulfed in his daughter's arms. He quickly explained about John's illness and Nan's face changed expression so vividly that you could read her thoughts. By now Huw had also left the coach and was paying the driver, who was unloading their luggage. Huw received a similar embrace, but shorter lived, for Nan came to the carriage door and looked in at John. She made sounds that were in no recognisable language, but her meaning was plain. 'The poor man' She looked up at Amy, smiled and reached out her hand. They were immediately friends. Nan beckoned to Amy to come out of the coach, then the Morris menfolk helped the sleeping invalid out and carried him quickly into the house.

John was carried into the parlour, laid on an ancient sofa and covered with a blanket. The room was small and neat and obviously rarely used. The afternoon light coming up the valley, across the lake and through the small window filled it with a warm glow. John stirred briefly, then slept again, more deeply, as if the comfort of his situation was already combating the disease.

As soon as John was settled Nan began scurrying about again. She took Amy's hand and showed her where she would be sleeping, in another small neat room at the other end of the long, low house. All the windows seemed to face west and the same light from the sinking sun gilded the whitewashed walls. She was to share this room with Nan who had already placed Amy's suitcase on the second bed, which had probably once belonged to her sister. Now she pointed to the pretty jug and basin on a washstand and mimed the action of washing her face. Then she made a chuckling sound, pulled up her skirts and squatted, and indicated somewhere to the back of the house. Amy understood at once that the privy was outside. She smiled and nodded. Nan echoed her smile and left the room to busy herself elsewhere.

Amy poured water from the jug into the bowl and splashed some on her face. The water was so cold on this hot day that she imagined it must have come straight from the mountain. She unbuttoned her sleeves and let her hands and wrists rest in the water, wondered whether to change her dress but she had only brought the minimum of clothes and was not sure about the privacy of the room. She had noted that the door had no lock and she could hear Huw and Gwyn muttering away nearby. So instead of changing she sat on the bed and with, the aid of a comb and small mirror she had brought with her, tried to tidy her hair. This was always a chore because her hair was so long and thick. She wondered if women would always have this problem or would it one day be permissible for them to cut their hair short like a man's. Oh, how much more convenient that would be. But when she saw the golden lustre of her newly combed locks she decided that convenience was not everything.

Amy rose and looked out of the window. The walls of the house were so thick that the little windows were like those arrow slits in the castle she had once visited near her home. The view outside was wonderful, with small green fields, marked out with neat stone walls, rolling down to that lake – what did Huw call it? Tal-y-llyn? Yes that was it. She rolled her tongue around her mouth trying to get the sound right. And that almost perpendicular slope which began on the right hand side of the lake but soon disappeared out of her view from the little window, must be the lower part of Cadair Idris. For a moment her heart beat faster with the thought of how hard the climb would be, but she and John had climbed so many hills nearer home that surely they were well prepared. Then she remembered that her stepfather would certainly not be climbing anywhere for several days and that her chances of ascending that mountain were very slim. Her eyes misted briefly with disappointment, followed by the thought of how selfish she was being. She quickly wiped her eyes on her sleeve and went to see what she could do to help Nan.

But when she reached the kitchen, a small and dark room this time, with the window staring straight into the mountainside, she saw that Nan had already done everything. The table was laid, the kettle was burbling on the stove, ready to make tea, Gwyn was carving a leg of lamb and setting pieces on the plates. The freshly baked loaf smelt wonderful and Amy realised how long it was since she had last eaten. Huw was opening a jar filled with some dark brown contents. When he had lifted the paper cap he sniffed the contents. 'Nan makes the best pickle in Wales' The blush that suffused his sister's face made it clear that although she could not speak she certainly understood English as well as Welsh. Huw indicated a chair and pulled it out for Amy to sit, but before she sat, she said, 'Perhaps I ought to look in on John'.

Nan grunted and shook her head, then tilted it to one side and closed her eyes. Amy knew at once what she meant. Huw moved on round the table to help his sister into her place. Nan looked up at her brother with such obvious love that Amy felt a tinge of guilt that she did not have such strong feelings for her little brother. 'Perhaps,' she thought, 'if we were closer in age…'

There was a moment of stillness around the table. Amy noticed that the others had closed their eyes. Gwyn said a few words in Welsh, and then they set about their meal. While she ate Amy kept glancing at Huw. He seemed so content in his home, so at peace with himself, that his face shone with happiness, which made him seem more handsome than ever. Suddenly he glanced up, saw her studying him, and gave her a secret smile that made her blush. Then she saw that Nan had noticed their exchange and gave her a look which said, 'So that's the way it is.'

After the meal Nan mixed some herbs in a glass, poured in hot water, stirred vigorously, wrapped the glass in a napkin and handed it to Amy, with a nod towards the parlour. When she looked in on John he was awake. She put the glass on the mantelpiece to cool and knelt beside her stepfather.

'How are you feeling, John?'

'A little better, my dear. The sleep has done me good.'

'Nan has prepared a potion for you.'

'Nan?'

'Huw's sister. She's quite wonderful. So clever and caring. She makes me feel like a spoiled child.'

'Life must have been hard for her. Since her mother died.'

Amy nodded. 'Will you try her medicine?'

'Yes. And perhaps I ought to take another of McKenzie's tablets.'

John tried to turn so that he could take the tablets from his pocket, but he was obviously very weak. Amy helped him to sit up a little and extracted the packet from his jacket pocket. She unwrapped the stiff paper and popped one tablet into her stepfather's mouth. Then she took the glass from the mantelpiece and held it to his lips. The water had cooled slightly and he was able to take a few sips. A puzzled look crossed his face.

'Strange,' he whispered, 'but not unpleasant.'

John took another sip, then tipped back the glass and drank the lot. He settled back onto the cushion which was pillowing his head and sighed deeply.

'Dear Amy. What a nuisance I am. You must forgive me.'

'There is nothing to forgive. You cannot help these 'sessions' as you call them.'

'An unwanted legacy from my African days.'

Amy took the glass from his hands, which were shaking, and asked, 'Is there anything else I can do?'

'No, my dear. Just let me...'

His eyes were already closed. Amy settled the blanket round him again, waited until he was obviously asleep again, then slipped out of the room.

When she returned to the kitchen she found it empty. The table had been cleared and she heard pots and pans clattering in the scullery. She tried to help with the washing up but Nan would have none of it, so she retreated to the kitchen. She decided to go outside and enjoy the last light of the day but just as she reached the hallway she heard Huw and Gwyn arguing outside and though she understood almost nothing she caught the words 'English girl' spoken scornfully by Gwyn and guessed what the argument was about. She had noticed that since they set out that morning Gwyn had behaved rather coolly towards her, though she could not think of anything she had done to deserve this attitude, and she was about to go to her room and sulk angrily, when Nan came into the hallway, took her arm and led her outside.

Huw and his father were sitting on a bench set against the wall, smoking their pipes and looking down the valley to where the sun was perched on a dark blue horizon. As she too gazed in that direction something made Amy think of the sea.

Huw came and stood beside her, saying, 'That's what the English call Cardigan Bay. If you swam directly westward you would come to Ireland. Some ancient stories in our language tell of a land that used to be out there but is now beneath the waves.'

Nan seemed slightly piqued by Huw's arrival, perhaps because he could talk to Amy, whereas she could only point and grunt. She took Amy's arm again and led her towards a stone building attached to one end of the house. A young black and white dog followed them, staying close to Huw's ankles, stopping when he stopped and moving on when he did.

'She wants to show you her beloved animals,' said Huw. 'That's the cow house she's taking you to.' He laughed and added, 'I hope you don't mind getting a bit of muck on your shoes.'

Inside the cow house smelt of sweet hay mixed with the sharper tang of soiled straw. There was only one cow waiting to be milked, its plump udder swinging as it flicked its tail. Nan took a bucket from a hook on the wall and set a little stool near the cow. She stroked the cow's black rump and crooned softly.

'She is called...how would you say it,"Midnight",' Huw said. 'We have only the one cow left. But she's a good milker and Nan has such a way with all the animals, which is a good job because Dad and I are so often away.'

Nan sat on the stool, leant into the side of the cow and by manipulating its teats with her nimble fingers sent a steaming gush of milk into the bucket. Then Nan worked another teat and soon there was a rhythmic swish, swish as two streams of milk spurted alternatively downwards.

Amy felt Huw standing close behind her and the room seemed suddenly too warm, though the heat of the day was fading rapidly. Part of her would have liked to lean back into his arms but another part wanted to rush away. Then she noticed that Nan was muttering something in her guttural manner and gesturing to her. Huw explained.

'She wants you to have a go.'

Again Amy had mixed feelings. She would love to try her hand at milking, but she did not want Huw to see her make a fool of herself. She was trying to decide when she saw Nan signal to Huw to go away.

'All right. I'll leave you to it.'

Nan stood up slowly and stroked the cow, crooning again. Amy took her place on the stool, almost toppling it with her skirts until she pulled the cloth up to her knees. She remembered how Nan had leant into the cow's flank so she did the same and was encouraged when the animal did not flinch. Then the Welsh girl took Amy's fingers in her own and showed her how to squeeze and gently pull down the teat at the same time and Amy was delighted when the milk came. She tried again, unaided this time, with another teat and was successful. She turned to Nan, smiling broadly and found that she was nodding and smiling too. Once or twice the milk failed to come but soon Amy got the hang of it and was successful every time. She became almost lost in the act of milking, until she heard Huw's voice.

'How's it going in there?'

At once her fingers fumbled and the milk failed to flow. She stood up crossly, though careful not to disturb the cow and indicated that Nan should take her place. Amy smoothed down her skirts and stepped outside. She was rather annoyed with Huw but was quickly placated when he said, 'Poor Nan. Since Mam died she must do everything. When we're at the quarry she's on her own from early Monday morning, till late on Saturday, 'cause they like to keep you waiting for your pay. There's the house to clean, the animals to see to, the garden to tend. There's our clothes to wash and mend. Shopping to do, and it's a fair walk to the shops. All on her own.'

'So where is this quarry?'

Huw pointed southwards where the road from Dolgellau climbed on into a steep pass between wooded hills.

'Three or four miles over that way. Quite a climb it is. Then there's a long day's work. And too tired we are to walk back after that. But either me or Dada tries to come back at least one evening in the week. Just to see how things are with dear Nan.'

At that moment his sister came out from the cow house, with the bucket filled with milk. There was a satisfied lowing and the cow appeared. Nan gave her a pat on the rump and she trundled off across the field. Huw took the bucket from his sister and carried it indoors. The dog followed him again.

Nan led the way across to a gate in a stone wall. Beyond in the small field half a dozen sheep, recently deprived of their fleeces and looking rather thin and white were munching away. Nan pointed at the sheep and began to grunt and gesture in an animated way, putting one hand over the other and moving it back and forth. Amy had no idea what Nan was trying to say, but Huw returned and began to explain, in a rather hesitant, embarrassed way.

'My sister is trying to tell you…each autumn we borrow a ram –that's a male sheep you understand…'

'Of course I know that. I live in the country too.'

'And it covers each of the ewes – do you know that too?'

'Of course,' Amy replied vehemently, trying to hide her own embarrassment.

'Then in the springtime the lambs are born.'

Nan opened the gate and walked across to the sheep. The dog lifted its head and whined, but Huw spoke in Welsh and the dog flattened itself on the ground beside him. Amy was glad to turn away to watch Nan and hide her flaming cheeks. The girl checked each sheep in turn, their mouths and feet especially. The animals let her handle them, almost as easily as the black and white dog when Huw bent to fondle it.

When Nan returned Huw handed her a small basket, which he had brought from the house, then walked away, with the dog close behind him.

'I'm going to stretch my legs and give the dog a run. Come Gelert!'

Amy watched Huw striding up the steep hillside, as swift and nimble as the animal beside him. She was admiring his broad shoulders and strong thighs when Nan tapped her arm and led her towards a wooden henhouse, surrounded by reddish-brown hens, scratching and pecking among nettles in the stony ground. She raised a flap at the back of the hen house, lifted the eggs from the nesting boxes and placed them carefully in the basket. A hen was still sitting on one of the nests. Suddenly it cackled in triumph and fluttered away. Nan took the egg it had just laid, held it in her hand for a moment, then raised it to Amy's cheek. The egg was smooth and warm and Amy smiled with pleasure. Nan placed the newly laid egg gently on top of the rest, put the basket on the ground, and began to make sounds and gestures that Amy could not at first understand. The girl repeated her little mime, pointing first at Amy, then placing her hand across her own heart, before pointing to the hills where Huw could just be seen standing on a high ridge. Finally she smiled broadly and nodded her head. Now Amy could not misunderstand but when she shook her head such a look of dismay filled Nan's face that Amy was forced to give a hesitant nod and whisper, 'Perhaps? One day...' Nan's pleasure was almost tangible. She picked up the basket of eggs, put her arm through Amy's and led her back to the house.

Whether it was McKenzie's tablets or Nan's potion John was much improved next day. He was able to sit up and take some soup and bread. Too weak yet to stand or walk he asked to be helped to a chair near the window so that he could enjoy the view.

Gwyn and Nan went out early to attend chapel near the lake but Huw stayed at home to do odd jobs around the house and fields. Amy would have liked to help him but did not feel she should leave her stepfather, so she sat on that bench outside the door and read a copy of Wuthering Heights which Miss Watson had given her as a leaving present. She had tried to read the book before but had found it too romantic –all those bubbling emotions pushing the characters to their tragic ends. However it was the only book she had brought with her so she read on. She began to recognise something of the dark strength of Heathcliff in Huw and surely it was a landscape as bleak as this one would be in winter that gave Cathy her tough spirit. Yet Amy still could not quite believe in the dangerous irrational passions that drew these characters together and destroyed them both. She felt herself to be far too sensible to let that happen to her.

About mid-morning she heard hooves on the dry track and looked up to see Philip arriving on a splendid chestnut horse. His pale hair was tied back and Amy could see that he was almost handsome in a rather effete way. He dismounted, tethered the horse and came towards her. Pleased to find her apparently alone he smiled, bowed slightly and asked about John. As soon as he spoke in that privileged drawl Amy's momentary admiration vanished. She looked around for Huw as she led him into the house.

'Is your stepfather comfortable in this place?' Philip asked. He had to bend his tall frame to go inside.

'Oh, he is much improved. Nan made some herbal potion which appears to have done him good.'

'Nan? Who's that?'

'Huw's sister.'

'Really! Surely that was dangerous. I mean, who knows what these old country remedies might contain. He should have been seen by a proper doctor.'

Amy felt her irritation with Philip rising again and there was irony in her voice as she replied.

'Well he can be seen by a *proper* doctor now'

'I am not quite fully qualified as yet,' said Phillip, looking around the dark kitchen and wrinkling up his nose at the smell of something cooking. 'So where is the patient?'

Amy led him into the parlour, where John had fallen asleep again slumped uncomfortably in his chair. Philip tut-tutted with obvious disapproval. She woke her stepfather as gently as she could.

'John...John...Philip is here.'

'Philip? Ah yes, Philip. Splendid. I was looking at that view. What mountains, eh! Must have dozed off. How did you get here, my boy?'

'I hired a horse in Dolgellau. Perhaps you would you allow me to examine you, Sir?'

'Examine? Ah yes, I'd forgotten. Medical man. Like your father.'

'Amy, would you help me to move your father onto that sofa. It looks rather rickety, but I'm sure it will be more comfortable than this chair.'

'That's a fine piece of furniture,' said Huw, entering the room. 'It belonged to my mother and will outlast us all.'

'Yes, well...Good morning, Huw. Look, would you both mind leaving me to examine the patient alone for a while.'

As Amy followed Huw out of the room she glanced back to see Philip taking some sort of medical apparatus from the small black bag he had brought with him.

Huw went straight outside again and strode away. Amy called after him, 'I like your home very much, Huw.' He paused for a moment then walked on.

Amy sat on the bench and took up her book again but was too unsettled to read. Soon Phillip came out join her.

'Your stepfather is suffering from some kind of tropical fever.'

'I know that.'

'I believe the best thing would be for him to return to Vyrnwy Hall as soon as possible and let my father treat him. He is rather an expert on such diseases which are often carried by the sailors into Liverpool.'

'But...'

'Don't worry about the journey. I can return to Dolgellau and arrange for a carriage to collect you both and return us all to the Hall.'

'I think it would be better for him to stay here until he is a little stronger.'

Philip did not seem to hear her.

'And you must not let him take any more of that…concoction. Do you understand?'

'No! Well yes. I mean I do understand, but I do not agree. John has been comfortable here. Huw and his father have made us very welcome. And Nan is the kindest person you could ever meet. She would never give John anything which might harm him. He has suffered like this several times before. The fever passes after a few days and soon he is quite well again.'

At that moment Amy saw the Morris family walking together up the track, Nan between the two men giving an arm to each.

'But this place is so cramped and dark. I'm sure it must be damp. And what can this…Nan…really know about medicine?'

Gwyn came over to Philip, shook his hand and spoke to him in Welsh. Huw explained that his father had asked if Philip would like to join them for a meal. Philip paused, perhaps trying to think of an excuse, then looked at Amy as he said, 'Of course, I would be delighted. Please thank your father for me Huw.'

Amy introduced Nan, who seemed shy for the first time and made no sound. Huw was quiet too. He always seemed to shrink slightly in Philip's presence.

Nan hurried inside to check on the fowl which was roasting in the oven. On special occasions, and she certainly considered John and Amy's visit to be one, she would ask her father or brother to kill one of the older hens, which was no longer laying quite so well. Huw had brought in such a hen and she had plucked it last night and set it in the oven this morning before going to chapel. Gwyn came in with potatoes and carrots from Nan's garden and soon the meal was ready.

The invalid felt well enough to join them at the table. Phillip was forced to agree that John should stay at Tynygraig for a few more days, but that he should rest as much as he could.

'So I shouldn't try climbing any mountains just yet?' John said with a smile. Philip was about to protest when he saw that John was in jest. Eventually it was planned that Philip would arrange for a carriage to collect John, Amy and Gwyn on Tuesday morning. They would go back to Llanwchllyn on the train and collect Gwyn's cart for the last part of the journey over the mountains. Huw explained that he could not go with them. He had some friends to meet and business to attend to up at the quarry, especially since he and Gwyn would soon be forced to seek work there again, now that they were almost finished in the Vyrnwy Valley.

Amy noticed that Nan was not her usual bustling cheerful self. Ever since Philip arrived she had been subdued. Perhaps she was intimidated by his fine clothes and citified manners. Philip hardly touched his meal and seemed ill at ease in this simple home. But he was prepared to put up with any inconvenience so long as he could sit beside Amy. Huw, on the other side of the table, hardly spoke a word. At the end of the meal Amy looked across at him.

'Huw, would you please make sure that your father understands how grateful we are for the way you have made us welcome. Nan as well. I have really enjoyed coming to your home. My only regret is that we are not going to be able to climb that mountain.'

Huw whispered in Welsh to Gwyn who nodded at Amy, then went to get his pipe. John had been observing Philip throughout the meal. His feelings for Amy were obvious, but it was also obvious that she did not return them. 'What a pity,' he thought. 'Such a fine young man. Perhaps if he and Amy could spend more time together...' Suddenly he had a plan. 'I've been thinking about that climb,' he began. 'Obviously I cannot go, but I know how much you were looking forward to it, Amy. Why don't you make the ascent with Philip and Huw? I'm sure that they would look after you very well. I really think it would be for the best. You are all young, and strong. An old man like me would probably have been a nuisance anyway. What d'you think?'

He saw a glow of pleasure suffuse his step-daughter's face, but he found it more difficult to read the expressions of the two men. Huw replied first, 'Well, if Amy would be happy with that plan?'

'Oh yes,' said Amy. 'What about you Philip?'

He did not seem particularly enthusiastic, but he agreed to go.

'You would need to be back here early in the morning,' said Huw, thereby making it clear that Philip would not be able to stay in his home overnight.

'Very well. What time should I arrive?'

'About eight oclock. And you will need boots or strong shoes.'

'I had anticipated that,' said Philip with a touch of irritation.

'And warm clothes. Because it is always colder as you go upwards. Even if the weather is still good down here in the valley. And all the signs are that this weather will be with us for another day at least. Nan will prepare some food for us to take.'

'Wouldn't Nan like to join us?' asked Amy.

Nan shook her head vigorously and Huw explained, 'Nan won't go up there. Her head's too full of the old tales.'

Amy would have liked to ask what these old tales were, but Phillip interrupted.

'Your sister has no need to provide for me, Huw. I shall bring my own refreshment.' He stood up. 'I thank you for the meal, but now I should be on my way. It is obvious that John is recovering. Though I still think he should take great care and be examined by my father as soon as possible.'

Gwyn went out through the back door to smoke his pipe. Nan began to clear the table. Amy and Huw went out to watch Philip mount his horse set off for Dolgellau.

'Goodbye, Philip. Until tomorrow.'

'Eight oclock!' said Huw. Amy could almost feel him relax as Philip rode away. She thought about what Huw had said to him about his shoes and began to wonder if her own shoes would be suitable for the climb. But she generally wore light boots for any outdoor activity and when she thought how many times she had worn them for similar climbs with her stepfather, though not quite as steep as that mountain, she decided that they would do well enough.

When Philip had disappeared Amy lifted her eyes to the upper slopes of the mountain. She thought she could just make out some climbers crawling slowly along a high ridge, like tiny black insects against the background of the cloudless sky. Tomorrow she would be climbing right up there herself. She could hardly wait.

The Stolen Valley

7

Cadair Idris

Amy was still half asleep when she felt Nan shaking her shoulder and heard her mumbling. She sat up and asked, 'What time is it?'

Nan held up seven fingers. Amy was puzzled.

'But it's still quite dark?'

Nan pointed to the window, then left the room. The air felt chill. Amy pulled her shawl over her shoulders and went to look, but there was nothing to see. It was if they were in the middle of a cloud.

'Oh no!' she said out loud. 'We can't climb a mountain in that!'

But she still got dressed, in her simplest, shortest, navy blue skirt, which almost showed her ankles, a white blouse and her warmest jacket. She tied her hair back and fixed a straw bonnet on top. Then she went back to the window. The mist was still thick but seemed to be filling with golden light.

When she entered the kitchen Huw was drinking from a large mug and Nan was making sandwiches. Huw saw Amy's anxious look and smiled.

'No need to worry about the mist. All be gone in an hour or so.'

He stood and pulled back a chair for her.

'Have some tea. There's plenty in the pot.'

When she was sitting down he placed a pretty china cup and saucer in front of her. Nan muttered something and Huw laughed.

'She's saying you must be honoured 'cause that's the last of Mam's best tea set.'

Amy watched Nan efficiently slicing the bread and filling the sandwiches with some kind of meat and lettuce leaves.

'I still don't see why Nan can't come with us. It seems so unfair,' said Amy.

Nan seemed to shudder and shook her head.

'Oh, it's some nonsense an idiot told her when she was a little girl.' said Huw, 'Apparently, a long time ago, the people of Tal-y-llyn and Llanfihangel used to meet somewhere up on the slopes each Sunday for games and dances and perhaps other things. Well one Easter Sunday they were all having a really good time when the Devil appeared in the shape of an ass. They say he reared up on his hind legs and made a terrible sound which made the mountains tremble. Everybody fled and the villagers never met up there again.'

Amy noticed that Nan had covered her ears.

'It's just silly superstition. Anyway someone needs to stay here and look after your stepfather.'

Amy almost dropped her cup. 'Oh, my goodness! Poor John. I'd quite forgotten.'

'Don't worry,' said Huw, bringing a canvas bag with leather straps to the table, 'I looked in on him a while ago and he was sleeping soundly.'

He put the sandwiches and a bottle of tea into the bag, closed the top and fixed it over his shoulders with a leather strap. Amy could not help but study him for a moment, admiring his sturdy physique, his strong features and those thick dark curls. He became aware of her gaze and tried to divert her attention.

'We use these bags up at the quarry. To carry the explosive and our meals in them.' He smiled. 'We try not to get them mixed up.'

Gwyn appeared from the back door, adjusting his braces. He took a watch from his waistcoat pocket, studied the face, and said something in Welsh to Huw.

'He is saying we must be on our way. Glad to be rid of us perhaps. Oh, and he tells me I must take good care of you for your stepfather's sake.'

They were about to leave when Nan ran round to Amy and gave her a firm hug, which probably meant she never expected to see her again. At that moment there was a knock on the door and when Huw opened it they saw Philip standing outside. He had obviously taken the idea of mountain climbing very seriously and was immaculately equipped for conquering an alpine peak, in a thick tweed suit, heavy boots and a silly hat with a long feather stuck in the band. He must have gone shopping in Llanfyllin since he had decided to come with them. But the bigger surprise was that the mist had already thinned sufficiently for the nearest stone walls to have appeared.

'Well, well,' said Huw, sounding almost surprised, 'there's right on time you are. Gwyn will put your horse in with the sheep and Nan will give it some oats and water.'

Philip doffed his felt hat and thanked them both. He also had a bag across his shoulders, larger than Huw's and obviously quite new.

The three mountaineers set off. When they reached the gate where Philip's horse was tethered he unstrapped a folded tripod and took his camera and equipment from the saddle bag. Huw laughed.

'You're not thinking of lugging that lot up the mountain are you?'

'Oh yes. The camera and a few plates will go in my bag. And the tripod will fit across my shoulders under the straps.'

'But this is Cadair Idris we're climbing, boy. It's near enough three thousand feet.'

'Exactly. So I cannot miss the opportunity to take some photographs.'

'Well don't expect Amy and me to help you with that stuff when you get tired.'

'Of course not.'

'Oh well, come on then. And be it on your head...or back rather.'

They crossed the road from Dolgellau to Machynlleth and went on down a lesser road towards the lake, then turned right onto a narrow path leading into a wood. Beside them ran a shallow river. Huw told them it was called the Nant Cadair. The water was clear and still as glass.

When they reached the wood it was cool under the trees and a few wisps of mist still curled around the tree trunks. The path crossed the river over a small stone bridge, turned sharp right and began to climb steeply into a narrow wooded cleft, where the water dropped down over a jumble of boulders piled here by the river as it had thundered down in winter spate over the centuries. Even after several weeks without significant rain the water still cascaded in a series of miniature cataracts, each one boiling white where it hit the rocks below. Trees, mostly oaks, clung to the sides of the gulley by means of their exposed roots and the boughs met above so that the air was cool and damp under a green roof and everything, the trunks and roots of the trees and the rocks to which they clung, was coated with thick green moss.

The path itself was just a series of natural steps from boulder to boulder and Amy often found it difficult to stretch upwards from one to the next, but she struggled on, too proud to ask her companions to assist. Huw leaped upwards with ease, but Philip was already lagging behind, in spite of his long legs. After climbing for half an hour or so Huw paused on a flat rock to wait and called out, 'Don't worry. This is the worst part,' then added ominously, 'for a while.'

At last the path levelled out. The trees were less dense now and had changed from oak to birch. They reached a gate in a stone wall, which Huw explained was to keep the sheep out of the steep gulley below, where they might slip on the wet rocks. He held the gate open for Amy to pass through, and called to Philip, who had fallen behind again.

'Keep up, Philip, or the giant might get you.'

Amy would have liked to ask Huw what he meant but she was still getting her breath back. When Philip finally joined them he just managed to gasp out, 'What giant?'

'The giant is called Idris. This is his mountain. Cadair Idris means the chair of Idris.'

'Surely you don't believe in that sort of guff, Huw. I mean, we are living in a scientific age. Practically the twentieth century.'

'Perhaps,' said Huw. 'But they say that if anyone spends a night up on this mountain they wake up as either a poet or a madman.'

This time Phlip did not pour scorn, but merely smiled, as if perhaps he would quite like to wake as a poet.

Their path moved away from the river and the valley widened out into a great green bowl rimmed entirely with rocky cliffs. Stones, dislodged by frost and rain, had tumbled into screes down the steep slopes and streams like thin strands of white cotton rushed down as tributaries to join the river moving more sluggishly now across the boggy valley floor. There was a majesty and loneliness about the whole scene that made Amy feel that giants might well inhabit such a place. Then she laughed inwardly at her own silliness and hurried on.

They were walking together now. Their path kept to the drier bank on the left of the valley where ferns rose thickly to head height and sometimes the path almost lost itself amongst gorse bushes. Suddenly Huw stopped, picked something up from the ground and exclaimed angrily.

'There was a time when we Welsh had this mountain to ourselves. Now the English come in their droves at weekends and leave their filthy litter behind.'

Amy saw that what he had picked up was a brown paper bag, with the name of some Manchester grocer printed on the side.

She felt momentarily affronted by Huw's remark. She may be English, but she would never dream of dropping litter anywhere, let alone up here. She saw that Philip was equally offended. His face flushed as he said, 'It's only one small piece of paper, Huw. Then he asked, 'What is all this resentment of the English?'

Huw noticed their reaction.

'I'm sorry. I didn't mean you. You're my friends. But...let me try to explain.'

He stopped, removed his bag and placed in on a patch of green turf, like a little glade among the ferns. Philip also removed his bag, and the tripod, glad to be rid of the weight for a while. Amy realised how warm it had become. The mist had entirely cleared, there was no breeze and the sun was already burning down from a cloudless sky. She removed her jacket, placed it on the dry ground and sat on it, smoothing out her skirt around her.

'My 'resentment' as you call it, Philip, is because I live in a conquered country. You cannot know how that feels. You live in one of the most powerful nations in the world. Your Empire keeps spreading across the globe.'

'But surely,' said Philip, 'it is your Empire too. It is the British Empire and Wales is part of Britain.'

'Yes, that is how you see it. That is how it has been for centuries. But once Wales was a nation too, quite separate, with its own language and law and history. Then those Norman ancestors of yours came and conquered us, and built their castles everywhere to keep us under control.'

'But that was all ages ago. Nowadays...'

'We are still under your English rule. Did you know that although most of us Welsh attend chapels we have to pay tithes to your English church to keep the minister in his posh house? And that minister is usually English of course.'

Amy interrupted, 'I read something about that in our newspaper. They called it a Tithe War. Rioters with sticks and staffs, bulls let loose, auctioneers and tithe-collectors severely beaten.'

She had quoted almost word for word what she had read. It had not meant much to her at the time but now she began to understand.

Philip had been lounging on the grass. Now he sat up. He was astonished that Amy should have read about such things.

'That's the wrong way to go about it. I mean rioting and violence. Surely it is better to use your elected representatives...'

Huw was becoming animated now, 'Tosh! Most of our 'elected representatives' don't even live in Wales. They don't give a damn about us Welsh'

Huw apologised to Amy for his language. He opened his bag and took out the bottle of tea. He removed the cork and handed the bottle to Amy. The tea was cold but sweet and refreshing. She passed the bottle on to Philip.

'No thank you. I have something of my own. And I think Huw needs that drink to cool him down.'

'Perhaps? But there are some I know who would do much more than grumble, which is all I do really. They are ready to take real action to make their feelings known. They despise me because I won't join them. And believe me there have been times in the quarry when I have been tempted.'

He paused while he sipped from the bottle of tea, then wiped the top and refixed the cork.

'Let me tell you about the quarries. Who owns them? Englishmen! They grow rich on our backs. The work is very hard, the pay pitiful and the working conditions are scandalous. I have seen men crushed by falling slate because they were made to hurry by the overseers and the proper precautions were not taken. I have heard the old ones coughing up the dust clogging their lungs. But do you think the English owners care? Not a jot. They take our coal and iron, our slate and even our gold...'

'Gold!' said Amy. I had no idea there was gold in Wales.'

'Oh yes. It has been mined for centuries, and not so far from here. And where do you think most of that gold has gone. To England to make jewels for the English aristocrats! Now of course in Vyrnwy they are stealing our land and covering it with water.'

'I don't approve of that myself, but my father thinks it necessary.'

Philip paused as if to consider the pros and cons, then stood up and shouldered his bag.

'Don't you think we should be getting on, Huw. You said this climb would take us most of the day and it's already getting quite warm.'

Amy could see the sweat on Philip's brow. She wondered why he didn't take his jacket off and that silly hat. Huw had removed his jacket ages ago and tied the arms about his waist. Amy was glad she had removed hers and after the short rest and cold tea felt quite refreshed and ready to go on again. She had decided to copy Huw and tie her own jacket around her waist. Suddenly he jumped to his feet, picked up his bag and strode off.

The path began to climb again and wind its way around huge rocks which seemed to have been dumped there by some giant hand. Amy thought of Idris clambering around his mountain and throwing rocks about in a bad temper. She smiled as she thought Idris might look much like a larger version of Huw striding angrily ahead. She ran a little to catch him up.

'I'm beginning to see what you mean, Huw. It doesn't seem fair.'

'I'll tell you the worst, Amy. They want to destroy our language. I know that I can talk to you in English, and I am glad of that, but I love my own language. We have so much splendid poetry and stories and songs in Welsh. But they want to force us to give it up. Keeps us backward they say. When I was at school I had a wooden plaque tied round my neck with the words 'Welsh Not' because I dared to speak my own language in the playground.'

Amy was shocked to hear that. For a moment she felt almost ashamed to be English and lowered her head as she followed Huw around yet another enormous boulder. Then she stopped and gasped. In front of her rose an enormous cliff of bare grey rock and at its foot a circular lake, half in deep shadow while the other half glittered in strong sunlight.

'That's Llyn Cau. The lake is very deep. They say there is a monster living in it. Dragged here by King Arthur.'

Philip, who had just caught up, exclaimed, 'Oh, not King Arthur again! He seems to have lived everywhere, from northern France, to Cornwall, various parts of Wales and right up to Scotland. I wouldn't be surprised if he got to America as well. It's all nonsense. He never really existed.'

'How do you know that?'

'It's just makes good story. You know...knights and round tables, Merlin the magician, Lancelot and Guinevere. Chap called Mallory got the whole thing started. But Tennyson's version is superb.'

Amy could not keep the sarcasm out of her voice as she replied, 'Well it would be, wouldn't it.'

'And looking at that lake I find it easy to imagine Sir Bedivere casting Excalibur across the water and an arm rising from its surface and taking the sword away. I think it's time I took some photographs.'

'Very well,' said Huw. 'We can stop here for a while. Philip can take his pictures and I'll tell you another story about King Arthur, Amy.'

So Philip unpacked his photographic equipment and set it up while Huw and Amy walked down to the edge of the lake and sat on some wide, flat stones. All they could hear was the soft slap of ripples on the pebbly beach and the cries of some large birds wheeling high above them.

Huw asked, 'Do you believe in King Arthur, Amy?'

'Up here I think I could believe in anything. Giants, monsters, even dragons. But how do you know about these old stories?'

'From my mother. She was an educated woman from a well-off family. My father met her when he went to work near Aberystwyth for a while. Bit of a come down really, a woman like that marrying a poor hill farmer. Her family would have nothing to do with it. Cast her off they did. But it was a love match. Mam always seemed so happy till she got ill. And Gwyn is half the man he was when she was still alive.'

Amy thought about her mother and step-father. She remembered how happy they seemed when they were first married. But now John appeared almost happier when he was away from home. She looked at Huw from under the brim of her straw hat. He was an attractive man and she wanted to be close to him. Was that what it meant to be in love?

'This story of yours, Huw. Is it a love story?'

'Oh no, not at all. Well, except love of money. I suppose.'

Amy looked away to where Philip was trying to set up his tripod on the uneven ground. She knew she could never love him. She wished he was not with them. Huw began his story.

'A young Welshman, the seventh son of a seventh son, set off across Wales to make his fortune. When he reached Punlumon mountain which is a bleak and desolate place he found it hard going across the boggy ground so he cut himself a staff from a hazel bush and went on his way more easily. Soon he met an old man who greeted him saying,

"That's a fine staff you have, my friend. Do you remember where you cut it?"

"Oh yes," replied the young man. "I have a very good memory for things like that."

"Well if you can lead me back to the exact place I will show you a great treasure."

'So the young man led the way back to the windswept mountain top and showed the old man the exact place where he had cut the staff. Beside the hazel bush was a huge slab of stone. When the two men lifted the stone they saw a tunnel going down into the earth with a faint gleam at the end of it.'

Amy thought perhaps she had heard this story before, or one like it, but she was happy just to listen to Huw telling it. There was something hypnotic about his voice. Or perhaps it was the heat of the sun and the silence of this place. She would have liked to lie back next to Huw and close her eyes.

'The two men went down into the tunnel and came to a great cavern where many knights were sleeping and in the centre was their king. It was their gleaming armour which had lighted the way down into the earth. Also in the cavern were two enormous piles of coins, one of gold and the other of silver. But to get to the coins you had to squeeze past a large bell.'

The old man said, "You may take coins from one pile or the other, but not both. And do not touch this bell, for if any of the knights should wake it might be fatal to us both. But if for any reason you do accidentally sound the bell and one of them wakes, he will ask, 'Is it day?' and you must answer, 'Not yet. Sleep on.'"

'So the young man went forward and stuffed his tunic with as much gold as he could carry. But when he tried to get past the bell his chest was now so wide with golden coins that his elbow touched the bell and sent a great clang echoing through the cavern. The nearest knight woke and asked, "Is it day?" The young man replied, "Not yet. Sleep on." '

'Fortunately the knight lay down and slept again. The two men hurried out of the tunnel and replaced the stone.'

'The old man said, "Use that wealth wisely and it should last you all your life. But if you do need to return to the cavern and you wake one of the warriors he will ask, 'Is Wales in danger?' then you must answer, 'Not yet. Sleep on.' But I advise you never to return to the cavern for third time.'"

'Of course,' said Amy, smiling, 'he soon used up all the gold coins.'

'Yes. So he went back to the cavern and took as many of the silver coins as he could carry and when he passed the bell he accidentally set it clanging.'

Amy laughed and said, 'And the nearest warrior woke and asked, "Is Wales in danger?"'

'Look you now, which of us is telling this tale,' said Huw, with a smile. For a moment they looked at one another in silence and Amy felt her heart beating rapidly. She could hardly bear it and said, 'Go on'

'Of course it wasn't long before all the silver was spent as well and the foolish young man returned to the cavern. This time he took coins from both piles and was unable to pass the bell without setting it ringing more loudly than ever. All the knights woke, picked up their swords and asked, "Is it time?" '

'But Arthur, for that is who their king was, shouted above the clamour of his knights, "The time is not yet. Would you fight for this miserable specimen, who has spoiled our sleep and stolen our coins?" '

'So they took the coins back from the young man and kicked him out of the cave where he lay bruised and cold and penniless in the bog.'

Huw paused briefly, then went on again.

'For many years he told no-one about his adventures but at last he could not resist. Of course his friends in the tavern wanted to know where the entrance to the cavern lay. But when they went with him to that place the hazel tree and the large stone had disappeared. So he received another beating and was left once more, cold, bruised and penniless in the Pumlumon bog.'

When Huw had finished the story Amy sighed and said, 'How true that is. We humans always want more than we have.'

'Yes,' said Huw, 'And sometimes in taking what we want we may wake things before their proper time.'

Amy was puzzled by that and looked up at Huw and saw that he was looking at her. She had not realised how close together they were sitting. The day had become very hot and there was no shelter from the late morning sun. She removed her straw bonnet to readjust her hair and Huw leaned over and touched a strand of her hair to push it away from her brow. Amy would have liked to take that hand and press it to her cheek. But she remembered Philip, looked around and saw that his camera was aimed at them. He was hidden under that black hood from where he shouted, 'Don't move. I want you in the picture to give it scale.' But Huw suddenly got to his feet.

'I can't stand this any longer.'

He began to unbutton his waistcoat. Amy blinked and moved away slightly. What on earth did he mean?

'I am going behind that rock to undress. I cannot stay out of the water any longer.'

Philip put the cover back over the lens and put in another plate. He was not sure whether the exposure had been sufficient to make a proper photograph but if it had it might help him to be rid of Huw once and for all. He had known for some time that while Huw was around he had no hope at all with Amy. But if John saw that photograph...He had been waiting his chance and if only Huw had not leapt up at just that moment. What on earth was he up to now? Philip had thought for a moment that Huw was going to attack him and break the camera, but instead he had gone dashing off behind a rock.

He left his camera set up and was walking towards Amy, still sitting at the water's edge, when he heard a loud splash. Seconds later he saw Huw swimming out towards the centre of the lake.

'Perhaps he will drown,' thought Philip and he stood above Amy and watched the flash of white flesh disturbing the dark water.

Amy said, 'Oh, if only I was a man. I could just take off my clothes and jump in like Huw. It must be so lovely and cool.'

Philip was so stirred by the idea of Amy taking off her clothes that he could not answer for a moment.

'Why don't you join him, Philip?'

'Do you really think I would do that when a woman is present? Anyway, I have never learned to swim.'

'How typical,' thought Amy, then she said out loud. 'Well, at least I can paddle.' She turned away from Phillip, quickly removed her boots and thin stockings, then stepped into the icy water. She gasped. But then pain turned to pleasure as a delicious coolness spread through her limbs. She looked out again at Huw. He had swum back towards them and was standing waist deep in the lake, shaking the water out of his curls. His chest was covered in a thinner mat of that same dark curly hair and water droplets glittered in the sunlight on his wide shoulders. He shouted, 'Come on in, Philip. The water's wonderful.' Then he turned and swam back towards the centre of the lake.

Philip did not reply, but Amy saw him smile before he walked quickly towards the rock behind which Huw had shed his clothes.

'Perhaps, after all, he is going to join him in the lake?' she thought. Anyway with Huw far away and Philip hidden behind that rock she was able to lift her skirts even higher and step a little further into the lake. The water had almost reached her knees when she saw Philip emerge from behind the rock with a pile of clothing in his hand. But he was still fully dressed in that thick jacket and stupid hat so what was he up to? Then she heard him laughing as he ran back to where his camera stood and dumped the pile of clothes on the ground beside it. Now she guessed what he had done and was amazed to discover that he had a sense of mischief.

She heard Huw calling behind her, 'I'm coming out now, Amy. Please turn the other way for a moment.'

So Amy turned and at the same time stepped out of the water. Her feet were beginning to ache with the cold. Huw must be thoroughly chilled. She wondered what he would do when he discovered that his clothes were missing. She didn't have to wait long to find out. She heard him shout, 'You English bastard! Give me back my clothes.' It would seem that now that Philip had discovered his sense of humour Huw had lost his. There was a pause, then Huw dashed out from behind the rock and made his way towards Phillip, growling angrily. Amy turned away to avoid Huw further embarrassment but she had already seen enough to learn what an adult male looked like without his clothes, though the cold water had shrunk his manly parts. She was delighted and disturbed in equal measure.

With the recovery of his clothing Huw's equanimity returned. He covered his lower body with the clump of clothes and laughed as he pointed at Philip's camera.

'I hope you didn't take my picture.'

'Of course not,' said Philip, quickly refixing the lens cover, 'I've used up all the plates.'

Huw went back behind the rock and soon emerged almost fully clothed. He crossed to Philip and held out his hand.

'I'm sorry about what I called you. Please forgive me.'

The men shook hands. Philip folded the tripod and put the camera back in his bag. Then both men joined Amy at the lake's edge.

'That swim has given me an appetite,' said Huw, opening his bag.

Just then they heard voices and saw another group of climbers going on past the lake and on towards the summit. They waved but did not speak. Huw laughed and said, 'Thank goodness they didn't arrive a few minutes earlier.'

'Yes,' said Amy with a grin, 'They might have thought that the monster had come out of the lake.'

There were no more interruptions as the three of them ate and drank. Nan's simple sandwiches were soon consumed. Philip unwrapped the splendid meal the hotel had prepared for him and persuaded the others to share it. He passed a bottle of ale to Huw and opened another for himself while Amy preferred to finish off the tea.

They all lay back on the turf for a while and Amy felt her eyes closing when Huw announced, 'Time to move on. If we are to get to the top.'

Amy sat up reluctantly. Philip remained prone.

'I don't think I'll bother, Huw. This is such a beautiful spot and I've brought a book. I'm not used to all this strenuous exercise. You and Amy go on by yourselves'

Amy was delighted, but did not want to show it.

'Are you sure, Philip? You'll miss the view.'

'Yes, I suppose. But I don't think I could carry my camera right to the top and I can hardly leave it here.'

'You're probably wise,' said Huw, eager to be on his way and alone with Amy. 'The path is steep from now on.'

So Huw picked up his bag, Amy turned away from the men and put on her stocking and boots, then refastened her bonnet and the Welsh man and the English girl set off again. The path was indeed steep. It followed the side of the great cliff and Amy hardly dared to look down at the lake below, but when she did she could see Philip stretched out on his stomach reading, then the path turned away from the edge and he could no longer be seen. Huw was not hurrying ahead this time but climbing more slowly and frequently waiting for her. When the path grew even steeper and the stones shifted under her shoes Huw held out his hand and she took it gladly. When that particular difficulty was past he reluctantly released her hand.

When they reached the top of the cliff the path levelled off and they were walking along a wide ridge, with chunks of exposed quartz glinting among the heather. Suddenly Amy turned back towards the cliff, perhaps to see whether Philip was still lying where they had left him, but when she looked down she almost swooned as she saw how high above the lake they were and how the cliff dropped straight down. She shuddered, stepped back and found herself in Huw's arms. He drew her away from the edge before releasing her.

'Don't worry. I wouldn't let you fall.'

Amy had already forgotten about her moment of fear and was still feeling his arms around her. She wanted them around her again.

The view from up here was magnificent. Mountains, mountains, in every direction, with green valleys between them and far, far below them in one of those valleys she could see that other lake, called Tal-y-llyn, and she thought about Nan busy with her chores and John perhaps feeling well enough to step outside. But that was another life. She felt momentarily giddy with the knowledge that her own life was changing rapidly. She turned to Huw who was standing beside her.

'Is this the summit?' she asked.

'No, we have a way to go yet. Over there.'

They set off again away from the cliffs above the lake and towards the summit. The path once more became steep and rocky and Amy began to feel that she had done enough mountain climbing for one day, but at last Huw pointed to a rise of bare rock just ahead and announced, 'There it is! That's the summit!' Now all Amy's weariness disappeared. She hitched up her skirts and ran off, laughing.

'I'll race you to the top.'

Huw pretended to be tired and let her reach the summit first, but when he joined her she fell into his arms and whispered, 'Huw! Oh Huw!'

Amy did not know how long they embraced, but she knew that she wanted it to last for ever. She wanted to go on pressing herself against this man and feel his heart beating almost as fiercely as her own and sense the warmth of his hands on her back through the thin material of her blouse. After a while he turned her round and put his arms about her waist.

'Look!'

Amy snuggled against his chest, felt his chin in her hair and the heat from his breath. Her eyes were shut but at last she opened them and saw an astonishing view. In front of her the mountain dropped steeply down to another lake and beyond that was a broad valley where a river grew wider and wider until it met the sea. Where river met sea Amy could see a long bridge with a train, like a tiny mechanical toy, puffing its way across the water towards a small town on the other side.

'That's Abermaw,' explained Huw. 'The English call it Barmouth. They like to take holidays there. Perhaps one day we will go there together.'

'I'd like that very much.'

Suddenly she heard a voice somewhere behind them.

'Damn!' said Huw, rapidly removed his arms from around her, stepping back and pretending to be pointing out features in the landscape. Amy was distraught. What had she done? Then she recognised the voice.

'There you are. I thought I'd never catch you up.'

Amy knew that her cheeks were burning. How long had Philip been watching them? What had he seen?

'We were admiring the view,' said Huw, in a voice that was trying to sound calm.

'Yes. Magnificent, isn't it. After you'd gone I thought, well, to come so far and not reach the top. So I hid my camera under some stones and followed you.'

Amy's heart was still thumping. She stepped away to tidy her hair and pick up her bonnet which had fallen into the heather during that embrace. She felt a sudden chill. The sun had gone behind a cloud and a cold breeze swept across the summit. When she looked up again she saw that other clouds were bubbling up over the sea, thickening and darkening minute by minute; the first clouds that had appeared for days.

'Quick!' said Huw. 'We must get down. There's a storm brewing.'

Amy was glad of the urgency which took the edge off her feelings. She was almost afraid of the emotions which had surged through her in Huw's arms. Now she was worried about Philip seeing that embrace and telling John about it. Well at least he hadn't had his camera with him. But in the practical business of getting down the mountain as quickly as they could she temporarily forgot these concerns.

The light dimmed rapidly and the temperature dropped so that soon Amy was glad to put on her warm jacket again. Strangely the descent seemed almost more arduous than the ascent, though it was obviously quicker. She allowed both men to assist her at times as they scrambled down towards Llyn Cau.

'Perhaps,' she thought, 'if I pretend to show an equal interest in Philip he might forget what he had seen.' She felt astonished at her deviousness.

They did not stop to rest at the lake. Philip retrieved his camera and Huw offered to carry the tripod. Perhaps guilt was making him devious too.

By the time they reached the oaks in the gulley it seemed more like night than day and a strong wind had begun to disturb the upper branches. There was a distant grumble of thunder. In the narrow cleft beside the tumbling river the air seemed very warm. Amy's legs were aching now, her feet felt sore and she was sweating inside that jacket, but there was no time to take it off. The men handed her down from boulder to boulder like firemen passing a water bucket but she was too tired to care.

At last they were on the level again. The clouds had hidden the mountains and rolls of thunder echoed round the valley. They ran as fast as their weary legs would allow up the lane towards Tynygraig just as the first drops of rain began to fall.

The Stolen Valley

8

Testing the Sluice

George Owen sat on that rocky outcrop above the dam feeling very sorry for himself. Amy had left him and gone off to Huw's home in western Wales. Huw had said that there would be no room at his house but surely one more person would have made little difference and he would have been quite happy to sleep on the floor if that had been necessary. Amy had given him a brief kiss when she left but it had been no more than a parent pecking the cheek of a child. Now he imagined her climbing that mountain with John, Huw and Philip. He was already aware that Amy favoured Huw and he was inclined to agree with her choice.

He was unsettled at his new home. His grandmother was always asking him to help her move a piece of furniture then almost immediately deciding that it had been better where it was before so he had to help her move it back. While he was staying with Mrs Owen, John was using the room that would eventually be George's so he had not even untied his piles of books. He could not get used to the fact that the new house was just one of a terrace and that he could hear his neighbours arguing and their children running about, screaming in their games. He had always been a rather solitary child and was used to making his own entertainment, which largely consisted of reading, especially about inventions and discoveries or drawing his own inventions with accompanying explanations neatly written at the side. He forced himself occasionally to join in the games going on in the street, but because he was away at school most of the time, he hardly knew the other children and felt that they considered him to be different from them. And in many ways he was. His grasp of Welsh was not yet perfect and his Lancashire accent still slipped through at times.

Something else was bothering him. He had heard his grandmother telling Mr Noble that the legacy she had received from her brother was almost used up and she was not sure how much longer she could afford to keep George at Oswestry School. That would be a disaster because he had done so well in his studies and had expected to go on to one of those new technical colleges where he would learn to be an engineer. He was very grateful to his grandmother for using her inheritance to benefit him, but if he had to leave school now it would be difficult in this district to find any work other than farming which did not interest him at all. He wondered how soon the money would run out and what on earth he would do when it did. Perhaps he should discuss this problem with Amy when she returned or even with Mr Noble though he did not find it easy to talk to that tall stern man.

One advantage of their new house was that it was much nearer to the dam, but work on this had been completed and the workmen were packing up and moving on. George had watched the last stones being laid on the parapet and the few remaining pieces of scaffolding being removed. He had seen the misshapen or unused blocks of stone being loaded onto wagons and the steam cranes being dismantled and taken away to be used elsewhere. Then the engineers and their assistants began carefully inspecting every inch of the finished structure and he had overheard them saying that the sluice gates were to be tested soon, perhaps that very day. There were two of these sluices, through one of which the river would flow and the other was to relieve the strain should the dam become overfull. The mechanism operating the second sluice was not yet complete – a part for the mechanism had been delayed – so the sluice remained closed. But there had been no rain for so long that the river was not much more than a shallow trickle and it would take ages for even the smallest hint of a lake to form.

So he sat disconsolately on his rocky viewpoint and tried to imagine what the lake would look like when the water lapped against the stone work and perhaps even rose so high that it would overflow through those tunnels on the sill and down the other side. His daydreams were disturbed by a voice calling from below.

Testing the Sluice

'Hello there! George isn't it?'

George looked down to see a large, rather portly man, with a dark beard hiding most of his face so that it was difficult to tell whether he was smiling or scowling. But George knew that the man was Doctor Lever, Philip's father and Amy's stepfather's friend, and from their former brief meetings he knew that the man was friendly and interesting, so he slithered down from his rocky perch and shook the man's proffered hand.

George noted that Doctor Lever was overdressed for the hot day and that his broad forehead was covered in sweat which he was busily wiping away with a large white handkerchief. There was something about the man's appearance that made George wonder if he was not particularly well.

Joseph had been pleased to see the boy up on the rock. He too had been feeling out of sorts that morning. The walk from the lodge in the morning heat had exhausted him but he could not bear the thought of remaining in the house and having to discuss country sports. After working so hard to make sure that the dam was built and looking forward to its completion it had been rather an anticlimax to realise that water from the lake would not reach Liverpool for another couple of years.

Joseph was not really missing his son. He and Philip had never had that much in common anyway, and he could not share Philip's increasing interest in art and photography. But he was missing his new friend, John Noble, and also John's beautiful daughter, who had caused feelings to flow through his old man's veins that he had thought extinct many years ago. And there was another thing beginning to concern him. He knew that his health was deteriorating, mainly because he had never bothered to look after himself, but so long as he had work to do this had hardly mattered. His medical practice and his tireless work for a better water supply for his adopted city had occupied him completely. Both of these were coming to an end. What on earth was he going to do with his remaining years?

Now that the dam was finished it was possible to walk along the road across the top, so the old man and his young companion did just that, stopping occasionally to study a detail in its construction or admire the view of the valley which would soon be lost under a lake.

'What do you think of this dam, George?'

'I think it a splendid piece of engineering.'

'And what of its purpose?'

'If it improves the lives of so many then I am pleased that it has been built.'

'Even though your home and your village had to be destroyed?'

'Well there were only a few hundred of us, compared with the many thousands who live in your city. And we have been given new homes. I believe in progress.'

'Then why were you so glum when I saw you sitting up there?'

'Oh that's another matter altogether.'

'Can I help in any way?'

George sighed.

'Ah, I see. A matter of the heart. Someone you love who does not return your love. Am I right?'

George nodded.

'Is it a girl who lives in your village? A neighbour's daughter perhaps? '

George shook his head.

'Well, is it a girl you met when you were away at school?'

George shook his head again. He was not sure about having this conversation at all, but the old man seemed so understanding.

'Well then…let me think…Oh, not you as well?'

'What do you mean?'

'It's the lovely Amy, isn't it? My poor son is besotted with her. So too I would guess is that young Welshman. Even I have fallen a little for her charms.'

George looked astonished.

'You?'

'But the truth is George, that I am too old for her and you are too young. And we must both be sure of that. Otherwise our lives will be full of pain. Amy is not for us George. In fact I suspect that at the moment she is not for any man. She is too full of her own ambitions to have time for love.'

George thought about this.

'Well perhaps when I am older?'

'Possibly? But I suspect that by that time you will have suffered the pangs of love for at least a dozen more young ladies. I know I did at your age and I suspect that you are going to be a handsome rascal and will probably cause a similar amount of heartache in a many a young lady as well.'

George smiled, partly with the thought that he might turn out to be handsome, but also because the old man had made him begin to glimpse for the first time a possible future beyond his infatuation with Amy.

They had reached the other end of the dam. The day had become very hot indeed. Joseph led the way to a stone seat that been erected under the shade of a large tree.

'My advice to you, young man, would be to forget Amy for the present, or any other young woman, and concentrate on achieving your ambitions. What are they, by the way?'

'I want to be an inventor. First I must become an engineer, and study how things are made. Then one day...You see I have these ideas...'

'Such as...?'

'Well, do you see that carriage being pulled by those two horses?'

'D' you mean that big one carrying pieces of timber?'

George nodded and explained, 'Well I think that it would be possible to fix some sort of engine to the front of that carriage which would pull it along instead of the horses.'

'Like a steam locomotive?'

'No I think it will be powered by another sort of fuel and will not need to carry great quantities of coal or water to make it go. In fact the fuel might be some sort of gas. I have read that there have been attempts to make such a vehicle in Germany.'

Joseph did not have the imagination to see such a thing for himself, but he saw the fire of such a vision in George's young eyes.

'And then,' George continued, 'if the machine could be made light enough it might even lift a carriage with wings up into the sky.'

Now that was a step way beyond anything that Joseph could possibly imagine. A flying carriage indeed! He smiled at the thought. George did not notice. Instead his face became glum again as he said, 'But…'

There was a pause.

'But?' asked Joseph.

'No. It isn't fair to lumber you with all my problems. You probably have enough of your own.'

'Possibly? But I know that my problems have no solutions, whereas I might well be able to help you with yours.'

'Very well. When my grandmother's brother died he left her a legacy – not a large one, but enough to send me away to Oswestry School. I have been studying there for the last two years. My teachers have been pleased with my progress. They say that I could go on to a university. But I don't want to do that.'

'Why not'

'Because learning for its own sake does not interest me.'

'So what would you like to do?'

'Well, one day I was talking to one of the engineers building the dam. He told me about this place – actually it is in Liverpool- where you can learn to be an engineer.'

Testing the Sluice

'Ah yes, I believe I have heard of it. So if that is what you want to do, why not do it?'

'Because the money is running out. I heard my grandmother telling John Noble about it. I could not possibly pay the fees and be able to live in Liverpool.'

Just as an idea was beginning to form in Joseph's head his thoughts were interrupted by the clatter of hooves and the screech of iron-rimmed wheels on the road across the dam. A group of important looking men stepped down from a carriage and walked towards one of the stone turrets. They were talking loudly and gesticulating, as if they had just had a good lunch in a Llanfyllin hostelry. They were met at the turret by two other men, less expensively dressed. George recognised one of these as an engineer he had spoken to earlier. The men from the carriage gave some orders and these two opened a door in the turret and went inside.

'What is happening?' asked Joseph.

'I do believe they might be going to test the sluice. The mechanism is down inside the dam. They can only close one of the valves because a piece of the mechanism for the other one has not arrived. Come on! Let's have a closer look.'

George led the way to the centre of the dam. He showed Joseph how there were two outlets for water at the base, one at each end, which joined a little way downstream. Even as they looked one outlet ceased to flow. A great cheer went up among the men at the top, glasses were passed around and a bottle of wine was opened with a pop. The engineers returned from the bowels of the dam and three cheers were raised. Then the party from the carriage was taken to the other side of the dam, where the lake would one day be formed. Already a small muddy pool had formed against the huge wall. There was another cheer and another clinking of glasses before the men returned noisily to the carriage and drove away.

When the dust of their departure had settled Joseph spoke softly.

'Look George. I wonder if we might visit your grandmother's cottage. I am in need of a drink myself and a cool place to rest for a while.'

'Of course,' said George and led the way.

Megan welcomed Joseph into her home, sitting him down in the coolest spot while she fetched a glass of water from the scullery. She had had the same thought as George, that the man did not look too well.

Joseph took the glass and studied the water inside it, before taking a sip, then commenting, 'Such cold, clean water. And soon the people of Liverpool will be sharing it.' He drank again.

'Yes, indeed. It is very good water,' said Mrs Owen, 'We no longer have to draw it from a well. In these new houses the water comes from a tap.'

'I am sorry to impose upon you like this. But the day is so hot and I fear I am not as fit as I was.'

'Any friend of John Noble is a friend of mine. He was very kind to me at one time.'

'I have heard something of that. A terrible, terrible thing!'

Mrs Owen put a finger to her lips and nodded towards George but he was already absorbed in a book.

Joseph understood and changed the subject.

'Are you getting used to your new house?'

'Well, of course it is much smaller and I am still struggling to make everything fit, but usually there will be only me and George living here, and only me when he goes back to school, so it will be quite big enough.'

Joseph returned to the thought that had come to him just before those men had arrived in their carriage on the dam. He spoke to George.

'I wonder, young man, if you would do me a favour.'

He turned back towards Mrs Owen.

'I believe there is a shop in the new village.'

'Oh yes. And very well stocked it is.'

Joseph took some coins from his pocket and handed them to George.

'Would you please get me an ounce of tobacco for my pipe? And spend the change on something for yourself.'

'Of course...And thank you.'

When the boy had left Mrs Owen smiled and said, 'I suspect you have plenty of tobacco in your pouch. So what did you want to say while the boy is gone?'

'Well, I know that I am not talking to a fool, so I will come straight to the point. George tells me that the money for his schooling is running out.'

'How did he know that?'

'Apparently he overheard you telling John.'

'Well, even so, he shouldn't have bothered you with such a thing.'

'He has been worrying dreadfully and it just slipped out. Do you mind if I ask you if it is true?'

'Unfortunately it is.'

'Well I think I might be able to help. You see, I believe the boy has considerable ability and I would not like to see it go to waste. '

'Yes, he is a clever boy. He takes after his poor mother in that respect.'

'Well, I am more than comfortably off. My son is almost independent now. When he has finished his studies I will be handing over my practice to him. Soon I shall be rattling around alone in a large house and wondering what to do with myself.'

'You have no other children?'

'No, my wife died many years ago, giving birth to what would have been our daughter. The child was stillborn.'

'Oh, I am sorry...You never thought to remarry?'

'Never! Yourself?'

'No, I never considered it. I had enough to do looking after George. So what are these thoughts of yours?'

'I would like to help with the cost of George's schooling and when he is ready to take up a place at the technical college he can stay with me during the term times and come back here for the holidays'

Mrs Owen took a handkerchief from her pocket and dabbed at the tears which had sprung to her eyes.

'Oh, that is the kindest thing I have ever heard, Mr…'

'Lever. Joseph Lever.'

At that moment George returned and saw the tears in his grandmother's eyes.

'What on earth is the matter, Gran?'

'Nothing at all is the matter, George. Give Mr…Joseph his tobacco and then sit down here. We have something to discuss.'

To give some credence to his ruse Joseph took out his pipe and filled it with some of the tobacco George had purchased. The boy sat down and watched Joseph light his pipe. Then with a puzzled expression he turned to his grandmother and asked, 'What is it?'

'You should not have bothered Mr Lever with your troubles, George.'

'Yes, I know but…'

'But I have been telling your grandmother that I am more than willing to help out with your schooling.'

'And when you go on to that college in Liverpool you keep telling me about, Mr Lever would let you stay at his house. What do you think of that?'

A grin began to spread across George's face, almost from ear to ear. 'I think that would be wonderful.' Then the grin shrank. 'But what about you Gran? Would you manage without me?'

Mrs Owen laughed. 'Oh, I think I could just about cope. After all you're only a nuisance really.'

Testing the Sluice

George was about to be upset when he realised that his grandmother was only joking. He got up and put his arms around her. Then he turned to Joseph and held out his hand.

'I cannot thank you enough, Sir.'

Joseph shook the hand and said, 'You can thank me best by becoming a successful inventor. I cannot wait to see your flying carriage taking to the sky.'

There was much detail to sort out so Joseph was invited to stay and eat with Megan and George. Much later that evening George accompanied him back to the Hall. As they crossed the dam and took the road past the straining tower they were aware that the sky had clouded over and they heard the distant rumble of thunder.

Joseph was quiet as they walked along. He had begun to see a future for himself again and a reason to take more care of himself. He resolved to begin tomorrow by drinking and smoking less and taking more exercise. The young man striding beside him would be a worthy cause.

When they reached the Hall George said goodnight to Joseph, thanking him again for his kindness, and set off back to the village. As he passed the tower again a sudden flash of lightning split the sky and heavy rain began to fall. George was too excited to care. He ran through the deep puddles that quickly formed on the half-finished road. When he reached the dam he looked down just as another flicker of lightning lit up the scene and saw that the pool in front of the closed sluice was growing rapidly and was pleased that the sluice gate was to have a proper test.

As he stood looking down into the blackness in front of the dam he realised that this storm was coming from the west and he thought of Amy for the first time in many hours, but already his heartache had eased a little.

'If this rain continues through the night,' he thought, 'we shall have the beginnings of a little lake by morning.'

The Stolen Valley

9

Return Journey

Philip had not slept well. It had been impossible for him to ride back to Dolgellau in such a storm, so his horse had been put in the pony's stable for the night. Huw had courteously given up his bed to the visitor and joined his father in the marriage bed, but still Philip had spent a fitful night. The storm had not helped, with thunder crashing round the hills in a way that you never heard in the city and a gale of such force that he expected the slates to be ripped from the roof at any moment. Partly it was the bed which was too short for his long limbs and very hard, then there was Gwyn's snoring, which rumbled through the house, almost equalling the thunder at times, but mostly it was the proximity of Amy in the very next room. Philip was more or less certain of what he had seen on the summit of Cadair Idris and he knew that he must find a way to drive a wedge between her and Huw before it was too late.

Well at least they would be leaving this ghastly place in the morning and without Huw, thank God. John was almost recovered. He had greeted them warmly when they returned from the mountain and wanted to hear every detail of the climb. He had sat with them to share the strange tasting greasy stew that Nan had prepared and he ate with the gusto of someone whose appetite had suddenly returned. Philip had not eaten much at all. The meal did not suit his finicky digestion, and he still mistrusted Nan's use of local ingredients. In fact he was suspicious of the girl altogether. There was something about her dark looks and her unfortunate impediment that disturbed him. He would not have been surprised to discover that she kept a black cat. And the girl was obviously equally disturbed by him. She still blushed and lowered her eyes whenever she caught his gaze.

The Stolen Valley

When morning came at last the rain had thinned to a light warm drizzle oozing from a grey blanket of low cloud but the air crackled with a tension that presaged further storms. After they had breakfasted Huw set off for the quarry and Philip felt relief flood through him as his rival strode away. Huw and Amy had said goodbye in such a formal manner that Philip wondered if he had misinterpreted that scene on the summit. Then he heard Nan mutter something, pick up a Huw's canvas bag and point to her brother's disappearing figure. Amy took the bag at once and hurried after Huw. Apparently he had left behind the food his sister had prepared for him. Philip could not help but notice the way Nan smiled as Amy rushed away, but when she saw Philip watching her she quickly turned away.

'Ah well,' said John, who had also observed the little scene, 'It will give her a chance to thank him again. He has been very kind.'

After a while Amy returned and she and Nan went off grinning to attend to the stock. Philip paced about for a while, looking towards the girls who were just making their way from hens to sheep, then saddled his horse, carefully loaded the camera and tripod and set off for Dolgellau.

'We'll meet again at the station,' called John, admiring the way the young man sat his horse, and wondering why his daughter seemed to prefer the far less polished young Welshman. He was listening to the hooves of Philip's mount as horse and rider disappeared into the low cloud when he heard other hooves and the rumble of wheels on the metalled road. Gwyn came out of the house, heard the same sound, called to Nan in Welsh and both girls hurried back to the house.

While the luggage was loaded onto the carriage each in turn said farewell to Nan. Gwyn gave his daughter a brief hug, John shook her hand and Amy embraced her warmly. The Welsh girl's dark eyes were filled with tears as she watched them leave.

'Poor Nan,' said Amy as they drove away. 'She must get so lonely'

'Well, she will have her brother for one day more.'

'Oh yes,' Amy replied, smiling briefly, then suddenly she felt quite forlorn.

The journey back to the Vyrnwy valley was not to be as simple as they had hoped. When they reached Dolgellau station they were informed that the train from Abermaw would not be arriving as a flash flood had washed away the ballast under the rails near Arthog and the line had become unsafe. Now they must wait for a train to arrive from Llanwchllyn and that would not be for a couple of hours at least, so they all sat under the station canopy while the rain descended heavily again. It seemed that after so many weeks of drought the weather god was determined to make up for lost time.

John wondered if this weather had reached Shropshire yet and, if so, had the harvest been safely gathered in. He remembered the dreadful harvests of his early days back in Hope Underhill, when everlasting wind and rain had knocked down the crops and caused the tumbled grain to rot. Thinking of that time reminded him of his first meeting with Ella: for a moment he almost missed her and their little son. As if she had read his mind Amy asked, 'Have you decided when we might be going home, John?'

'I thought perhaps at the end of this week. Would that suit you?'

It wouldn't, but she could hardly say so. She heard the heavy rain hissing into the ballast and watched it bouncing off the shining rails and thought about her parting from Huw.

He had taken a path across the fields that met the road to the quarry higher up. Amy ran after him across the field, lifting her skirts out of the damp grass, nimbly climbing a stile and following the path around a rocky outcrop, which leaned like a huge buttress against the base of the mountain. There he stood waiting, firm and solid as the rock itself. As she ran towards him he had opened his arms and crushed her against him. She twined her arms about his neck and lifted her face until their lips met. She could have stayed there forever, feeling his hard body pressed against hers, the moisture of their lips mixing, their hearts thumping in unison, but suddenly he had broken away from her and gasped.

'You must go back now,' he said, 'before they suspect. I will see you in Llanwddyn tomorrow evening.'

He took a few hurried steps away, then turned grinning and touched the bag he had shifted onto his shoulder.

'That was a clever idea of Nan's.'

It was hard to watch him go, but they must not arouse John's suspicions and the parting would only be for a day and a half. How things would progress beyond that she neither knew nor cared. But now, as she stood on the platform the large clock over her head seemed to have slowed and the first hours of those days had become interminable.

When Philip appeared at the station, clean shaven and neatly dressed, she had risen from the bench and left her step-father's side, explaining that she had become tired of sitting. Now she glanced back and saw that he and John were deep in conversation, although the younger man seemed to be glancing towards her from time to time. She became worried that he might be telling her step-father about the scene on the summit. But surely he had been too far away to really know what had happened. And John's face showed no sign of his being upset.

She looked further along the platform and saw Gwyn chatting away to a porter, but then a whistle sounded and she turned to see a locomotive appear from the east, shrouded in smoke and steam as the brakes were applied. Soon they were all aboard and the engine began to labour back up the line towards Llanwchllyn.

Gwyn sat away from the others, to smoke his pipe. Perhaps he thought the smoke might bother them or perhaps he felt awkward in not being able to communicate. Amy and John had again taken the window seats. Philip had chosen to sit next to John and their conversation continued as if they were the oldest of friends. But Amy was aware that Philip was still watching her surreptitiously so she turned to look out of the window. Once again they were travelling through that narrow gap cut into the thick woodland on the lower slopes of the hills but now it seemed like a dark tunnel. The rain had stopped and the black background of crowded trees turned the window into a mirror in which Amy saw the pale reflection of her face. Behind her she could see Philip watching as ever and she shivered a little, then forced herself to look beyond the mirror image at the scene outside. As her eyes adjusted to the gloom she became aware that the gentle trickle of water running beside the rails that had accompanied their outward journey was now a foaming torrent, tumbling over spray saturated boulders in its haste to get to the sea.

Thoughts and feelings began to tumble inside her like that rushing water beside the line. She was no longer the sensible, clear thinking girl who had set out to help Megan with her move. Where had she gone, that girl who calmly discussed politics and scientific theories with her stepfather, and planned her future life in logical steps? Now she was simply a mess of emotions. All she wanted was to be with Huw again, her body pressed against his, her lips moistened by his, her heart banging almost painfully in her breast. Was that love? She thought it must be, but what was to become of that love. In less than a week she and Huw would be miles apart and it was most unlikely that their paths would ever cross again. She did not know how she could begin to tell her parents what she was feeling. And if she did manage to tell them there was little chance that they would allow the relationship to continue. Just over a week ago she too had her future planned. It probably did not match the future her parents had planned for her but it had certainly not included the way she felt now.

'Oh, Huw! Huw!' she whispered to herself.

'What's that, my dear?' asked John.

'I was saying how slowly the train is going,' she said, avoiding Philip's gaze.

It was true. The train was moving at less than walking pace, each joint in the rails jolting the carriage as the wheels passed slowly over it. The rain had begun again, a strong wind spattering it against the window where it ran down the glass in crazy rivulets.

'Well, if it still raining like this when we get to Llanwchllyn we certainly cannot cross the mountains in that cart of Gwyn's,' said Philip. 'We must hire a carriage.'

'What,' Amy exploded, 'And leave poor Gwyn to make the journey alone. After he has been so kind?'

'Well,' said John, ever the pragmatist, 'Let us wait and see.'

Suddenly the train eased forward again and they saw workmen sawing up the branches of a tree which had partly fallen across the line. In the gloom the new cut wood looked golden. One of the men raised an axe and brought it down on one of the smaller branches. His strength and the skill with which he handled the axe reminded Amy of Huw and she felt blood flowing into her cheeks.

John looked across at his step-daughter and smiled.

'I must say, my dear, the Welsh air seems to have done you good. You are positively glowing. Philip was just saying how fine you look.'

'Was he?' replied Amy.

'In fact he has a proposition to put to you.'

'Oh, no,' thought Amy, panicking, 'He's going to propose!'

John continued, 'He and Joseph will also be leaving Llanwddyn at the end of the week and returning to Liverpool. He would like to invite you to go with them and see that city for yourself.'

Well it wasn't a proposal of marriage. But almost as bad.

'And I thought,' said John, 'that as you have several weeks of your vacation left and I know how much you like to visit new places...'

'Of course I must ask my father, but I'm sure he will agree. Our house is quite large,' added Philip. 'You would be very comfortable there. We have several servants. And I could show you all the splendid buildings in our city. And the many fine works of art.'

'Yes,' she thought. 'You could show me your grand house and fine manners and ogle me to your heart's content.'

She had no intention of accepting the invitation but now was not the time to speak her mind. It would only upset John who was obviously impressed with Philip, so she said simply, 'That's very kind.'

'There we are then,' said John, as if the matter was settled.

When they left the train at Llanwchllyn the rain had ceased and the thinning clouds revealed small patches of blue but the atmosphere was still very humid. John, Phillip and Amy left their luggage at the station, except for Philip's camera which he insisted on carrying with him, and lunched at a local hostelry while Gwyn fetched the pony and cart from his friend's stable. When he returned Amy noted that Gwyn had fixed the tarpaulin more firmly on the poles, so that they could shelter under it if the rain returned. Philip was scathing about this inadequate roofing and still thought that they should have hired a carriage for their journey across the mountains, but when John joined Gwyn on the driver's seat – preferring to travel that way- and he saw that he would be sharing the rest of the cart alone with Amy, he was soon persuaded to get in. The luggage was safely stowed under a canvas sheet fixed firmly to the cart.

So their journey began and for the moment everything was fine. The pony was rested and pulled well up the gentle incline out of the village. There were even short bursts of sunlight as they climbed past the farmsteads and cottages that clung to the mountainside. In one of the small fields a middle aged man and a boy, probably father and son, were lifting sheaves back into stooks, after they had been blown down in last night's storm. The boy reminded Amy of George, with his round cheeks and dark curls. She had become aware during the last week that George's feelings for her were no longer those of an innocent child and that she would probably have to be cruel to him to be kind.

'Poor George,' she thought. 'He thinks I am so wonderful. He follows me about like a faithful dog. If only he knew what I am really like.' But she still enjoyed his company because of his lively interest in everything. When she snapped out of her reverie she realised that Philip was talking to her.

'St George's Hall is particularly fine and there are many masterpieces in the Walker Art Gallery nearby.'

'But I thought your father said that there was a great deal of poverty in Liverpool.'

'Well, of course in any large city...'

'What about the docks? I would love to visit those. It must be exciting. All those ships coming in from foreign parts and setting off for places far away.'

'Well, of course, we could visit those if you wished. But the docks are not really the place for a woman.'

'There must be women among the passengers.'

'Yes, but most of them are poor immigrants from Ireland or refugees making their way to America.'

'I want to travel when I am a little older.'

'But I thought you wanted to teach.'

'Oh, I don't want to do that for ever.'

'No, I suppose you would like to marry eventually and have...'

The thought of Amy's firm young flesh swollen in pregnancy and his medical knowledge of the way such pregnancy was caused made him blush. He turned away, as if to admire the view.

'There are many things I want to do before I settle down like that.'

'I see,' said Philip, with a sigh.

At last the long slow climb brought them out of the valley and they could see their road winding ahead across the bleak plateau. Heavy clouds had gathered again in the west and were sweeping inland. Gwyn saw the change in the weather and clicked his tongue to urge the pony forward, but the animal was tired from the long climb and only slightly increased its pace. Soon the clouds began to engulf them, the sun was obscured and the air grew cooler. Amy wrapped a shawl around her shoulders and Philip buttoned up his jacket, saying, 'We should have hired a carriage as I suggested.'

'We'll be fine, so long as the rain doesn't get any heavier.'

But at that very moment the wind rose again and drove the rain into her side of the cart. Instinctively Amy moved to the other side closer to Philip. He gallantly removed his heavy jacket and put it over both their shoulders. Amy's gratitude overcame her repugnance and she was content to stay in that position.

'I knew this was a mistake. If we get another storm while we are up here...'

They reached that fork in the roads, turned left and began to cross the exposed mountain top. Last night's storm had laid the dust on the road and the ditches on either side were full. When they had crossed this mountain a few days ago the only sound had been wind among the dry grasses, now Amy could hear water running everywhere. The clouds thickened and swept across the mountain top so that it was only possible to see the road immediately ahead. Raindrops began to drum on the tarpaulin above them and a strengthening wind sent flurries into their faces.

'This is most unwise. We have no waterproof clothing. And your father is still recovering...'

Amy wanted to tell Philip to shut up but in fact she was beginning to think that he was right. She saw how exposed her stepfather was on the seat beside Gwyn but the Welshman suddenly surprised them by bringing out an oilcloth from under the seat and wrapping in around them both. John smiled and turned to his stepdaughter.

'How are you back there?'

She tried to smile reassuringly but was actually feeling rather alarmed. The road ahead, hardly visible now, began to descend quite steeply. The pony increased its speed, splashing though the deepening puddles and sending spray from the wheels high into the air. Suddenly a flicker of lightning split the clouds above them and a great crash of thunder followed almost immediately. The terrified pony leapt forward down the hill, dragging the cart in a mad career behind it. Gwyn shouted and pulled hard on the reins but another flash of lightning sent the pony into a frenzy. Philip pushed Amy down onto the floor and held her tight with one arm while the other held onto the side of the cart. Amy was far too terrified to care about their proximity. She did not even care what part of the man she was holding onto as long as she could avoid being thrown from the cart.

The cart bucked and swayed but kept to the road until they came to a sharp bend where its weight dragged the front wheel on Gwyn's side into the ditch and dashed it against a boulder. There was a loud crack as the wheel collapsed, the cart swung over and Gwyn was flung off into the heather. The sudden stopping of the cart and the terrified strength of the pony caused the harness to break and the pony went plunging on down the hill.

Incredibly the other occupants of the cart had managed to remain on board. John not being hampered by holding any reins had clung to the front boards. The weight of Philip's body had held Amy safely on the floor, where she lay battered and trembling. The tarpaulin roof had blown off and the rain came down on her unhindered. She became aware that her legs were cold and wet and when she looked down she saw that her skirts had risen to her hips and that Philip lay unmoving across her revealed underwear. She sat up and tried to push down her skirts. Philip did not stir.

'Are you all right, Philip?' she asked.

He groaned, opened his eyes and saw Amy's body beneath him. For a moment he wanted to stay like that, pressed close, with her lovely face pale and wet in the crook of his arm, but then politeness overcame the pleasure of their compromising position and he rolled to the side of the cart, pulling down Amy's skirts as he went. She realised that he had probably saved her from serious injury and for a moment she was so overcome with gratitude that she could have kissed him.

John clung to the sloping seat, looking at the broken cart, feeling the rain soaking through his clothes – the oilcloth Gwyn had wrapped around them had been blown away- and seeing nothing but the thick clouds sweeping past.

'Oh, my God! Are you all right, Amy?'

He glanced back and was relieved to see that his stepdaughter was apparently unharmed, then he called out, 'Gwyn! Gwyn!

A faint voice called in Welsh from somewhere in the clouds and although none of them could understand the words, they knew that the speaker was in pain. Philip got down from the cart, leaving his jacket around Amy's shoulders. He and John followed the Welshman's cries until they found him lying in the heather, with his leg twisted awkwardly beneath him. He moaned again and pointed to his leg. Philip guessed that it was broken, but quickly used his medical knowledge to confirm the fact. He turned to John and spoke angrily.

'I knew something like this would happen. We should never have trusted these Welshmen and their stupid cart. You and Amy could have been killed. Now here we are stuck on top of this damned mountain in a storm and no shelter for miles. That son of his should not be trusted either. When we were on the mountain I saw...'

Amy had joined them. Her recent warmer feelings for Philip cooled instantly when she heard his words. She burst out.

'There's no time for that now, Philip. We have to find some sort of shelter and make Gwyn comfortable as soon as possible. Then one of us must go and find help.'

'You're right of course, my dear,' said John. 'Perhaps Philip and I could carry Gwyn to the cart. If we could find that oilcloth we could lay it on the ground and get under the cart. At least then, we would be out of this awful rain.'

'Very well. And I do have something in my bag that might help with the pain. Do you think you could find my medical bag, Amy, while we deal with Gwyn?'

She nodded and went back to the cart. Philip found the oilcloth on the road a few yards behind them. He laid it on the ground under the cart, then he and John lifted the Welshman between them and carried him across to the cart, crying out with every painful step. They laid him as gently as possible on the ground and pulled him under the cart, out of the rain. Amy handed the medical bag to Philip. He took out a small bottle.

'Now, we must find some suitable wood for splints. I wonder if Gwyn has a sharp knife on him.'

John and Amy looked at him with alarm.

'It's all right. I'm not going to operate on him. But if I could cut some pieces of leather from the harness, they would hold the splints in place.'

They found a well-used pen-knife in Gwyn's jacket pocket. Philip cut several short pieces of leather from the harness. John brought two spokes from the shattered cart wheel.

Amy watched, fascinated, as Philip unstoppered the small bottle, poured some of its contents onto a piece of cloth and pressed that to Gwyn's face. He struggled briefly then became unconscious.

'Now...' said Philip. 'I want you both to support him while I straighten this leg...'

Amy and John each held an arm while Philip pulled at the leg until the broken bone snapped back into place; then he applied the splint. She noticed that Philip's forehead was covered in sweat and realised how difficult it must be for him, as a tall man, to work in such cramped conditions under the cart. Her admiration for his skill had made her forget his recent threat to expose Huw. For a moment she felt almost angry with Huw for allowing them to get into this situation.

The wind had died down and the rain eased a little but suddenly Amy began to shiver and tears sprang into her eyes. Her stepfather took her in his arms. For a moment she seemed like his little girl again.

'Philip explained, 'You're suffering from shock. We must bring your luggage under here and find you some warmer clothing.'

He struggled out from under the cart and soon returned with her suitcase. He opened it and was about to search for something suitable when Amy grabbed it from him, saying, 'I'll do that.'

She found a dry shawl and a thicker jacket. She handed Philip his own jacket, then said, 'We ought to bring all our cases under here, before the rain soaks through. Perhaps we could find something to put under Gwyn's head?'

Philip went out again and brought back the rest of the luggage, including his camera which he was relieved to find had survived the crash. He changed into a dry jacket and carefully pushed the damp one under Gwyn's head. The Welshman stirred, then slept again.

'Now I must be on my way,' said Philip. It's a few miles to the Hall but I'll walk as quickly as I can and bring my father back in one of their carriages to deal with Gwyn.'

Amy was surprised and pleased at the complete change in Philip. Even his lazy drawl had gone as he stated his plans.

'You seem to have managed pretty well without his help,' she said.

'Well, I have almost completed my studies...' he replied with unusual modesty. He brought out another container from his medical bag and handed it to Amy.

'When Gwyn wakes up he will feel the pain. Give him some of this brandy. And perhaps you should take a sip yourself. To keep out the cold.'

He got out from under the cart and stood up.

'No time to waste!' he said and strode off down the road.

Watching him go Amy realised that most of her animosity towards him had faded. Then she remembered Huw's arms around her that morning and his lips pressed to hers. She remembered the warm surge that had filled her body in his embrace. Yes, Philip could be admired for his medical skill and the way he had behaved in this emergency but he did not have that physical effect on her.

Gwyn woke almost before Philip was out of sight. He cried out with the pain. Amy moved away from John and took the top off the flask. She asked her stepfather to lift Gwyn's head, then put the flask to his lips. She thought how like Huw's lips they were, so similar in shape though less full. The Welshman swallowed, almost choked, then closed his eyes, as John lowered his head down onto the makeshift pillow.

'I think you should take a little of the brandy yourself, my dear,' said John, 'as Philip suggested.'

Amy held the flask to her lips and swallowed. She had never drunk brandy before and the harsh taste of the liquid shocked her. It was like drinking flames, but soon she felt a welcome warmth spreading through her limbs.

'Such a fine young man. Thank goodness he was with us. I do not know how we would have managed without him…'

'Yes.'

'Of course I don't want to lose you yet, but one day…'

'One day, perhaps.'

'What did he mean about not trusting young Huw?'

'I don't know. I'm sure it wasn't important.'

'No, you're probably right.'

Through the long afternoon and into the evening they kept their vigil beside Gwyn. He was awake now most of the time. Sometimes his face would crease up with pain and they gave him more sips of the brandy. But when the pain eased he smiled at them and began to sing something in Welsh, quietly but in perfect tune.

'Holl amrantau'r ser ddywedant,

Ar hy dy nos.'

Dyma'r ffordd i fro gogoniant,

Ar hy dy nos'

Of course neither John nor Amy had the faintest idea what the song was about, but it seemed somehow appropriate and comforting.

The low clouds swept by and there were several short, sharp showers. Again Amy heard water running everywhere, as if the earth had become totally saturated. John began to feel weary and maudlin.

'I should never have brought you to Wales. Look at you. Lying under an old cart on top of a mountain. And it might have been worse. You might have been thrown out and injured like Gwyn. Or worse! What on earth will your mother say?'

'She will say that it was my decision. And no real harm has come of it. In fact I have had a splendid time. I really liked Tynygraig and dear Nan and climbing that mountain was wonderful. I wouldn't have missed that for anything.'

Amy looked at her stepfather and thought that he had suddenly aged. She had always looked up to him, measured other men against him. She had always been proud to be seen with him, to take his arm and walk beside him, admiring his stern handsome face and listening to his liberated ideas. But after this last bout of that disease and their calamitous journey he seemed somehow shrunken, his shoulders drooping, his hair more grey, his face pale and lined. She thought of Huw's youthful strength and the glitter of his dark eyes and knew that she too had changed considerably during the last few days.

In all the hours they lay waiting nothing else passed along the road, but at last they heard hooves and the rumble of wheels and the carriage arrived. Amy was pleased to hear Joseph's voice, with its energy and warmth. He and Philip had brought a stretcher which they pushed under the cart, carefully eased Gwyn onto it, and carried him to the carriage, where they laid the stretcher on the floor. Then Joseph brought two large warm capes from the carriage. He gave one to John and wrapped the other around Amy's shoulders, giving her a paternal hug. Meanwhile Philip and the driver had lifted the luggage onto the roof of the carriage, secured and covered it, before pushing the cart to the side of the road. Then they all squeezed into the carriage, carefully avoiding the injured Welshman, who seemed to be sleeping again, and went on their way. Amy suddenly remembered the pony, but Joseph told her not to worry, he would ask his friends at the Hall to send someone to fix a new wheel on the cart and search for the pony next day.

Squashed between John and Joseph in the sudden warmth of the carriage and inside that thick cape Amy soon fell asleep. When she woke again she heard Philip's voice.

'I stayed to take some photographs, so Amy went on up the last part with Huw. I know now that I was wrong. I should have gone with them. Then it would not have happened...'

Suddenly Philip saw that Amy was awake and looking straight at him. He paused.

'What wouldn't have happened?' asked John in an anxious tone.

'Well...'

Philip was finding it hard to continue, with those green eyes glaring at him, but having begun he had to go on.

'I saw them high up on that cliff above the lake. Huw seemed to take her right to the edge. She could have fallen to her death at any moment.'

Amy's look of contempt made him almost squirm. He tried to smile, as if to say, 'You see, I didn't betray you.'

Amy wondered what he might have said if she had not woken at that moment. She pulled herself upright.

'Actually it wasn't Huw's fault at all. I stupidly wandered from the path and suddenly found myself right on the edge of the cliff. He pulled me back just in time.'

Philip looked embarrassed and said, 'Well of course I was some distance away.'

There was moment of quiet, then Joseph said, 'It seems to me that this wild Wales is a dangerous place.'

'Perhaps,' said Amy, staring defiantly at Philip, 'but quite wonderful too.'

As the carriage made the last part of the descent down the narrow gorge into the Vyrnwy valley Amy thought she could hear a low continuous thunder rumbling towards them again, but when she looked out of the window into the gathering dusk she saw the cause of that sound. The stream where they had begun their journey out of the valley a few days ago was now a savage beast, rushing in great white gouts from boulder to boulder, and beating against the pillars of the new bridge. Huw was right about the Welsh rain. If all the streams flowed into the valley with this force, and those valves George had told her about were closed, the lake would soon begin to fill.

When they reached Vyrnwy Hall Gwyn was carried into one of the servant's rooms and put to bed. Joseph checked his leg and congratulated his son on the splints he had made in such difficult circumstances.

'You'll make a fine doctor yet, my boy.'

But Philip was still smarting from Amy's look of scorn. He cursed his stupidity at trying to tell John about the scene on the mountain top. He knew that he had risen in Amy's opinion during that dreadful journey. Then he had ruined it all. Oh well, at least his camera had survived the journey so his trump card remained intact.

After a welcome supper at the Hall, John and Amy got into the carriage for the last few miles of their journey back to Llanwddyn. At last the rain had stopped and when the clouds parted a bright moon shone down on the valley. It was John who had dozed off this time, when Amy woke him and pointed out of the carriage window.

'Look!'

He opened his bleary eyes and followed her gaze. They were just passing the straining tower which in the moonlight looked even more like a fairy-tale castle. But then he realised what it was that had caused Amy's excitement. Between the tower and the dark mass of the dam lay a great stretch of shimmering water.

The Stolen Valley

10

Betrayal

Just the faintest glimmer of daylight forced its way through the thick curtains so that Amy had no idea what time it was. She had woken feeling uncomfortable and out of sorts and wondered whether her monthly period was due but a quick calculation determined that this was a while away yet. Then she remembered yesterday's dreadful journey and knew why her limbs ached and why she wanted to drop back into the forgetfulness of sleep. But a sudden burst of sneezing kept her awake and she wondered if she had caught a cold, which was very possible after her drenching on the mountain top. When she had woken3 she had heard the wind driven rain rattling against the windows but now it seemed to have stopped. Soon she would have to get up but for the moment she snuggled back down in her warm bed.

There was no sound from the rest of the house. Mrs Evans had probably gone out. Amy felt a slight flicker of guilt about lying in bed while the rest of the world went about its business, but not everyone had been soaked to the skin, thrown dangerously about a cart, lain under that same cart for hours on a wet road, listening to Gwyn's moans of pain, while they waited to be rescued. Yes, she decided, she had earned a lie in. If her stepfather had any sense, he would be doing the same.

They had arrived late last night and after a warm drink in Mrs Owen's house Amy had gone next door, washed her face, brushed her hair, dropped into her bed and slept soundly. She vaguely remembered George telling her that he had some important news but she had told him that it must wait until the morning. Now she wondered what his news might be. But whatever it was he had seemed mightily pleased about it.

She thought for a moment about Philip. He had shown unexpected skill and determination in yesterday's emergency, but had spoiled everything by giving his biased version of events on the mountain to John. Amy had made sure that her stepfather had been given another version, though that had been equally biased and did not mention how gladly she had fallen back into Huw's arms or the emotional turmoil that his embrace had sent flooding through her. Philip had not mentioned their renewed embrace on the summit, so perhaps he had not seen it or had not understood what was really happening. No, she thought with relief, I think that crisis has passed.

But remembering Huw's body close to hers sent thrilling signals through her limbs. She explored her own body as if he was with her now and wondered what would happen if he was. She knew that he had made her aware of her body in a way she had never been before. On the one hand she was happy to surrender to these new feelings but on the other she felt as if she was moving towards the edge of a precipice just as dangerous as the one above that lake. She longed for this dreary day to pass so that she could be with him again. She worried that if she had caught a cold he might be put off by her sneezes, but these seem to have stopped. She thought about the moment of farewell they had shared yesterday morning, when he had almost squeezed the life out of her with his fierce clasp. Her body began to writhe almost of its own accord and a fine flush had come to her cheeks when there was a sudden knock on the door.

George had been awake for hours. He had been too excited to eat his breakfast and wanted to rush off to see Amy and tell her about Joseph's plan. But his grandmother insisted that Amy should be allowed to rest after yesterday's ordeal and that he must not waste the bacon she had placed before him. So George grimly chewed the thick salty rashers, dipped the bread in his tea and tried to be patient. He had developed a new attitude to Amy, based on Joseph's advice. She would no longer be an idol on a pedestal to be worshipped but an old friend with whom he could share ideas while they enjoyed a healthy jaunt together. It had been easy to adopt this new attitude last night when Amy had returned, looking quite ordinary, her eyes dulled by weariness, her hair draggled and tangled, her face and dress smudged with mud, and he was determined to maintain his new attitude when he saw her again today.

At last his breakfast was finished. He had dressed carefully that morning and checked that his hair was neat. Joseph's comments about his good looks had surprised him but now when he squared his shoulders and looked in the mirror over the mantelpiece, he decided that perhaps there was some truth in the old man's words. He realised now that, at fifteen, he was too young for Amy, but there would be others soon, more suitable and perhaps even more beautiful. He was momentarily shocked by this almost sacrilegious, rather thrilling idea, but he was still keen to share his good news with her.

'Don't go disturbing the poor girl yet,' said Mrs Owen.

'Of course not, Gran'

It was raining again as he hurried next door. There had been brief periods of sunshine between heavy showers all morning. There was no answer when he knocked on the door but he remembered that Mrs Evans was rather deaf. The door was unlocked so George walked in and looked around the downstairs rooms. They were empty. The widow must have gone out. He waited for a while in the kitchen to make sure she had not gone to the privy, then began to climb the stairs. There were only two bedrooms. The door of the larger one was open and there was no-one inside, so he knocked on the door of the other room.

'Just a moment', said a voice, obviously Amy's, but with a strangely husky tone, then after a longish pause, 'Come in.'

The room was rather dark, but he could just make out Amy sitting up in bed.

'Oh, it's you, George. I thought it was Mrs Evans come to scold me for staying in bed so late. Would you open the curtains for me, please?'

George did so and the soft light of the grey day fell on Amy's face. Her eyes had regained their brightness, her cheeks glowed rosily, her hair tumbled in golden strands over her breasts that were visibly rising and falling under her thin nightgown. All George's resolutions crumbled: he could have knelt there on the rag rug and made obeisance.

Amy smiled and indicated that he should sit on the bed.

'Tell me about your news.'

Being so close to Amy had made him almost forget what it was, then his pleasure at the thought of it returned and he burst out.

'Doctor Lever has promised to pay for the rest of my schooling and when I go to study engineering I am to live with him in Liverpool.'

'Well, that is wonderful news, George. Have you told John?'

'No. I didn't want to disturb him last night and he has gone out now.'

'Oh, where did he go?'

'A carriage came from the Hall. There was a note from Joseph. He left as soon as he had finished his breakfast.'

Amy was puzzled, then worried. Perhaps Philip was going to tell John something else about that climb. And she would not have the chance to put her own side of the story. But it was not fair of her to lessen George's pleasure with her own worries.

'Do you think you will be happy in Liverpool?'

'Of course! Though I do worry a little about leaving my grandmother.

'I am sure she will be pleased for you.'

'Now it's your turn. What was it like?'

'What was what like?'

'Your visit to Huw's home. The mountain. Everything!'

Amy looked at his dark eyes, bright with curiosity and smiled.

'Huw lives in this deep valley, near a lake called Tal-y-llyn. His house is built almost into the foot of a mountain. He has a sister called Nan, who is pretty and kind but not able to speak.'

George was puzzled, 'She can't speak English you mean, like Gwyn?'

'No. She cannot speak at all. It is how she was born. She can only make strange sounds and yet you always know what she means.'

While George thought about this Amy went on.

'They have a cow, two pigs, a few sheep and lots of hens. Nan looks after the animals and keeps the house clean and tidy while Huw and Gwyn are away.'

'Where is Huw now?' asked George.

'He is visiting some friends at the quarry where he and Gwyn used to work. I think they are hoping to work there again now that they have almost finished here. He will be back at their camp this evening.'

'And the mountain? What was that like?'

'Very high and very steep in places. It is called Cadair Idris, which means the chair of Idris. Idris was a giant. Half way up there is a mysterious lake.'

In her mind's eye she saw the lake again and Huw standing there, shaking off the freezing water. Then he was running towards Philip and showing the whole of his trim, strong body. A warm glow suffused her body. She hurried on.

'And when we got to the summit the view was amazing. You could see mountain after mountain and other lakes and even the sea. But then we had to hurry down again because a storm was coming.'

'Tell me more about Nan,' said George, but before she could begin the door opened and Mrs Evans stood gaping at what she saw.

'You naughty boy,' she shouted. 'Leave this room at once. How dare you come into a young lady's bedroom and sit on her bed. And you, Miss, I'm surprised you allowed it. I don't know what Mrs Owen will say when I tell her.'

'Don't worry Mrs Evans. George and I have been friends since we were both children. He was just telling me some very good news.'

As she spoke she gestured to George to leave and he quickly understood. Then Amy changed the subject to distract the formidable widow.

'I'm sorry I'm so late in bed. The journey tired me so. I'll get up now. Is it raining still?'

'No, it stopped as I was coming from the shop. I'll leave you to get dressed while I brew some tea.'

'Thank you. George meant no harm. He's just a boy. Surely his Grandmother does not need to know.'

'Hmm. Well, I suppose...'

And with that grudging acceptance Mrs Evans left the room.

When the carriage dropped John at Vyrnwy Hall his first surprise was to find that Gwyn had gone. Joseph explained.

'When I went to check his leg this morning he started gabbling on in Welsh, so I fetched one of the servants to interpret. Apparently he was demanding to be taken to their camp so that he would be there when Huw returned so I wrapped some thick cloth around his leg and found more comfortable splints. We gave him some food and off he went with the men who are to mend the cart and find the pony. I hope the animal hasn't come to any harm.'

'So do I,' said John. 'It will not be easy for them to buy another pony or a cart. But you did not ask me to come here so early to tell me about Gwyn.'

'No'

John saw that Joseph's face was unusually sombre, but that Philip seemed rather pleased with himself as he spoke.

'I couldn't get to sleep last night, after all the day's adventures, so I developed negatives from the plates I took on Cadair Idris. This morning I made some positive prints onto prepared paper when the sun shone briefly. I thought you would like to see them. This way.'

John was puzzled. Surely he had not been called so urgently to the Hall simply to see some photographs. But he followed Philip down a narrow passage towards the back of the house with Joseph, silent for once, following behind.

'I have made a temporary dark room in a disused pantry,' Philip explained. 'The pictures are in there.'

The little room had no natural light so the photographer lit an oil lamp which stood on a folding table. This revealed a large stone slab fixed into the back wall which had kept things cool when the pantry had been in use. Standing on it now were various pieces of photographic equipment, which Philip quickly explained.

'The smaller lamp goes inside that box with the red glass sides to make a safelight, so that I can handle the sensitive plates and paper without them being exposed.'

John had never been much interested in the process of photography, though he liked to see the finished photographs, but he nodded sagely. On the same slab there were some shallow dishes, perhaps normally used to feed animals, but which had been thoroughly cleaned, and several dark glass bottles filled with liquid and labelled with chemical names. Next to the slab there was a sink with a large water jug inside.

'The sink is used for washing the plates and prints when the process is completed. Then I peg the prints up on this line to dry. These should be ready now.'

Philip took down four of the photographs and laid them on the folding table. There was barely room for the three of them in the tiny room and John could hear Joseph's laboured breathing behind him.

When John studied the photographs his first thought was of regret that he had been unable to climb the mountain himself. Phillip had managed to capture the grandeur and wildness of the place. The sharp contrast of light and dark clearly showed the structure of the great bowl beneath the lake, where streams flowed down into the river, and beyond that the mountains which rose up all around. He was obviously a skilled photographer but like his pictures of the Vyrnwy valley what they lacked was any sign of humanity.

'The photographs are excellent,' said John, 'but I am surprised that your companions do not appear in any of the pictures.'

He heard Joseph sigh. 'My son has not shown you all the photographs. He knows that the others are rather disturbing. They are the reason why I asked you to come here so urgently.'

'What do you mean?'

'It's no good my boy. You must let John see those pictures. Then he must make up his own mind what to do.'

Philip pretended great reluctance as he unpegged the other two photographs and laid them on the table. The first one showed Huw and Amy sitting close on the shore of the lake with Huw apparently caressing Amy's cheek. The second was a picture of Huw facing the camera in angry nakedness and in the background Amy was watching with a smile on her face.

'My God!' gasped John. 'The scoundrel!'

He looked again at the photographs, then turned to Philip.

'Tell me exactly what happened?'

'When we reached the lake I left those two sitting at the water's edge and went to take those other pictures. When I returned to the lake Huw was sitting very close to Amy. I had set up my camera to take a photograph of the lake and I thought their figures might give my picture a sense of scale. They had not seen me return. Huw leaned across almost as if to kiss Amy, then he saw me with my camera and leapt away. Next thing he had taken off all his clothes and was swimming in the lake.'

'You mean he just leapt into the lake quite naked? With Amy sitting nearby?'

'Well, it was very warm. I almost felt like swimming myself, but with Amy...'

'What happened next?'

'I decided to play a silly trick and moved Huw's clothes away from the water. I know it was a stupid thing to do, but I did not like the way he had started to make love to Amy as soon I was out of the way. I wanted to keep him in the cold water for a while. I thought he would wait in the water until I returned his clothes. But instead he came charging out of the lake and ran towards me. I was so shocked that I accidentally operated the shutter on my camera and took that photograph.'

John studied the incriminating photographs again.

'To think I trusted him with my stepdaughter.'

'Well he did seem a pleasant enough young man,' said Joseph.

There was a moment's pause, then Philip spoke, 'There is one more thing you ought to know. When they left the lake and began to climb again I got left behind. You see I was not as fit as the others and I had to hide my camera before I could follow them. When at last I reached the summit they had been standing there for some time. And Huw's arms were encircling Amy's waist. Of course he released her when he saw me approaching, but I could not help wondering what would have happened if I had not arrived just then.'

'This gets worse and worse.'

'Perhaps the Welsh do not have the same sense of propriety,' suggested Joseph. 'After all he is only a simple quarryman.'

'That is no excuse. Amy is just a young girl. How dare he try to seduce her?'

'I partly blame myself,' said Philip. 'I should have stayed with them all the time.'

'That should not have been necessary. The man is a blackguard. I do not want to see him ever again. And I will make sure that he has no further contact with Amy.'

'Well, I think I might be able to help you there,' said Joseph. 'Philip tells me that he has invited Amy to stay with us in Liverpool for a while. Of course I agreed at once. We were due to leave in a few days, but frankly I have had my fill of this place. What I suggest is that we bring forward our plans and leave tomorrow. We can collect Amy early in the morning and be in Liverpool by evening. Then we can make sure she has so much to see and do that she will not have time to even think about Huw. What do you say?'

'I think that is the perfect answer. I cannot thank you enough, my friend. I shall go straight back to Mrs Evan's house and tell Amy to prepare for the journey. And I shall make sure she does not attempt to see that young man when he returns to the valley this evening.'

Joseph led John back to the hallway. He had decided to walk back to the new village. It would give him time to reflect on what he had learned and perhaps he would be a little better tempered when he saw his stepdaughter. After all from what Philip had told him she had hardly rejected Huw's advances.

Philip stayed in the little dark room and began to pack away his photographic equipment, while humming a tune from his favourite work by Gilbert and Sullivan.

'None but the brave deserve the fair.'

The sky had cleared by the time Amy and George began their walk. They left the new village and began to cross the dam. In the few days that Amy had been away the landscape had changed dramatically. Now the filling lake stretched away along the valley, past the straining tower and towards the ruins of old Llanwddyn. A north westerly wind ruffled its surface and little waves slapped against the lower wall of the dam, where a trail of flotsam lifted from the drowned valley bobbed about. There were boughs torn from the trees by the recent storm; straw that had been caught in the hedges after the harvest; bottles left behind by the harvesters and several corpses of beasts trapped in burrows by the rapidly rising water.

'The men will come soon and close the valves. They have certainly passed their test.'

'I suppose it was lucky that we have had all this rain.'

As she said this Amy glanced up at the sky. She was wary now of sudden showers and she had brought an umbrella just in case. At the end of the dam they turned left and followed the new road towards the tower, where the water had already covered the base and turned the walkway into a proper bridge.

'So the water will rise into the tower as the lake fills and be strained through those wire grilles you were telling me about,' said Amy. 'But how then does the water get to Liverpool? I mean water cannot climb over hills.'

'It won't have to. They are making a tunnel right under the hill. Like a long pipe through which the water will flow. The tunnel is already well started.'

'You mean they have to cut right through the solid rock.'

'Yes. They use explosives to break the rock. Then they bring out the rubble.'

'That sounds very dangerous.'

'It is. There have been several accidents already. You have to use just the right amount of explosive and put it in exactly the right place. Huw told me that it is the same at the quarry. You have to know what you are doing.'

Amy had not thought about Huw for a while. Now she saw him in her imagination standing on a huge rock, holding a lighted fuse and smiling. She shuddered.

'Will you be seeing Huw tonight?' asked George.

'It depends what time he arrives. It may be too late for him to visit.'

George looked at Amy and saw how her eyes shone when she talked of Huw, then he remembered Joseph's advice and was determined not to be jealous. Amy smiled and put her arm through George's.

'But I don't need to think about Huw when I have a handsome young man beside me. And one who is going to be a famous engineer.'

George felt suddenly several inches taller. Then he looked at the sky, which had begun to cloud over.

'I think we should go back now. It looks as if it might rain again soon.'

When they reached the dam they saw a group of men, standing near a carriage, some wearing dark suits and others in simple working clothes. As they approached they overheard one of the working men, who held a large spanner in his hand, explaining something to the others.

'It just won't shift. Something seems to have jammed.'

One of the better dressed men studied a sheaf of papers, then turned to the others.

'Perhaps we underestimated the force of the water.'

'So what do we do?'

The group of men blocked the road on top of the dam. Suddenly one of them noticed Amy. He smiled admiringly.

'Sorry, Miss. Do come past.'

He made a way for her and George followed. He knew that all eyes were on Amy and he felt very proud.

As they walked on slowly George strained to hear the continued conversation.

'Nothing we can do, till we can get one of those diving suits up from Bristol and send someone down in the water to have a look. '

'Meanwhile the lake keeps filling.'

'So it seems...'

Then George was out of earshot, but he had heard enough to know what was happening. Just as they reached the end of the dam George heard another voice, calling loudly, 'Amy! George! Wait for me!' They both turned to see John hurrying towards them, his face set like a mask and his skin purple with temper. They waited until he reached them.

'George, go home. Now! I need to speak to Amy alone.'

George stared at John's angry face. How his pupils must fear him, thought George, when he spoke to them like that. He was reluctant to leave Amy, whose face had turned crimson, alone in the company of this man who seemed full of fury, but the tall school master lifted his walking stick in a threatening manner and practically shouted, 'Go!' so George did just that.

Amy was not afraid of her stepfather. She had seen his moods before, though not usually directed at her, but she was afraid of the reason for his mood. It was too much of a coincidence to imagine that his anger had nothing to do with his recent visit to the Hall. She wondered what Philip had told him? But she had always been able to change her stepfather's mood with a soft smile and her hand placed gently on his.

'What on earth is the matter, John?'

'The matter is you and that damned Welshman. How dare he! And how dare you encourage him.'

'I don't know what you mean.'

'Oh don't pretend to be innocent. I have seen the evidence.'

Then Amy remembered. The photographs!

'You are never to see that young rogue again.'

'But...'

'There will be no buts. You are to go straight back to Mrs Evan's and pack your case. You will be leaving for Liverpool first thing in the morning.'

Now Amy was angry as well. Her stepfather had never, even when she was little girl, spoken to her in this manner or treated her like this. She looked up at John, her chin jutting forward and her eyes ablaze.

'I don't want to go to Liverpool. I won't go to Liverpool.'

'You will do exactly as I say. You are still a child and you will do what your father tells you to do.'

In her anger Amy said something she had never said before, or even thought of saying.

'But you are not my father!'

John was momentarily shocked by this response, then he grabbed Amy's arm and began to pull her towards the house.

'I am in loco parentis. You will obey me. I know that your mother would say the same.'

John's grip on her arm increased. He was actually hurting her. All her love and respect for him was fading rapidly as he dragged her along.

'Do you think that Ella and I would want you to be involved with an ignorant quarryman. You are too young to be involved with any man. It is obvious that Huw has played upon your innocence. He planned it all. Invite you to his home. Take you up that mountain. Wait till Philip was out of the way. Thank God that young man saw what he did and informed me.'

It began to rain. Amy pulled away from her stepfather and put up her umbrella.

'Philip is a pompous tell-tale. I hate him.'

'He is exactly the sort of man of whom your mother and I would approve.'

Amy stood still and looked at her stepfather. The rain was falling heavily on his uncovered head and flattening his thinning hair. So for all his splendid talk he was just as conventional as the rest. His opinion of Huw and his admiration of Phillip were simply based on class. At bottom he was a snob. For the first time since they had known one another Amy felt contempt for her stepfather and at the same time she realised that open defiance was not the way to proceed.

'Very well. I'm sorry I spoke as I did. I will do as you say. Now let us get back to Mrs Owen's house before you catch your death of cold.'

But her mind was busy with plans as she linked arms with her stepfather and hurried him along in the rain.

11

Rising Waters

When they reached the new village Amy went into Mrs Evan's cottage, telling her stepfather that she needed to sort out her clothes. He went next door to inform Megan about Amy's imminent departure and found a letter waiting for him.

Dear John,

I wonder when you are coming home. It is obvious that you prefer the company of my daughter and your new friends to that of your wife and son but we have found new company as well. Robert Moreton came to visit. I explained your absence to him but he did not rush away. He seemed quite taken with little John and has offered to teach him to ride when we visit the Manor House. We are to go there on Saturday.

I hope that you enjoyed your visit to your Welsh friend's home. Did you climb to the very top of that mountain? I expect Amy is blossoming in all that male company. I wonder sometimes if she is not too much aware of her attractions. There was a time, John, when you seemed quite satisfied with mine. I know that I do not look as I did then, but that is also true of you, my dear. We cannot stay young for ever.

You will be pleased to hear that little John is quite well at present and is making progress with his reading. He has told me that he feels too nervous when you are with him to concentrate on the words. Perhaps you expect too much of him. Anyway you will be able to judge his progress when you return.

Megan must be quite settled in her new home by now. Would you please pass on my best wishes to Megan and George. My only regret about not coming with you is that I shall not be seeing them.

We do miss you and would like you to come home soon.

Your loving wife,

Ella

John felt a mixture of jealousy and guilt as he read this letter. He remembered that Robert Moreton had been very taken with Ella before he, John, had come on the scene. Mind you in those days Robert had been a profligate womaniser. But why should he take an interest in little John? He had children of his own. And little John was hardly the outdoor type.

He wrote a brief note to Ella, explaining about Amy's visit to Liverpool – though it was possible he would reach Hope Underhill before the letter, then he penned an equally brief note to Huw.

Mr Morris,

I must thank you, your father and your sister for your hospitality when we visited your home.

However I have since learned that certain events occurred during our stay that would make any further contact with me or my stepdaughter very unwelcome. Amy will be leaving for Liverpool tomorrow morning and I shall soon be returning to my home.

John pondered for while about how to end his note but finally decided to simply sign his name. When he had found envelopes he addressed the letter to Ella and wrote 'Huw Morris' on the other. Then he looked about for George and Megan informed him that the boy had gone to his room as soon as he came in.

When John knocked on George's door the boy asked, in a surly manner, who it was, then grudgingly admitted him. George was sitting on the narrow bed, reading. He was angry with John for the way he had spoken to Amy and for sending her away so soon. But he agreed to post the letter and deliver the note, partly because he wanted to see Huw again but also because the shilling he was promised as a reward would enable him to buy a farewell gift for Amy.

The rain had stopped as George set out for the post office but the low grey clouds promised further outbreaks so he hurried on his way to the Morris's encampment. This time he did not cross the dam but took the road on the western side of the growing lake. He was astonished to see how the water had spread even since his walk with Amy but when he crossed one of the streams coming down from the wooded hills in a fierce cascade he could see the cause of the lake's swift rise. There were innumerable streams bringing water down into valley as well as the river itself and if each of these was as swollen with the recent rain as this one then unless the valves could be opened again soon the whole valley would be submerged.

At last the water ended and he was able to cross the fields towards the old village. But even here the ground was sodden and his boots squelched as he walked. When he reached the ruins and looked down the valley towards the dam he saw how little inlets were already filling each depression like the groping fingers of a watery hand.

It was strange walking along the old road, seeing the foundations of the buildings he used to know so well. The larger trees had been felled for timber and lugged away, and without these familiar landmarks it was sometimes difficult to remember which pile of stones had been which house. Beyond the village he passed his old home, which had been the last to be demolished, but George did not feel particularly nostalgic. After all he had not lived there for very long and for much of that time he had been away at school. Anyway he was at an age when the future always seemed more exciting than the past.

When he reached the camp there was smoke rising from the chimney of the shepherd's hut and he could hear Gwyn singing. He called out and when he was admitted he found Gwyn sitting on a bed with his splinted leg stretched out in front of him and an almost empty bottle gripped between his hands. He had enough Welsh to ask when Huw might be back and to understand that Gwyn did not really know, before the man slumped back, closed his eyes and slept, snoring loudly.

George wondered what he should do. Huw might not return for hours. He liked the young Welshman and enjoyed being in his company but did not want to stay in this hut with Gwyn for too long. He was curious about the note that John had written but he did not have the courage to open the envelope. He had just decided to leave the letter where Huw would see it and make his way home when the rain began to fall again, beating heavily on the tin roof of the hut, so that Gwyn stirred, groaned and slept once more. If George attempted to walk back in this rain he would be soaked to the skin so he lay back on Huw's bed and dozed off.

He woke to the sound of men's voices, raised in argument, just outside the hut. The rain had stopped so that the voices were clear but the Welsh was being spoken too rapidly for George to follow. After a moment of silence Huw shook out his cape and came into the hut, looking flushed. When he saw George sitting on his bed he was surprised but then he noticed his father's leg in its splints.

'What the devil's been going on?'

'There was an accident. The cart wheel got smashed and Gwyn was thrown out. His leg is broken.'

'Oh, my God. What about Amy?'

'A few bruises but nothing worse. I believe Philip was able to protect her. He also dealt with Gwyn's leg. Then he set off to find help.'

'Well, well. So our Philip was the hero of the hour.'

Huw was considering the implications of this when the pony outside neighed impatiently, waiting to be fed.

'But I saw the cart outside. It did not look broken.'

'No, Joseph's friends sent out some men to mend it and find the pony which had run away.'

Gwyn woke briefly, smiled at Huw, mumbled incoherently and went back to sleep..

Huw eased the bottle from his father's hands and threw it out of the hut.

'Who were those men outside?' asked George.

'Just people I know'

'Why were they shouting?'

'Because I would not do as they asked. I am not such a fool.'

George was puzzled and wanted to know more but Huw changed tack abruptly, 'So what are you doing here?'

'I brought a letter for you. From Amy's stepfather.'

George handed him the letter.

'I had forgotten about Mr Noble. Was he injured?'

'No. But for some reason he is very angry with you and with Amy.'

Huw opened the envelope and read the letter.

'Well, I can guess who is responsible for this.'

George did not really know what Huw meant but he saw a look of distaste spoil that handsome face. Just then a shaft of sunlight filled the hut and when George looked out he saw that the sky was clear again.

'I ought to be getting back before the rain starts again. Is there a reply?'

'Yes, but not to John Noble.'

Huw found a pencil and wrote on the back of John's letter. Then he returned the note to the envelope and sealed it as well as he was able.

'Would you take this to Amy? And don't let anyone else know'

He brought a shilling out of his pocket and handed it to George. He took the envelope with a sigh. He was growing tired of being a postman but now he wanted to get back to the village shop.

The shopkeeper made it obvious that she was waiting to close for the day, by fixing the shutters and tidying the shelves, while George deliberated. Finally he chose a prettily embroidered handkerchief.

'Just the thing for a sweetheart,' said the shopkeeper with a smirk. George blushed and fumbled with the coins in his pocket.

'It's for my Grandmother.'

'Oh, yes. Well I'm sure that Mrs Owen will appreciate it.'

She handed over the wrapped handkerchief.

'That will be one shilling and nine pence.'

George handed her the money, collected his change and hurried from the shop.

He made sure that John Noble was not watching as he knocked on Mrs Evan's door. It was Amy who opened it, smiled to discover it was George rather than her stepfather, and put a finger to her lips.

'Mrs Evans is asleep in the kitchen. Come in,'

George held out the present.

'I brought you a farewell gift. Oh, and a note from Huw.'

Amy gave him a quick kiss on the cheek and took the gift, but it was obvious that she much more interested in the note.

A voice called from the kitchen, 'Who's there?'

She pushed the note into her bosom, pocketed the little parcel and ushered George out of the door.

Later that evening they all gathered in Megan's kitchen for their last evening meal together. Amy thanked George for his gift but seemed preoccupied. John harped on about Philip and Joseph, saying how kind it was for them to invite her to Liverpool and how exciting it would be to explore that city. Amy nodded and smiled but said little. Usually she loved to talk, asking Megan about her early life in the old village, questioning her stepfather about some event in the world and listening with unfeigned interest as George outlined his plans for the future. Tonight she hardly said a word and barely touched her food, so that Megan asked if she was ailing. She replied that she was fine, but perhaps just a little nervous about the long journey tomorrow. George sensed that she was lying and did not much like this new aspect of her personality. He wondered what the note from Huw had said, but he did not mention it, because John was not supposed to know of its existence.

After the meal Amy helped Mrs Owen with the dishes but when she returned from the scullery she began to yawn rather obviously and told them that she wanted to check her luggage and have an early night, so she returned to Mrs Evan's house. Megan always went to bed early so John invited George to play a game of chess, but the school master did not seem to be able to concentrate and George won easily. John said that he would retire as well, as it had been a long and rather disturbing day, so George was left downstairs by himself.

The Stolen Valley

He turned down the lamp, lifted the glass, blew out the tiny blue flame and sat in the darkened room, until his eyes became accustomed to the gloom. His feelings were confused. He wondered why John had been so angry with Amy and why she had agreed so easily to go to Liverpool. He had been hurt that she had hardly mentioned his gift and wondered whether she had even looked at it. He did not understand what was going on but felt uncomfortable about the whole atmosphere that evening.

Suddenly he wanted to get out of the house. He drew back the curtains, looked out at the moonlit scene and gasped. The ghostly form of woman in a white dress stood just outside, gazing up at the moon, her long loose hair shimmering silvery in the moonlight. Then she settled a shawl about her shoulders and walked away towards the dam.

At first George thought that the figure was some insubstantial spectre, whose grave had been disturbed in the recent exhumations, come back to haunt the valley, but as soon as the figure moved he recognised Amy's walk. He put on his jacket, opened the door as quietly as possible and began to follow, keeping sufficient distance behind so that she would not know he was there. She was walking quickly, in spite of the small suitcase she carried, in fact almost running at times, and had soon crossed the dam, where she took the road towards the straining tower. George kept to the wooded hillside, moving stealthily from tree to tree. A small cloud passed across the moon and for a moment he was blinded by the sudden darkness. When the moonlight returned he could not see Amy at first, but then spied her some way ahead, running towards another figure standing on the roadway, waiting. Even at that distance and in the semi-darkness he recognised the sturdy form and particular stance of Huw. Using the shadows George crept closer and watched as Amy rushed forward, dropped her suitcase into the tangled vegetation at the side of the road, and ran into the Welshman's arms. They remained in that embrace for a while, then parted and moved off arm in arm along the road towards Bala.

George stayed where he was. He was disturbed by Amy's deviousness and by the way she had flung herself into Huw's arms. Suddenly she was not his Amy at all. It seemed that everyone was using him. He had spent the day taking messages from one person to another, as if he had no importance in himself. He turned back to the new village, noting as he crossed the dam that the water had continued to rise, slipped quietly back into the cottage, went straight to bed and wept into his pillow.

When they neared the tower Huw leant back against a tree and drew Amy close again. She relinquished all control and simply melted into his arms. She felt the roughness of his unshaven face rasping against her cheek, then his lips sought hers and pressed gently at first then more fiercely until their teeth meshed and she drew away, gasping for breath.

He tightened his grip around her waist and she felt the hardness of his muscled thighs pressing against hers. The night was cool, but warm blood was pulsing through her limbs from her jolting heart. The world, her life, had shrunk to this place, this moment. Suddenly she remembered that there was another world where not everything was perfect.

'What are we to do?'

'Well you cannot go to Liverpool with that...'

'I have no choice, unless...'

'You could come back with me to Ty'ngraig.'

'You mean marry you. That's not possible. I am still under age. I would need my parents' permission.'

'If we go now we could take the cart and be there by tomorrow afternoon. I am to start at the quarry again soon.'

'They would guess where I had gone. We would be pursued. You would be arrested for abduction.'

'Then what can we do?'

'We must go somewhere else. Where we will not be known. Take new names. Start a new life.'

'But how would we live?'

'Oh, you're strong and skilled. You would soon find work. And I could work too.'

'Never!'

'Do you want us to be together?'

'Of course.'

'Then forget all this nonsense about me not working. I know I have lived a cosy, privileged life so far, but I am not afraid of work, if it would allow us to be together.'

Suddenly the sensible Amy returned.

'Do you have any money at all, Huw?'

'Yes. I have just collected the wages for our work at Llanwddyn.'

'And I have money too. John gave it to me for my visit to Liverpool. It is enough to buy us railway tickets to wherever we choose.'

It all seemed so possible. An adventure. A step into the unknown. Perhaps in her heart of hearts Amy knew that it was not going to be as easy as that, but she had wanted change and now she saw her chance. Of course she would miss her mother, though they had often been in conflict of late, and perhaps her little brother, but she could not go on living with John now that he had shown such a narrow minded view of life. She put her arms around Huw's neck and leant her head against his shoulder, then pulled away.

'What about Gwyn?'

'Joseph is to visit him in the morning. When they discover that I have gone they will surely help him to get home.'

'Poor Gwyn.'

'And I will write to Nan and post it from somewhere on our way.'

'Then we must start our journey. Where will we go first?'

'To Bala. If we walk all night we will be there in time for the first train towards England.'

'Then let's get going.'

'But it's not going anywhere you are,' said a low voice in a Welsh accent, and three figures emerged from the darkness. They encircled the couple and Amy felt Huw's fists clench.

'Who are you?' she asked.

'Old friends, of Huw.'

'This is Tom,' said Huw. 'He speaks English. Owen and Daffydd speak only Welsh. I worked at the quarry with them. But they have stupid ideas.'

'Are you going to introduce your pretty little friend?' asked Tom. 'Before she leaves us and goes back to England.'

'My name is Amy and when I go it will be with Huw.'

Tom spoke in Welsh to the others and the circle closed slightly.

'I think not, my fancy English girl. We need his help with something that is not your concern.'

Huw turned to Amy. 'It would be better if you went back, Amy.'

'And if I refuse?'

'Then you must suffer the consequences,' said Tom, then he spoke to the others in Welsh.

Huw called out, 'Run, Amy. Run!'

But the other men, both large and strong, grabbed Huw and held him, in spite of his fierce struggling, while Tom pulled Amy's shawl over her face and grabbed her wrists.

Amy could not see what was happening and the men spoke only in Welsh, but she felt one of them, Tom she thought, grasp her arm and force her forward, stumbling along a stone path. She was angry with this man for touching her, for insulting her, for being stronger than her, for being a man. She heard water lapping, apparently beneath her, then the sound of an iron door opening and clanging shut. She sensed that they were now inside somewhere. There was still the sound of water, but different now, as if it was at the bottom of a deep well. Amy was afraid to move in case she fell into that water.

Now Tom, or whoever it was, took hold of her around the waist and carried her down some iron steps, which rang bell-like under his heavy boots. She wanted to scream and lash out at him, but her voice was muffled by the shawl and her wrists were tightly held. And she felt so insecure being bundled down those steps that she was almost glad he was holding her tightly.

At last they reached a lower floor. The men were speaking now always in Welsh; their voices raised in angry dispute and echoing around whatever building they were in. Huw kept repeating a single word in Welsh, then groaned as if he had been hit in the stomach but he still repeated that same word with increasing vehemence. At last the argument ended. Amy was forced to sit. Then she heard footsteps going back up those iron stairs, the iron door opening and shutting again, followed by the dull screech of metal fitting into metal, a firm click, then silence.

She called out, 'Huw!' and heard him groan again. At last she was able to shake the shawl off her head and saw, in the light of a single candle, which their captors had left behind, that Huw was lying nearby, clutching his stomach. She looked around and saw that they were on a small wooden platform fixed to the side of a large circular room of stone. The flickering candle flame was reflected from a wide black pool of water swirling a few feet below them. She shivered, not with cold, but with fear and called out again to Huw.

'Where are we? What has happened? Are you hurt?'

Huw managed to sit up.

'It's all right, my lovely. We're safe now.'

'Safe?' She meant it to sound ironic but the tone of his voice did make her feel a little safer. 'But what is this place?'

'We're inside the straining tower. They have locked us in so that I cannot stop them carrying out their stupid plan or give a warning. But they have promised to come back when it is done to release us both.'

'How long will that be?'

'A couple of hours. Three at the most.'

'But what is this plan?'

'Wait.'

Slowly and painfully he managed to shuffle over and sit beside her.

'I am so angry with myself for getting you involved in this.'

'Involved with what?'

'Do you remember, when we were climbing Cadair Idris, Philip asked me why I was so resentful of the English? I gave you my reasons and I said that some of my friends were prepared to do more than merely grumble. Well, Tom and the others are like that. They are men of action. Foolish but determined. They are planning to blow up the tunnel under the mountain to stop the water reaching Liverpool.

'My God!'

'Of course it is stupid and dangerous. And in the end it will only hold up the supply for a while. But they feel so strongly about the way the English steal everything from Wales...

'What did they want you to do?'

'They found out where I kept my supply of explosive. But they are not experts with the stuff. They do other jobs in the quarry. They wanted me to show them how to use it. How much explosive to use? The best place to put it. How long the fuse should be? That sort of thing'

'And you refused. So they hit you and shut us both in this tower.

'Exactly'

'Oh Huw! Well at least we are together. And when they release us we can still go on our way.'

'Yes. If that is what you want?

She snuggled as close to him as she could get.

'It is what I want most in the whole world.'

The Stolen Valley

12

Missing

At eight o'clock next morning the carriage arrived. John, Megan and George were waiting outside and most of the inhabitants of the new village stood watching at a distance. A carriage like that was a rare sight in Llanwddyn; with the coats of the two black horses rubbed to a shine and the black lacquered bodywork of the carriage gleaming. The driver, in his black and gold livery, climbed down and opened the door. Philip stepped out, his face shining with happiness. Joseph got out more slowly. He was having a bad day.

'Is Miss William's ready?' Philip asked.

Mrs Evan's told him that she hadn't seen Amy yet that morning but she'd go now and knock on her bedroom door. George moved a little away from the group. He knew what was about to happen and did not want to be involved.

Mrs Evans was white faced when she returned.

'She's not there. Her bed hasn't been slept in. I found this on the coverlet. It's addressed to you, Mr Noble.'

She handed the letter to John who tore open the envelope, read the brief note and exclaimed, 'I'll have him roasted alive for this!'

Joseph took the note from him and read it aloud.

Dear John,

I am going away with Huw. I love him very much and he loves me. Do not try to follow us. Please tell Mother that I have chosen as she once chose, with her heart.

Your stepdaughter,

Amy

Philip burst out, 'He has enchanted her. Probably with the help of that witch of a sister. I was suspicious of her from the start.'

John looked round for George. He grabbed him by the shoulder and looked him in the face.

'D'you know anything about this, George? You and Amy were the best of friends.'

George might have said something but he did not like the way John hurt his shoulder. It reminded him of the way he had treated Amy yesterday. He was beginning to see her stepfather as a bully. George was on the side of the underdog.

'Of course I don't know.'

Even Megan joined in.

'Are you sure George? Did she say anything?'

Philip had been pacing about. Now he turned back to them.

'Let us be practical about this. Where are they most likely to have gone?'

'Well, they would probably have taken the pony and cart and made for that home of his in the mountains,' suggested John.

'Yes, and taken Gwyn with them,' added Philip. 'That's the first place to look.'

Joseph called out to the driver, 'The old village! As quickly as you can!'

John, Joseph and Philip jumped aboard, but just as the carriage was turning round another of the servants from the Hall came running towards them, and gasped out.

'Doctor Lever. Come you at once! There's this man! It's terrible hurt he is! On the road he lies. By that tower.'

Philip pulled the servant up into the carriage.

'Come with us. Show us where he is. If he is capable of being moved we'll take him to Hall. Then you can deal with him, father, while John and I go on to that damned Welshman's camp. We have to find Amy before it is too late.'

George ran behind the coach for a while, then stopped and sat on the wall of the dam. It had rained heavily again for most of the night and the lake had continued to rise. He had been woken in the early hours by what he thought at first was a single clap of thunder, but the sound wasn't quite right.

The injured man was in a dreadful state. He was lying on the ground near the entrance to that tunnel which was being cut into the hillside and would eventually be connected with the tower for the water to begin its journey to Liverpool. A strong door had been fixed over the entrance to this tunnel to keep out intruders but this had been blown off its hinges. Joseph guessed that the man had crawled out of the tunnel so that someone might see him. His face was blackened with soot mixed with blood from some gashes on his head and his clothing was torn to shreds. He kept trying to point to the tunnel entrance and muttering something in Welsh. Joseph told him to lie still and when the driver translated this the man did as he was told. It was easier for Philip to bend and inspect the man's limbs, which he did quickly and expertly before declaring.

'No obvious damage to his body. It is the head which has suffered. Not just those cuts but some dreadful bruising. We must get him to the Hall as soon as we can.'

John had some sympathy with the injured man but he was eager to be in pursuit of Amy. As the driver and the other servant lifted the poor man he began to gabble again in Welsh and point to the tunnel. The driver translated.

'He may be delirious of course, but I think he is saying that there is someone else in the tunnel. Perhaps more than one.'

'Well judging by the state of this man, who has managed to get out, anyone still in there is likely to be dead,' said Philip.

Joseph held the man's head as they placed him carefully on one seat of the carriage, where the driver had placed a blanket, perhaps to protect the immaculate carriage as well as provide the injured man with some comfort.

'When we reach the Hall I will ask my friends to contact the engineers. It would be far too dangerous for any of us to go inside.'

'Yes,' said John, eager to be on the way. 'But what on earth was this man doing in the tunnel? I thought the work had stopped until the valves could be opened again. In case of flooding.'

He looked into that battered face as if seeking an answer but the man's eyes were shut. Joseph explained.

'He has slipped into a coma. We shall be lucky if he lives to tell the tale.'

When they reached the Hall the man was taken to the gun room where Joseph and one of the maidservants cleaned him up as best they could. He did not recover consciousness and Joseph was not surprised when he saw the terrible blows the man's head had received. He dressed his wounds and made him as comfortable as he could, while his friends contacted the engineers.

Meanwhile Philip and John went on to the Morris's encampment, where they were surprised to see the cart still in its place and the pony tethered nearby. Gwyn had managed to move a little and was sitting on the steps of the hut smoking his pipe.

The driver asked Gwyn in Welsh where they might find Huw. The quarryman shrugged and told them, through the driver, that Huw had gone off somewhere last night and not returned. Philip checked Gwyn's leg and asked how he was going to manage without his son to help him. Again the quarryman shrugged.

Philip suggested to the driver that he should return later with some provisions for Gwyn and attend to the pony. He nodded and explained to Gwyn.

John was pacing about impatiently.

'So what do we do now?'

'We contact the police,' said Philip decisively. 'This is now a very serious matter. Abduction at the least, and what else, we do not know.'

They returned to the new village, where they learned that the engineers had discovered serious damage inside the tunnel and two bodies among the rubble, but even in their mangled and disfigured state it was obvious that neither of the bodies was female. John sent a telegram to Ella, 'Amy missing - come at once.' Philip went to the Police Station and told them what had happened. They were connected to the new-fangled telephone system and immediately contacted the nearest railway stations at Llanfyllin, Llanuwchllyn and Bala and gave them descriptions of Amy and Huw.

There was nothing else that they could do for the moment so Philip returned to the Hall and John went into Megan's cottage. Mrs Evans was there as well and the two widows were sitting at the kitchen table sharing a pot of tea. Megan looked at John's anxious face and said, 'I do not believe that Huw would harm young Amy, you know.'

'You have been taken in by his charm like the rest of us, Megan. I blame myself. I should have seen what was going on.'

'It is all the fault of that wicked dam,' said Mrs Evans. 'Ever since they started building it things have gone wrong. It's interfering with nature and that always leads to trouble.'

'It's just progress, Mrs Evans,' said John, rather impatiently, then he asked, 'Where's George?'

'He went out for a walk. He's worried about dear Amy.'

'I think I might do the same,' said John.

George sat on his rock above the dam looking across the swelling lake and wondering what he should do. His mind was in a mess. Obviously he was the one who had last seen Amy and Huw and his information might help to find them but he was not sure that he wanted them to be found. Well, not yet. He did not approve of what Amy had done but it was her choice. He did not like the idea of anyone being forced to do what they did not want to do and it was obvious that Amy had not wanted to go to Liverpool. He liked Joseph enormously and not just because he had promised to help him with his future plans but there was something about Philip that aroused his antipathy.

He wondered where Huw and Amy might have gone. When he had last seen them their most obvious route would have been towards the old village where they would have taken the pony and cart, but that was almost too obvious. The other possibility was to walk to Bala, but if they had done that last night they would have been totally drenched before they got there.

There was also the mystery of the tunnel. He had seen the men arrive to investigate. He knew now that there had been an explosion –it must have been what had woken him in the night- and he knew that some men had been killed and injured. Everyone was talking about it. But was it just coincidence that the explosion in the tunnel happened on the same night that Huw and Amy disappeared? He thought back to that incident at the Morris's encampment, when he had woken from his snooze to hear Huw arguing with some others outside. What had Huw said? 'I would not do as they asked. I am not such a fool.' But who were 'they' and what was it they wanted him to do?

George knew now that his feelings for Amy were foolish. To her he was a mere boy. Huw was a man, and a handsome one at that, and he remembered how Amy had flung herself into his arms, but was he really a suitable match for Amy. After all he was just a man who worked in a quarry and would probably never be anything else, but Amy was about to go to college and become a qualified teacher. And George knew that she had all sorts of plans, as he had, to travel the world and do important things. He could not imagine her simply living with Huw in some dreary little cottage somewhere.

George thought it most likely that the couple had gone off together, but what if something had gone wrong. Perhaps Amy was in danger. Should he tell John what he knew? Well, perhaps, but not yet.

George was getting hungry. He had waited to say farewell to Amy before having breakfast and then in all the excitement he had not felt hungry. Now he needed to eat but he did not want to be confronted by John Noble, whom he liked less and less. He climbed down from his rocky lookout and took a path below the dam. With the closing of the sluice the river had shrunk to a mere trickle and he knew a place where a tree had fallen from bank to bank making a bridge for those with enough courage and a good sense of balance to attempt it. Once across he climbed the steep wooded slope leading up to the back of the houses on his side of the street, entered the yard and carefully opened the back door. He grabbed some bread and cheese from the pantry and was about to leave when he heard a familiar voice in the front room.

'The police will be arriving soon to begin a search. They will be asking for volunteers to join them. No-one of Amy's description has been seen at any of the stations. I am convinced that George must know something. I must talk to him again. Do you know where I might find him?'

George did not wait to hear more. He shoved the bread and cheese into his jacket pocket and slipped out of the house again.

Back on his rock George watched two wagon loads of policemen arrive. They were joined by some of the workmen still left at the camp. Most had already moved on now that the main work on the dam had been completed, but some had stayed, to work on the tunnel or the road, in the hope of finding some other employment, or because they had nowhere in particular to go. A score or more of villagers offered to help as well and of course a crowd of children followed, glad to be out of school and involved in any adventure.

A large, ruddy-faced policeman, with a smattering of silver on his uniform and a very loud voice addressed the gathering in Welsh and English and divided them into two groups; one would search the west side of the valley and the other the east. Someone asked what they were looking for and the policeman explained that a young woman had gone missing- he briefly described Amy- and that she might be in the company of a young man. Someone laughed at this and the policeman's face turned livid as he shouted, 'It is possible that she did not go willingly with this man. You are looking for any evidence of their whereabouts. Anything! However small!'

George thought about the way Amy had rushed into Huw's embrace. It seemed to him she had gone willingly enough. The groups began to move apart. George waited until he saw John Noble join the group moving to the west side of the lake, then joined those going to the east. He merged with the adults, keeping his cap down, and not speaking to anyone as they moved along the bank of the lake.

Soon they reached the tower. George noticed that the lower part of the structure was already submerged and that water was flowing through the arches of the bridge that joined the tower to the bank. The policeman leading their group held up his hand to halt the search, crossed the bridge, discovered that the padlock was still firmly fixed across the door, took a quick look around, shook his head and rejoined the search party.

George noticed that on the other side of the road the door at the entrance to the tunnel had been closed again and boards had been fixed across the frame. It would not be safe to clear the rubble in the tunnel until the sluice was open and the level of the lake began to fall.

The policeman rejoined them and was about to wave the searchers on again when someone shouted, 'Wait!' He had been examining the bushes at the side of the road and now brought his find to the leader. It was a small suitcase. George recognised it at once but said nothing. Now he became worried. If Amy had gone away with Huw, why had she left her suitcase behind? What had happened? He wondered whether he should now tell someone what he knew. His passion for science and engineering had long replaced any interest in religion but George began to pray silently and earnestly that Amy was safe.

The policeman examined the suitcase, noting the initials 'A. W.' cut into the leather. He took a notebook from his pocket and read, 'Amy Williams.' He stroked his chin. 'Tis hers, by God.' He handed the case to one of his subordinates. 'Take that back to the place she was staying' He consulted the notebook again, 'Mrs Owen. Number three. Next the chapel.'

As the constable moved away, the Sergeant turned to another colleague. 'That don't bode well, Jenkins. Don't bode well at all.'

He waved his hand and the searchers moved on again, slowly, in a long line that reached from the edge of the water up onto the steep slopes of the valley where the recently planted trees were growing fast. As the day progressed, and nothing else was found, people began to leave the line, as they remembered they had other things to do and most of the children soon became bored and drifted away, so the spaces between the searchers gradually widened. George was glad of the food in his pockets, which he surreptitiously slipped into his mouth as he walked along. When they crossed a stream tumbling down into the lake he cupped his hands and drank some of the cool, clear water, thinking how lucky the people of Liverpool were soon to be having such water delivered to their very doors.

The day became hot and the line slowed again. They had reached the end of the lake. The leader decided that they should concentrate on the demolished village until they met up with the other search party, when further plans could be made. As they approached the ruins, George noticed that the water had now reached the remains of the houses at the lower end of the village and was lapping among the piles of stones.

The two groups now came together. George made sure that he kept well away from John, but he saw the horror on the schoolmaster's face when he was told about the suitcase. Again George wondered if he should tell someone what he had witnessed, but perhaps Huw and Amy had dumped the case in order to make more rapid progress. He longed for Amy to be safe but he could see no reason why she should not be while Huw was with her. And if she wanted to be with Huw she should be allowed to do just that. George knew that he had lost Amy for ever but he still wanted her to be happy.

A dog cart, driven by Philip, arrived from the Hall with food and drink for the searchers. The Bradshaws were used to dealing with dozens of beaters at a shoot so catering on this scale was not a problem. When John told Philip about the suitcase he shouted, 'The man is a monster! He is capable of anything. We have all been such fools.'

He explained to John that Joseph was doing his utmost to keep the injured man alive, in the hope that he might be able to help them. He told John to bring Ella to the Hall as soon as she arrived, so that they might decide what to do next. Then he drove away.

After a short break the search began again, with a careful examination of the ruins. Any possible hideout was scrutinised; the remains of a cellar, the crypt of the church, a crumbling pigsty and a leaning hen house. When they reached the Morris's camp a couple of men rudely pushed Gwyn aside and went into his hut, upsetting everything. George wanted to stop them, but did not dare reveal his presence. Gwyn saw John and shouted at him at him in Welsh. It was quite obvious that he was asking him for help but the schoolmaster's face showed nothing but hatred for the man who had so recently welcomed him into his home. George felt guilty and ashamed on John's behalf.

Clouds gathered again in the late afternoon and soon a light drizzle began to fall. The search parties began to thin again. John and some of the policemen stood together under a large umbrella. George managed to get close enough to hear their conversation without being seen.

'It's obvious they've left the valley,' said one policeman. 'We can't search the whole of ruddy Wales.'

'But...' began John.

'Face facts, Mr Noble. We haven't found a single clue, except that suitcase. I don't know why they left it behind but your daughter and this Welsh chap must be far away by now.'

The rain began to fall more heavily. The search party was dismissed. The face of a younger policeman suddenly lit up with morbid enthusiasm.

'Of course there's always...' he gestured towards the wide expanse of water, its surface seething under the downpour, 'the lake!'

'Nonsense!' one of his older colleagues announced. 'Why would they be in the lake?'

The younger man was enjoying the drama of his imagination.

'Perhaps he panicked and drowned her. Or perhaps they chose to die together. A lover's pact.'

'Oh, do shut up, Davies. Anyway, I have been informed that this diving suit thing is arriving soon, then the sluice can be opened and this unexpected lake will quickly disappear.'

George heard the terror in John Noble's voice as he said, 'You don't really think...' and knew that he had to speak. He left his hiding place and joined the group.

'They are not in the lake, Mr Noble.'

'George! What d'you mean?'

'I'm sorry. I should have told you. But I was angry with you. I was angry with everyone.'

'Told me what?'

'I saw Amy leave the house last night. I followed her. She met Huw. She was happy to be with him. I had delivered a note to her from him earlier. I think they had planned to go away together. She was carrying that suitcase. They met near the tower. I think they probably walked on towards Bala. That's all I know.'

The main policeman's face turned scarlet again.

The Stolen Valley

'D'you mean, you've let this whole search happen, when you knew what had happened? My God, if I was your father...'

'He has no father,' interrupted John. 'He is the grandson of an old friend.'

'Nevertheless...'

George threw himself at John and began to pummel him.

'I didn't know what to do. Amy didn't want to go to Liverpool. I was angry with you for forcing her to go. And I was angry with her for going away with Huw. I love her very much.'

The boy stopped hitting John and burst into tears.

'I still think...'

'Yes, Sergeant,' said John, 'the boy has caused much trouble and delay. But at least we know that my stepdaughter is alive. I am grateful for that. Let me deal with the boy.'

'Very well. But what will you do now about finding the girl?'

'I don't know. My wife will be arriving soon. Perhaps she will know what to do. Meanwhile, I cannot thank you enough for all the help you have given me today.'

By now the search party had dispersed, except for the policemen. The wagons arrived to take them back to their various stations. John and George were given a lift back to the new village. Neither man nor boy spoke as the wagon rattled along. But both were thinking the same thought. Where was their beloved Amy now?

13

Trapped

Amy lay back on the wooden boards of the platform and nestled her head on Huw's chest. She could hear his heart beating steadily and her head rose and fell with the rhythm of his breathing. For the moment the fact that they were trapped in this tower, with the light of a single candle, showing the impenetrable walls and the black water lapping ever closer to their platform, did not worry her. She was here, lying next to the man she most wanted to be with, and soon they would be released to go off and share a life together.

'When do you think they will come back?'

'Soon.'

'Will we still have time to walk to Bala and catch the first train?'

'Perhaps. Otherwise we may need to hide up somewhere and catch a later train.'

'Where will we go?'

'As far away as we can, Cariad. Where no-one knows us. Where we can begin a new life as man and wife. Well, at least as far as anyone knows.'

'Will we be married Huw?'

'When we can be, lovely girl.'

He stroked her forehead and took a strand of her long golden hair and tickled her cheek with it. She laughed and turned to face him.

'Oh Huw! Huw!'

She lifted her upper body onto his chest and pressed her lips to his.

At that moment there was a deep crump of something like the first rumble of distant thunder and even the thick tower shook slightly as did the boards of the little platform.

Huw released a long slow breath and whispered almost in awe, 'Well, I'll be damned. They've done it. Soon now, we shall be free.'

When they got back to Llanwddyn John was amazed to find Ella and little John waiting. Ella said, 'But surely this cannot be George. Why you're a young man.' He blushed as she kissed his cheek. She introduced George to her son. Little John lifted his hand for George to shake in such a formal way that it made them all laugh. John looked at his son and thought how much he had changed in the short time they had been apart. He seemed taller, had lost some of that babyish pudginess; his face shone with health and a new confidence. 'So that is what happens when his father is away,' he thought, guiltily.

George seemed to grasp at once that John and Ella needed to talk, so he asked little John if he would like to see the dam and off they went together. There seemed to be an immediate rapport between the boys, in spite of the difference in their ages. Neither parent had any qualms about letting their son go with someone who was, to the little boy, still a stranger.

John turned to his wife and was surprised again. He had forgotten how comely she was, especially in a pretty blue dress he had not seen before, which fitted her fuller but still shapely figure, and the colour of which matched her eyes that had something of the old sparkle in them. He was surprised that Ella did not seem particularly concerned about her daughter's disappearance. She put her arm through his and said, 'Let us walk a little, my dear. We need to talk.' So they set off towards the lake. When they reached the end of the dam they did not cross but walked straight on along the new road for a while.

For a while neither of them spoke, but then John felt the pressure on his arm as Ella suddenly stopped to look across the lake. He wanted to clasp her to him and kiss her and be man and wife again in more than name. But instead of responding she turned to face him, holding him at arm's length, and said, 'Oh, John...What have you done?'

'Me!'

'Yes, you, my dear! Do you remember so little what it is like to be young?'

'I don't know what you mean.'

'Do you think when we first met, if someone had forbidden me to see you again, I would have obeyed? Oh, John, what a big booby you are. How little you really understand?'

'But this Huw is just a quarryman who works for a pittance. He is not suitable at all for our daughter.'

'Megan cannot praise him enough. She has told me what a handsome young man he is. How hard he works. How much he cares for his father and sister. And how helpful he has been to her.'

John felt himself becoming angry. He had expected Ella to be as shocked as he was and to share his dismay.

'But we are talking about a man who has abducted your daughter and probably seduced her by now.'

'Oh, John! John! She is almost eighteen. She is in love for the first time. If only you had not interfered that love would probably have cooled as quickly as it came. Now you have forced her into an action she will probably regret.'

'Then we must find her as soon as we can.'

'How do you think we can do that? They must be miles away by now.'

'The police will help us. They will circulate their description to all forces. Surely someone will recognise them.'

Ella shook her head.

'Megan has told me that she will be quite safe with Huw. He may not be your choice, perhaps not mine, perhaps in time he would not be hers, I don't know. But Megan tells me that he is a good man, strong, honest and intelligent, that he has had some education and that he will probably do well in whatever field he chooses, especially with Amy's help. We have lost her John, because of you, but perhaps, once they are settled somewhere, she will let us know.'

'But all her plans. Her future. Her teacher training. Her career.'

'But whose plans were they really, John? You have made her the person she is. You have filled her head with your ideas. Now she is being herself. You must accept that.'

'I cannot believe you mean all this. She cannot marry him without our consent. She will be living in sin.'

Ella did not reply but took her husband's hands in hers, put them round her waist and looked up into his face.

'Do you still love me, John?'

There was a moment's pause, while he looked into his wife's pale blue eyes. The wind rose a little and the water of the lake lapped on the stones behind them. At last he whispered, 'Of course.'

'Then trust me. I know that I have not been myself of late. I have been too much occupied with little John, and with other things, while you have only had time and eyes for Amy. She has always admired you. It was always John says this and John thinks that. Now she has chosen to break away and be herself. You must accept that. Let her go, John. I need you. Your son needs you. Come back to us.'

He looked away from her for a moment, scanning the lake, as if he might see Amy, on the far side, beckoning to him. Then he turned back to Ella, hugged her to him and bent to kiss her forehead.

'You are right. I have been much at fault. I have been too much concerned with my own satisfaction and with wallowing in discontent. Will you forgive me?'

'Of course, my dear.' She broke away and put her arm once more in his. 'Now we must get back and see what those boys are up to.'

As they began to walk back towards the new village, John asked.

'But how did you get here so soon? I only sent that telegram this morning.'

'Ah, well you see, Robert had come to give little John his riding lesson when the telegram arrived. So he fetched a carriage and took us to Llanymynech, where we caught the train...'

'Moreton again!'

Ella stopped and looked into her husband's face and smiled.

'Are you jealous, John?'

He looked at that smile and the eyes above glinting with a merriment he had not seen for ages. For a moment he saw this attractive woman as other men might see her.

'Perhaps, a little,' he said.

'Then you really are a fool,' Ella replied, laughing, and reached up to kiss him.

When they reached the end of the dam John was amazed to see his son running towards him. He was almost worried by this new energy the boy showed.

'Papa! Papa!' the little boy gasped. 'George knows everything about the dam. He is going to be an engineer.'

George smiled and said, 'He has been full of questions. I have tried to answer them.'

This was new as well; an interest in, curiosity about something other than those toy soldiers. What a change in such a short time. Now the boy had got his breath back he began to tell them what he had seen.

'There were these men on the dam. One of them got dressed in a funny suit, and put on this big helmet, made of brass George says, and it had a little round window at the front and there was a long pipe coming from the back that went into a box thing on wheels.

Then the man in the funny clothes climbed over the dam holding on to a rope ladder and went down into the water, right into it...'

'It was a diving suit,' George explained.

'The other men turned these wheels on the box thing round and round.'

'That keeps the diver's helmet full of air.'

'He was down in the water for ages. Then some other men pulled him up again. And when they took off his helmet he told them something and everyone looked happy.'

George took over the tale.

'Apparently a big branch had floated down towards the dam and got caught in the gears that operate the valve. The diver will be going down again to attach a rope to the branch so that it can be pulled away. Then they can open the valve.'

'How long do you think that will take?' asked John.

'Well the diver will need to rest for a while, but I should think the water will be flowing again by the end of the day.'

Ella looked across the lake towards the tower.

'It seems a pity to let all that water flow away again.'

'But the tunnel is not yet completed and of course they will need to repair it now.'

'Yes. Megan told me about the explosion. Two men dead and one badly injured. How dreadful.'

'There are also things still to be done in the tower. Machinery to be put in place. Then the lake can be allowed to fill properly. They say it might be ready by November.'

'November,' thought John. 'I wonder what will have happened to us all by then. Perhaps...'

'We must get back to Megan,' said Ella. 'There may be some news.'

Trapped

Amy had fallen asleep where she lay half over Huw. Since that explosion the boards under them had not felt quite so secure. They were becoming hard to his back but he dare not move and wake her. At least while she was asleep she would not be worrying about their situation. Huw himself was very worried. Several hours had passed since they had heard the explosion, but his friends – some friends, he thought – had not come back to release them. Something had gone wrong. He knew that. He knew too that it was probably his fault. You had to be so careful with explosives. And he had refused to help them.

In fact everything had gone wrong. This girl, this lovely English girl, whose firm breasts rose and fell as she slept and whose long loose hair framed her pale face, perfect in sleep. Of course he was attracted to her. What man would not be? And he knew she was attracted to him, girls often were, but he had never intended things to turn out like this. Naturally he had wanted to hold her and kiss her and perhaps go even further, if she was willing. And it was one in the eye for that pompous, pampered Englishman, Philip Lever, because she had chosen him, a mere Welsh quarryman, but marriage! Huw did not want to marry any girl yet. That was not part of his plan at all.

When he had sent that note asking her to meet him he had no idea she would come prepared to leave her stepfather and go away with him. He knew it would never work. A girl like this, who had probably never cooked a meal or scrubbed a floor or spent a day at the washtub, and whose time had been largely spent reading books, making sketches and pressing flowers, would soon tire of being a labourer's wife. And he knew that if they were together it would inevitably lead to children and that would tie him to her for ever. That could not be. His father needed him, Nan needed him, and the little farm needed him. But he could not take this girl back there. It was too obvious and it would not be long before they came to arrest him. But meanwhile he must continue the pretence that once they were out of here they would go away together and live as man and wife. God, what a mess it all was.

He was not yet too worried about their present situation. The water in the tower had not risen much further. It continued to stir round a few inches below their platform. It should not be there at all. George had explained it all to him. The plan was that hydraulic machinery- this platform had been built so that the machinery could be installed - would lift the water up from the lake and then it would pour down through a filter of fine copper gauze before it left the tower and travelled through the tunnel towards Liverpool. There must be a fault in the tower wall or perhaps something had been left open so that the water had come in and risen inside the tower to the same level as the lake outside. Work had ceased on the tower until the sluice could be opened – perhaps it was being opened even now - and the water released. Surely that would happen soon and then the workmen would return.

Huw realised that it would not be easy for him and Amy. They had nothing to eat and more importantly nothing to drink, except the water below them and he was not sure how clean that might be. But so long as the water rose no further and that someone came to rescue them before too long they were in no real danger. When someone came he would explain about their capture and imprisonment. If his friends – he still thought of them as friends- were out of the tunnel and far away by now, he could make them the villains of the piece.

He wished he knew what time it was. His pocket watch had fallen off in the struggle with their captors and dropped into the water below. He knew that dawn had come, because a faint glimmer of daylight was shining through a tiny window far above them. He pinched out the candle, knowing that he always had some safety matches in his pocket, as was the habit of someone used to lighting fuses. He adjusted his aching limbs, without waking Amy, closed his eyes and tried to sleep.

He must have slipped briefly into unconsciousness because he had been woken suddenly by the scrape of metal on that door at the top of the stairs. Oh thank God, they had come at last. Soon they would be out of here. But the door did not open. The sound died away. Huw extricated himself from Amy and hurried up the stairway. He called out but he knew that his voice would never penetrate these thick walls. He thumped on the iron door but knew that unless someone was standing very close, they would hear nothing.

Of course the noise woke Amy.

'Huw! Where are you? What has happened?'

He hurried down the steps and felt the whole platform move slightly as he stepped onto it. He took Amy in his arms.

'Someone came to the door up there. I heard them move the lock. But they went away again.'

'Do you think it was your friends?'

'No. They would have released us.'

'So what has happened to them?'

'Perhaps they were caught as they left the tunnel. Or they might have had to run away before they had time to release us.'

Huw realised that Amy was trembling, so he pulled her close to him and whispered, 'Don't worry, lovely girl. Someone will come soon. They must.'

Philip was in a dreadful mood. His love for Amy had almost evaporated and for that young Welshman he felt only hatred. It was his turn to sit with the injured man, in case he woke and was able to tell them something about the missing lovers. It was a tedious business and he had read most of 'Idylls of the King' three times already.

He looked up when the man on the makeshift bed stirred, but it was simply an arm slipping further off his chest, nothing to indicate that the man was waking from his coma. The man's head was bruised and swollen, his nose was broken and so were several teeth. Philip suspected that the man had never been particularly handsome but now...Two dead and this one not likely to survive. What idiots! What can they possibly have hoped to achieve. He had already learned that the tunnel had hardly been damaged, the inexpertly handled explosion – with much too short a fuse - had sent most of its force outwards, so that loose rocks had been flung towards the men, like cannon shot, before they were far enough away. The tunnel would be cleared in a few days and the whole project would still be completed on schedule. What a waste!

He had also learned that some packaging from the explosive had survived. It was clearly marked as the property of the quarry where Huw and his father had been employed. That meant, almost certainly that Huw had been involved. He remembered the Welshman telling them about his more hot-headed friends and saying that he would not join them. But it was obvious that he had provided the explosive. So what did that make him, other than a coward who was prepared to pass the ammunition but not fire the gun.

Philip tried not to think of Amy but it was impossible. Unwanted images kept popping into his mind; Amy on that pony, riding round the valley with him, with her good seat and her fine profile thrown into relief by the morning sun; Amy sitting by that lake watching the brief flash of Huw's flesh and smiling broadly; Amy lying in that cart, after the accident, her skirts awry, revealing her underwear. He did not want to think about her. She had rejected him, probably she was at this very moment in the arms of that...

The door opened and his father entered.

'No change?'

'None.'

'My turn now. Go and eat.'

'I'm not hungry. Is there any news?'

'Nothing about Amy. But they think that the sluice may be opened by nightfall. Then the water will go down and at least our worst fears may be over.'

'You don't really think...'

'All I know is that once a woman's reason is drowned with passion anything can happen. If only we could have taken her to Liverpool, I am sure she would soon have got over this infatuation. Such a lovely, lively girl. She might have done anything. Now...'

'How is John taking it?'

'His wife has arrived. At least now he can share his burden. In fact I have sent a message inviting them to the Hall this evening. George too. The little one will stay with Mrs Owen. They will be here quite soon.'

Things had not gone as planned with the sluice. Eventually the diver had gone down again and attached a rope to the branch, but the wood had become so deeply enmeshed in the gears which operated the valve that the men above hauling on the rope could not pull it away. Then the rope had broken.

The diver was brought up again. The weather had changed. A strong wind had come from the north-west and lifted the waters of the lake into little waves that broke against the dam wall. It began to rain, in heavy bursts, blown horizontally at the men on the dam so that they were soon almost as wet as the suit of the diver.

Night fell before the diver could go down again so work on the sluice had to be abandoned until the next day.

It had been a long, long day inside the tower. Mostly Amy still enjoyed being close to Huw. As the day progressed his caresses had become less tender and his hands seemed to explore her body in a progressively intimate way. This caused involuntary warmth to spread through her limbs, especially her lower body, and her heart began to beat faster. She did not resist. But some misgivings had begun to form. It was like being married, she supposed, this concentrated time together and not all that she learned about her enforced partner was positive. She discovered that he had no knowledge of world affairs. His world was Wales and he saw everything from a Welsh perspective. He knew nothing of literature beyond Welsh poetry and stories. But why should this matter? She could pass on her knowledge to him as he passed his onto her.

The Stolen Valley

What worried her more was that he had stopped talking about their life together. Instead he seemed more and more concerned about his home, his father and his sister and how they would cope without him, especially now that Gwyn was unable to walk, at least for some time. The more she pressed him about their future the more he seemed to avoid considering it.

And sometimes his frustration at being penned up in this tower made him short with her. He would suddenly leap up and walk rapidly about the platform, causing it to shake disturbingly, stretching his arms and legs, breathing deeply and cursing in Welsh. She understood that Huw was a very physical person, used to striding across the hills and doing hard work with his strong arms. This confinement was beginning to get him down.

Amy too began to feel unsettled. She was becoming thirsty and felt hot and dirty. She wanted to wash and change her clothes and her bladder had begun to fill.

But most of the time they were happy in one another's company, embracing and kissing or simply lying close together on the small wooden platform, while Huw told her some of the stories his mother had told him or taught her some Welsh songs.

At last the dim daylight in the tower began to fade. Huw lit the candle again and they lay still for a while watching the light flickering across the walls of the tower. Suddenly Huw said, 'I am sure that we shall be rescued soon, probably in the morning, but we cannot go on much longer without drinking. Let us take a chance with the water in the tower and drink as much as we can. Then if we have other needs it will not matter so much if we pollute the water.'

Amy saw the sense in what he said.

'I'll go first. If the water is really bad I will know by the taste. And I have been drinking such water all my life without any harm. Will you support my legs?'

Amy agreed and Huw leant over the edge of the platform and drank from the water cupped in his hands. She held on to his legs, feeling the hardness of his calf muscles and remembering how sturdy they had looked when he was naked and how easily he had leapt up the slopes of Cadair Idris. He paused, then drank again. At last he sat up, wiping his face with his sleeve and laughing, 'Well, I'm not dead yet.'

Now it was Amy's turn. Huw gripped her thighs as she leant forward and drank deeply. The water tasted good, slightly bitter and very cool. When she had drunk enough she splashed water over face. She could feel Huw's fingers pressing into her thighs, almost to her buttocks and with perhaps more force than was absolutely necessary and she felt that warmth spreading through her own limbs again.

Now they both needed to relieve themselves. Amy turned away as Huw stood on the edge of the platform, unbuttoned himself and released a strong stream of urine into the water. Then he moved and turned away while she removed her undergarments, sat on the edge of the wooden platform and emptied her own bladder. There was something about this sharing of usually private functions that equally pleased and disturbed her.

She did not replace her drawers but lay down beside Huw again and let him encircle her in his arms. Suddenly he groaned and rolled over on top of her. He hugged her close, almost squeezing the breath out of her and she felt his hard manhood pressing against her. In a momentary panic Amy swept out her arm, catching the candle and sending it into the water.

In the sudden darkness her courage failed at last. For a moment all hope of rescue deserted her and she felt strangely calm. She whispered, 'Huw. If I am to die. Make me a woman first.'

Ella could see at once why John liked Joseph. It was the attraction of opposites. Doctor Lever was such a round smiling, extrovert, while John was tall, thin and dour. And it was obvious that the man from Liverpool liked women. She felt him appraising her and liking what he saw.

'Well, I can see where Amy gets her looks.'

'Her father was a good looking man,' said Ella teasingly, but she enjoyed the implied compliment.

She was not so sure about Philip. He was not at all like his father, either in looks or manner. He might be handsome one day but his face was as yet unmoulded and spoiled by a constant sneer. She had heard about the way Amy had rejected him. Perhaps he was tarring her mother with the same shameful brush.

'How is the invalid?' asked John.

'Not good,' replied the doctor. 'He is still unconscious and his pulse is very weak.'

John explained to Ella how the man had been found near the tunnel and they hoped if he woke he might be able to tell them something about Huw and Ella.

'One thing we do know now,' said Philip, 'is that Huw had a hand in all this. They have found evidence that the explosives were stolen from the quarry where he worked.'

'But the dead men have now been identified. They all worked at the same quarry as Huw,' said John. 'Surely any one of them...'

'No. Only a man with Huw's particular skill would have access to the explosives.'

Ella was suddenly frightened.

'Do you think Amy might have been involved as well?'

'They found no female corpse in the tunnel. And I believe that Huw would have made sure he was far away by the time of the explosion.'

Ella was relieved to hear this. She was also aware that Philip very much wanted Huw to be implicated. It was obvious that Amy's rejection had made him very bitter.

Joseph had asked one of the maids to keep an eye on the injured man while he greeted his guests. He went off to check that she was being diligent while Philip led the others into the dining room. When he returned he sat next to George and asked, 'Have you thought any more about my offer of help, young man?'

George always felt more grown up when he was with Joseph. He knew that he was being taken seriously.

'I've thought of little else...'he began, then added rather guiltily, 'Well except about Amy of course.' As he said this he knew that she no longer meant so much to him. He was over that at last.

They were just beginning the dessert when the maid who had been left to look after the injured man rushed into the room and curtsied in front of Doctor Lever. She could speak no English but she pointed at her eyes and fluttered her lashes. Her dumb show made it clear that something had changed in the sick room. They all followed her. The man was writhing on his makeshift bed and his eyes were now wide open. He looked at each of them in turn, then sat up and began to mutter something in Welsh. Suddenly George understood.

'The castle in the water! That is what he is saying. The castle in the water. I think he must mean the straining tower.'

'But they checked there. It was locked. You told me.' said John.

George asked the man in Welsh, 'Is that where they are? The man and the girl?'

The man nodded vigorously, but that was a mistake. It must have disturbed a clot in the brain. The man groaned, collapsed back onto the bed and lay still but with his eyes staring open and a look of horror on his face. After a pause Joseph put his ear to the man's mouth and shook his head. He felt the man's pulse, then closed the man's eyes. The maid wailed. Ella comforted her and helped her out of the room.

'You must go at once,' said Joseph. 'Find the chief engineer. He will have a key.'

'And inform the police,' added Philip. 'They will want to speak to Huw.'

'But Huw wouldn't...' began George but Philip cut him short.

'They must have had inside help to get hold of a key. For the tower and the tunnel as well. There were many Welshmen among the labourers. One of them could easily have been bribed.'

'That doesn't matter now,' said John, going across to Ella who had just re-entered the room. 'We must get to the tower as soon as possible. Please God, we are not too late...'

Ella smiled to hear her husband invoking the Lord.

'You go with them, Philip,' said Joseph. I will stay here with our poor dead man. Annie will help me. Go! Go!'

Rain was still falling heavily as the carriage took them to the Chief Engineer's house. He was not happy to be woken in the middle of the night, but at last grasped the urgency of the situation. He sent one of his men to fetch the key to the tower. They went next to the police station. The Sergeant and a couple of constables, in their own vehicle, followed the carriage as it made its way alongside the lake.

They had made love twice. The second time had given Amy more pleasure than pain. After the first time she had wiped away the blood with her drawers and thrown them into the water.

Huw had been gentle but determined. After the second time, when she had been more aware of his movement inside her, she had felt his release coinciding with her own. Any doubts about sharing a future with him had temporarily faded. The only doubt now was whether they had a future at all. Would they be rescued in time? Meanwhile they had fallen asleep in one another's arms.

Amy woke first. For a moment she did not know where she was. The darkness was complete and terrifying. Then she heard Huw's heavy breathing and was slightly reassured. But there was something wrong. She felt weak and shivery and her back and legs felt damp. At first she thought her bladder might have filled again and that the lovemaking had caused it to overflow, or perhaps she had begun to bleed once more. Then she realised what had happened. The water in the tower had risen and had just begun to cover the platform.

Trapped

In a panic she woke Huw. He felt the damp boards beneath him, stood up and helped Amy to her feet. As they stood up the platform begin to sway. The rising water must have loosened its connections to the wall of the tower. Huw carefully led the way in the total darkness to where he thought the iron stairs were located but each step he took seemed to set the platform swaying more dangerously and as his one hand grasped the rail at the side of the stairs the platform gave way completely. Amy slipped into the water and her cry for help was muffled as her head went right under the water but Huw had kept hold of her wrist and now he pulled her up onto the staircase, water dripping from her hair and soaked clothing. Just as they reached the top of the stairs they heard the lock being drawn outside and the heavy door swung open. They were dazzled by the light from several lanterns shining straight into their faces and Huw felt Amy collapsing in his arms. John left Ella's side and rushed forward, pulling Amy out of Huw's arms and carrying her, shivering with cold and fright, across the bridge towards the carriage. It had all become too much for the young English girl and she fainted in her stepfather's arms.

Huw hurried after John trying to explain what had happened but found his way blocked by the policemen. The Sergeant announced, 'Huw Morris, you are to come with us for questioning on several serious charges. Take him away.'

The Constables took an arm each and forced Huw over the bridge. As he passed through the little group at the other end he saw Philip's expression of triumph and George's look of concern before he was pushed into the police vehicle and driven away.

The Stolen Valley

Part Two

1895

'Ah, poor humanity! So frail, so fair,
Are the fond visions of thy early day,
Till tyrant passion, and corrosive care,
Bid all thy fairy colours fade away.'

Charlotte Smith (1749 – 1806)

The Stolen Valley

1

The Funeral

The last workman had long left the Vyrnwy valley. The dam was weathering into gentler shades of grey and the lake behind it was filled to the brim. Millions of gallons of good Welsh water were lifted each day into the tower, strained through the wire gauze and sent along the aqueduct to Liverpool, sixty-eight miles away. Thousands of trees which had been planted on the bare hillsides were maturing rapidly and a series of wooded slopes were now reflected in the slate-blue surface of the lake. The road around the lake was much used by well-off tourists from over the border, coming to stay at the fine hotel built on the hillside, and enjoy shooting and fishing. Day trips were organised from nearby towns so that the less well-off could enjoy the picturesque spectacle of the dam and the lake and spend their pennies at the village shop.

A few of the inhabitants of old Llanwddyn still felt bitter about their enforced move and some had left the valley altogether to start new lives in the cities of the North or Midlands. Some had even taken ship to new lands, but most of the villagers had settled quickly into their better built homes on the slopes near the dam. Children had become young adults, had married others from their own or nearby villages and some now had children of their own. These were children who would never see the dusty streets of old Llanwddyn. Most would find it hard to imagine that there had ever been such a place.

Death too had brought change to the new village. In the last five years more than a dozen villagers had succumbed to illness or accident or simply old age and had been taken in their coffins to the burial ground near the new church. Today it was to be the turn of Megan Owen.

As the coffin was carried out by the undertaker's men and loaded carefully onto the cart George thought it looked too small even for his grandmother's tiny body; more like that of a child. He was distraught; filled not so much with grief as guilt. His life during the last few years had been so interesting and fulfilling that he had rarely returned to Llanwddyn. But he knew that Megan would never have begrudged him the chance to use his brains and skill to make his fortune and her sudden illness was entirely a matter of bad luck. She had been visiting friends in Bala when an epidemic of whooping cough arrived in the town and spread rapidly. The symptoms soon became apparent and she knew she no longer had the strength, in her mid-eighties, to fight the disease so she insisted on being taken home. Eventually the disease turned into pneumonia and finally, when she knew that death was imminent, she had asked that her grandson be informed.

When he eventually arrived George was shocked by his grandmother's appearance. The last time he had seen her, several months before, she had been the same energetic and inquisitive person he had always known. Now she was shrivelled, shrinking daily, weakened by those frequent fits of coughing which left her gasping for breath. At first she did not seem to recognise him, but gradually their old closeness returned. To George she had been a mother rather than grandmother, since his actual mother's untimely death when he was six years old. Even now as a generally admired and well respected man in his early twenties the loss of the woman who had cared for him for most of his life hit him hard.

He had moved on from school to study engineering in Liverpool. Now he was working for a famous shipbuilding company, in a junior capacity, helping to design their next great ocean-going liner. His social life had developed too. Since his estrangement from Philip,

Joseph had treated George as his own son, so he was never without funds or friends. He had become a handsome young man as Joseph had once prophesied. He was pursued by young women for his looks and his prospects and had already broken several hearts.

The coffin was laid on the beribboned cart and one of the undertaker's men took hold of the single black-plumed pony's bridle and clicked his tongue. The pony jerked forward, apparently disconcerted by the light weight of the load, then steadied and moved on smoothly. George took his place as chief mourner immediately behind the cart as it rolled towards the dam which the funeral procession must cross to reach the church built on the tree covered hillside beyond. For a reason known only to herself, Mrs Owen had switched her allegiance from chapel to church almost as soon as she moved to the new village. Now the bell was tolling from that new church to call her to her final resting place.

John and Ella Noble walked behind George with little John, now nearly twelve years old, between them. He had grown quickly in the last year and there were indications that he was going to be as tall and thin as his father, and possibly of the same serious disposition. The poor health of his early years had long passed. Riding lessons at the Manor House and joining the hunt, whenever he could, had given him physical fitness and attendance at that school in Shrewsbury had made him an able and confident boy.

The Nobles had left Hope Underhill yesterday and stayed at a hotel in Llanfyllin overnight, determined not to be late for the burial service of such an old friend. They had not in fact had any contact with Mrs Owen during the last few years, because she bitterly disapproved of an action they had taken. Nevertheless, when George informed them of her death, they immediately made plans to return to Llanwddyn. There were no other family mourners so they occupied the next rank in the procession.

Ella thought how fine George looked in his well-cut suit, probably provided by Joseph. He had grown into a sturdy young man with dark brown wavy hair above a strongly moulded face. She remembered a photograph of his mother that Megan had once shown her.

The resemblance was obvious. Even in grief George walked upright with a determined stride.

They reached the dam and began to cross. There had been a great deal of rain that autumn and the lake was completely filled, stretching away far beyond the old drowned village into the distant hills, where its shoreline was lost in morning mist. In fact the lake was overfull and as they crossed the dam the mourners could hear the thunder of excess water spilling over the sill beneath them and pouring in a white sheet down the outer wall. The day was quite bright for November, with only a few small clouds scudding across a pale blue sky.

It was almost impossible now to believe that the view had ever been different. How completely the valley had changed and the past been obliterated. What he saw now seemed to George far more beautiful than it had been before; a perfect blending of wide, wind-ruffled water and steep wooded hills. Had there ever really been anything else? Had he really lived in a house just above the village with his grandmother and seen this magnificent dam rising huge stone by stone. Had he really watched Huw and Gwyn knocking down those houses in the old village? Had he and Amy and Philip really ridden their ponies across meadows that were now deep under the lake? It seemed impossible. The only real loss for him was that of his beloved grandmother who had brought him to live in this valley half a lifetime ago.

But George was not the only one looking back in time. When they reached the other end of the dam John looked northward, saw the tower and remembered that terrible time when his stepdaughter had been imprisoned there, but he had forced himself not to think of her for so long that she had almost ceased to exist. He shuddered momentarily, adjusted the collar of his winter coat and strode quickly on.

The cart began to slow as it climbed the steep lane towards the church and the two dozen or so mourners walking behind adjusted their pace accordingly. The tolling of the bell, brought from the old church whose ruins now lay deep under the lake, increased

The Funeral

in volume as the church came into view. The pony halted near the porch as it was trained to do, the men transferred the coffin from the cart to a bier and the mourners followed it into the church as the old bell ceased to toll.

The church was solidly built of the same blue, grey stone as the dam. Above its slate roof rose a small turret in which the bell swung silently a few more times, then stopped, so that the only sounds were a faint murmur from the organ within the church and the harsh calls of rooks from the dark pines which surrounded the churchyard. Inside the light from the brass lamps hanging above the pews was dimmed by the cold brightness of the November sun illuminating the stained glass windows as the mourners took their places behind George who sat alone in the front pew. The organ wheezed to a stop and the vicar began the service, which for the sake of the majority of the mourners was in Welsh.

The sound of that language reminded George of his Grandmother so that the tears he had held back all morning now flowed uncontrollably. Little John looked at his father, with a puzzled expression and whispered, 'Is that Welsh the vicar is speaking, father?' But John put a finger to his lips and his son had learned that his father was a man to be obeyed.

Some of the villagers smiled at the memory of an earlier service, when all those bigwigs from Liverpool had come to celebrate the formal opening of the water supply to their city. In the last few years some compromises had been achieved between the church and the people of Wales so that the bitterness of former days had faded a little and the arrival of frequent English visitors to admire the new lake and the dam had caused the vicar to give services in Welsh and English on alternate Sundays. So the grand ceremony had been fixed to take place on an English Sunday, but when the Mayor of Liverpool and his entourage had settled in the best pews the vicar arrived and began the service in Welsh - perhaps he had mixed up his Sundays? - and so it continued throughout, much to the bewilderment and increasing annoyance of the party from Merseyside.

After today's service the coffin was carried across the narrow road to the little steeply sloping cemetery on the other side, where many of the graves were filled by corpses that had been brought from the old church. The sun had gone in and a cold wind sprang up, causing the mourners to huddle closely round the open grave as the coffin was lowered into it. The familiar words of committal were obvious to John even in this foreign language. Then the service was over and the mourners made their way swiftly down the hill to get out of the wind and enjoy the funeral feast which George had arranged to be served at his grandmother's cottage.

When the last mourner had gone the gravedigger spat on his palms, picked up his spade and set to work: glad of the exertion to warm his chilled limbs. Soon the grave was filled and a little mound was formed from the soil displaced by the coffin. He patted down the earth, replaced the turfs he had cut and piled before digging the hole and set the few wreaths and bunches of flowers on the neat mound. He stood for a moment to light a pipe and admire his handiwork, then carefully cleaned his spade, returned it to the hut in the corner of the graveyard and made his way home.

As soon as the gravedigger was out of sight two figures stepped from the shadows of the surrounding trees. One was a woman, pulling a tattered shawl over her thin dress in a vain attempt to keep warm, the other was a child, perhaps four or five years old, clinging to her mother's skirts as she stumbled across the uneven ground. When they reached the new grave the woman stood still for a while, her eyes closed and her face contorted with pain. When she opened her eyes she reached down and studied the little card attached to one of the wreaths. She read aloud the message, 'From John and Ella Noble, and their son John, in memory of a dear friend.' and her eyes filled with tears.

The little girl turned her thin face up to the woman and asked, 'Are you crying, Mama?'

The Funeral

The woman quickly wiped her eyes with her sleeve, picked up the little girl and kissed her cold, pale cheek.

'It's only the wind my dear. It made my eyes water.'

'Can we go soon? I don't like this place.'

The woman looked again at the wreaths and sighed.

'That big one will be from George.'

'Who is he?'

'Someone I used to know. It is his grandmother who is buried here.'

'Was she a nice lady?'

'Oh yes, very kind.'

'Have I got a grandmother, Mama?'

Tears threatened again. The woman hugged the child to her and tried to keep a sob out of her voice as she answered. 'Yes, you have a grandmother. Perhaps you will meet her one day.'

The woman quickly grew tired of the weight of the child, which caused a pain in her abdomen, though she was very light, and lowered her to the ground, where she examined the wreaths herself.

'Why do people put flowers on graves? Surely they will soon die?'

'It's just something people do. To show their respect, I suppose.'

'Why haven't we got any flowers?'

'I'm afraid flowers like that cost much more than we can afford. And there aren't many wild ones at this time of year'

'So how can we show *our* respectacles?'

The woman smiled at the little girl's mistake, then an idea came to her and she said. 'I know. We'll borrow these.' She picked up a middle sized wreath. 'You take that small bunch over there. Now we'll go down the path a little way, then walk back to the grave and put our flowers on it. That will show our respects'

The little girl liked the idea of a game, so she picked up the smallest bunch of flowers and was about to join her mother when a

215

man's voice shouted angrily, 'Hey, you! Get away from that grave! What the devil do you think you're doing?'

The woman looked up and saw a red-faced man in a long black coat hurrying towards them. She picked up the little girl, helped her over the fence and ran with her into the trees.

At Mrs Owen's cottage her own and several borrowed tables were smothered with plates of dainty sandwiches and buttered chunks of bara brith. Mrs Evans had spent hours preparing her neighbour's funeral feast. The cold day and the long walk had given all the mourners a good appetite so the plates began to empty rapidly. Little John had soon got bored with the occasion and gone to look at the dam. John and Ella sat to one side as the only strangers in the room. They watched George circulating among the mourners and resurrecting his rusty Welsh to thank them for attending his grandmother's funeral. But at last the turn came for him to speak to them.

John asked him why Joseph had been unable to accompany him.

'Poor Joseph has not been well. He suffered a seizure a few months ago and has since been unable to walk properly. His speech is also slightly impaired and he is too embarrassed to be much in company.'

'Oh, I am sorry,' said Ella. 'He is such a kind and generous man.'

'Indeed. He has been my benefactor and my truest friend. I try to help as much as I can but he insists that I have more important things to do'

'But what of Philip?' asked John. 'Surely he could help. After all he must have qualified as a doctor several years ago.'

'We rarely see him and his visits are always short. After that dreadful time when your daughter was rescued from the tower...'

The Funeral

John was about to say that he did not have a daughter, but George went on...

'something happened between Philip and his father. By the time I moved to Liverpool Philip had left to live elsewhere. We do not even know precisely where that might be.'

'So he did not take on his father's practice?'

'No. When Joseph retired the practice was purchased by another doctor. I am told that it is rather in decline.'

'So who is caring for Joseph?' Ella asked.

'Oh, he is very well looked after. His housekeeper, Mrs Bruce, has been with him for years and a nurse calls in each day. Though she tells me he is very difficult patient.'

Ella smiled, 'I can imagine that'

'Of course Joseph was disappointed not to be able to come with me. He would have loved to see you both again. And I think he hoped he might see your daughter as well. I remember once he told me...'

John interrupted.

'We don't have a daughter.'

'But Amy...'

'She chose to go her own way. We have forgotten her.'

George was puzzled. He noted that as Ella turned away he thought he saw the glint of a tear in her eye. John's face remained as hard as stone. Now George began to understand why the letters he had written to Amy when they had first parted remained unanswered. Of course he had long got over that childish crush on her and so many other pretty faces had passed his gaze since then that he could not even clearly remember hers. John led him away and began to ask about his life in Liverpool. Ella was about to follow when little John rushed towards her, his eyes gleaming with excitement.

'Oh, Mother, it was quite amazing. I leant over the parapet and saw all that water crashing down. The noise was tremendous.' Then his face became serious. 'Oh, and as I was coming back a strange thing happened. I was just passing the turret at this end when I saw a woman and a little girl huddled in the doorway to keep out of the cold. I think they might have been gypsies or beggars. The woman's clothes were ragged and dirty and they both looked very hungry. But the strange thing is that as I walked past the woman smiled at me and seemed to say my name but I couldn't be sure because of the noise of the water. Anyway, something about them made me afraid so I hurried back here.'

Ella was about to ask her son to tell her more when little John suddenly saw the almost empty plates on the tables. His walk in the cold air had made him hungry again so he dashed across to grab a sandwich before they all disappeared. Ella thought about what he had said and for a moment wondered what it meant, but rapidly decided that he had been mistaken. The woman was probably simply asking him for alms.

But what her son had told her left her disturbed. She withdrew to a corner and watched the others in the crowded room enthusiastically partaking in the post-funeral feast. Perhaps, she pondered, it is the reminder of our own mortality at another's internment which lightens the hearts of those left alive.

The clatter of crockery and the clink of glasses grew ever louder and the voices rose accordingly to be heard above the din. Most of the voices were speaking Welsh and Ella was reminded of the harmonium they had just acquired for the school when it was played with all the stops out. The faces around her were becoming scarlet and sweaty in the confined space and within their bulky mourning clothes so that she thought some of the older ones might soon explode.

Suddenly she had to get out of the room. No one seemed to notice as she sidled through the crowd, or perhaps they assumed she was making for the privy. She collected her coat from the hallway and slipped outside.

She found herself running towards the dam. Her heart was thumping in her chest as she reached the turret and looked into the doorway but of course the woman and her child had gone.

The Funeral

Ella looked around but saw no-one. As she walked slowly back to the cottage she found that she was trembling. John was waiting for her at the door.

'Ella? Where have you been?'

'I had to get out. It was so warm and noisy.'

'Oh yes. And all that Welsh was beginning...'

Suddenly he noticed the strange look on his wife's face. She took his hands and held them firmly.

'John.'

'Yes?'

'I had the strangest feeling that Amy was nearby.'

'That's ridiculous!'

'It was something little John said...'

'We must stop calling him that. He'll soon be taller than me.'

'John, listen. There was a woman and a child.'

'No. You listen. Amy made her choice all those years ago. I told her then that she was no longer welcome at our house. I have not changed my mind. She made her bed, so she must lie...'

'And I agreed with you then. The shame she would have brought on us. Most probably you would have been removed from your post. It would have ruined our son's life too. But now... Oh, John, she is my daughter, and I felt that she needed me...That something terrible...'

'This is nonsense, Ella. Why would she be here? She's a grown woman now. If she had been absolutely desperate she would have got in touch. No. She doesn't need your help anymore.'

John put his arms around his wife and she grew calm. Of course he was right. Amy would now be twenty-four years old. It would have been her birthday two months ago. She might be married. She might have other children even. She had managed without her mother's help for all these years. Why would she need her now?'

'Come inside again, my dear. You're shivering. We must find out what our son is up to.'

The woman and the little girl were walking beside the lake at the beginning of their long journey home. Home for the woman was a damp room in a dockside court and when she returned to Liverpool she would have to give up her daughter again. Amy – for that is who it was- had hoped to be in time for the funeral but the old man who gave them a lift from Bala in his cart could not get his ancient nag to increase its pace. She had thought that if she joined the others around the grave there might have been some sort of reconciliation but by the time they had climbed all the way up to the church the mourners had gone. There was only that gravedigger and he left soon after. When the vicar had spotted them in the graveyard she had run through the trees, clutching her daughter, and then made her way down to the dam. Both were exhausted and very glad to find shelter in the doorway of that turret. Amy's sickness returned and she badly wanted just to lie down.

Amy had known her brother at once, though it had been several years since she last saw him, but when she called his name he had run off. She did not have the courage to go to the cottage and spoil Megan's funeral with a scene and she knew that if they did not begin their return journey to Bala soon they would miss the last train. So slowly, reluctantly, because she was disappointed, tired, and hungry and because her body was wracked with pain she had taken her daughter's hand and walked on.

When they reached the straining tower Amy paused for a moment, her memories stirred by those solid walls rising from the deep water of the lake. She shuddered at the memory of that tower's interior, flickering in the candle light and the black water swirling beneath her...and then that dreadful moment when she had woken to find the water rising and the platform had collapsed...

2

Aftermath

Amy had fainted as she was rescued from the tower and when she returned to consciousness she was in bed at Mrs Evan's house, with Ella sitting beside her, holding her hand. Whatever had caused the fever, the shock of imprisonment or her immersion in that water or the whole traumatic experience, she had felt its first stirrings even then. She remembered little of the journey back to Shropshire or the following weeks when she lay in her bed in the school house while the fever raged. At its peak she had terrible visions of being drowned or being locked in that tower for ever. Occasionally Huw's face would appear, but it was grotesquely enlarged and misshapen and his burning skin was covered in sweat. He had become part of her nightmares.

As the crisis passed she thought more kindly of him again, remembering his embraces and wondering vaguely what had happened to him, but she did not have the energy to pursue an enquiry. At last as she began her long convalescence she was finally able to ask, but all she got for answer was, 'He went away. We do not know where.' Sometimes she wondered why he had not tried to contact her. Perhaps his letters were being intercepted? But gradually, and thankfully for her future health, the memory of that whole Welsh episode began to fade.

When at last her convalescence was over she was allowed to take up her place at college. Allowance had been made for her illness and she was given some extra tuition to bring her up to scratch. At first, when she moved to the city where her college was situated she felt homesick and constantly tired but in the female, cloistered atmosphere of the training college some of her enthusiasm for study began to return. Her looks also improved a little. She had lost the radiance of extreme youth, her figure had not quite filled out again and her emerald eyes were less lustrous than before but the main change in her was not something outwardly apparent.

Soon she knew that all was not well. Her monthly periods had stopped – she thought at first this was due to her illness – but then other symptoms appeared which she could not ignore. Amy was an intelligent girl who was not ignorant of the facts of life and soon recognised that she was pregnant. What on earth was she to do? Who could she consult?

Of course she had heard those old wives' tales of gin, hot baths, spicy food or vigorous exercise and she knew that in the backstreets of any city there were women who would 'rid her of her trouble' at a price. But she also knew that these back street abortions could be extremely dangerous. And did she really want to lose the child? After all it was made out of her love for Huw, though she wondered now how much he had really loved her. After all he had still made no attempt to contact her. Twice she had written to him at Tynygraig but her letters had not been answered.

So she continued the routine of her studies, and most of the time was able to put her problem out of her mind. She had not yet begun to show and anyway her simple student clothes easily disguised any alteration in her physique. She found that her appetite became voracious but her companions saw that as a natural return to health. Her energy level had also increased, since the initial morning sickness had eased. Luckily the college was newly built and the sanitary arrangements were up-to-date so she had been able to hide that early symptom in the privacy of a cubicle. She found her studies fairly easy and generally rewarding, though she was careful not to partake too enthusiastically in the weekly drill. All in all she was enjoying herself but whenever she had time to pause her problem returned and at night she often cried herself quietly to sleep.

At last the end of term drew near and she was due to return to Hope Underhill. Well there was no other way. She must tell her parents. Surely at that time of 'goodwill to all men' centred about the birth of a child, they would be sympathetic to her plight and ready to help. She knew that her mother had been about the same age when she herself had been born. She was not so sure about her stepfather's response. He had shocked her with his attitude when he had discovered about Huw, and since that time their relationship had never recovered its old intimacy, though he had been solicitous enough during her illness. But surely it was just a matter of finding the right time to tell her mother and leave her to pass on the news to her husband. Of course it would come as a great shock to both of them and it would mean an end to her chosen career but surely...

So, she dressed carefully to hide her secret and went home. The Christmas holiday began. The last of the decade. The weather colluded with the festive mood and dropped a light fall of snow on Christmas Eve. Her brother was still young enough to be filled with excitement. She put her atheism to one side and went to church with her parents and actually enjoyed the sense of community as most of the village packed into the old church and sang those familiar carols with great gusto. When they returned from church on Christmas morning she gave her brother a gift she had found in the large bright shops of the city. He was delighted when he unwrapped that perfect model of a horse drawn gun carriage with its attendant gunners. John was pleased with her gift to him; a copy of 'The Study in Scarlet' by that popular new author Mr Conan Doyle. For her mother she had found a small locket which though not particularly valuable – after all she was living merely on her allowance from John – was very pretty and might perhaps one day contain a tiny photograph of her first grandchild.

In the whirl of Christmas it was easy to put off the moment, but in the post-festive lull it could be avoided no longer. The snow had melted and an unseasonably mild spell followed. Amy had noticed how much better her parents were getting on these days. The events in Wales during that summer seemed to have brought them closer again, but John was still a restless sort of man so as soon as the festivities were over he wanted to walk off the extra pounds he had put on during the recent sedentary days: though those pounds were more in his imagination than reality. He suggested that Amy accompany him and little John on a walk up to the Long Hill. But Amy saw her chance and asked to be excused so that she could spend some time with her mother. John was at first a little disappointed but these days his relationship with his son had much improved so they would enjoy a walk together and he thought it only fair for the ladies to be given the chance to discuss female things. So when the men had gone Amy sat beside the fire opposite her mother and began her confession.

'Mother, I have something to tell you.'

'Ah, I wondered when you would say it. John and I both noticed how much better you were looking and how much calmer you seemed. You have met someone haven't you? '

'No, mother... It's not that? Well not exactly...You see...'

'Oh don't worry. We expected it to happen. After all you are an attractive young woman. And so long as he is suitable, and has the means to support you, we would be happy for you both. Of course it would have to be a long engagement. And you would have to abandon your career.'

'Mother, please. Listen to me.

Amy looked at her mother's smiling face, rosy from the glow of the piled fire. The whole scene was the epitome of a happy home. She would have liked nothing better than to end the conversation there, to walk away, to pretend that nothing was the matter. Instead she must go on.

'Mother... I am expecting a child.'

Ella's face turned pale as milk. Her sewing dropped to the floor. Her mouth hung open.

'That is impossible' Suddenly, she realised. 'Oh my God! That Welshman!'

When the two Johns returned from their walk full of the things they had seen they found Ella sitting alone staring into the fire and no sign of Amy. Her husband was puzzled when she handed a letter to their son, saying, 'I want you to go to the Manor House and hand this letter to Squire Morton.'

'But I'm hungry, Mama.'

'Well, take some cake from the pantry. But hurry. It's urgent.'

'Very well.'

The thought of cutting a large slice of that splendid cake he had seen on the slab in the pantry made up for the tedious nature of his errand, so he was soon on his way. And anyway he enjoyed the company of Robert Moreton and his children. Perhaps they might go for a ride together.

When his son had gone John asked his wife, 'What on earth was so urgent?'

'Nothing. I simply wanted him out of the way. Sit down, John, while I give you some dreadful news.'

After her confession Amy had left her silent mother and gone to her room. She had heard her stepfather and brother return, then someone left again and for a few moments an ominous silence prevailed. Then came an awful howl from the room below, followed by heavy footsteps on the stairs. A fist banged on the door but John did not wait to be admitted. He was so angry that he spat out his words.

'You will pack your bags and leave this house first thing in the morning. And you will never return.'

'But...'

'What you have done will bring shame on the whole family. If it was known I would probably be dismissed from my post. Your mother would never be able to show her face in the village and your brother...'

Amy felt her own anger rising

'I do not believe you can be so cruel, John. Just when I most need your help. I am sure my mother...'

'She agrees with me entirely. You are not to leave this room tonight. We shall tell your brother that you are not feeling well. You must be ready for the carrier first thing in the morning. And you are not to try to say goodbye to your mother or your brother'

Amy burst into tears.

'But where am I to go?'

'That is for you to decide. I shall not send you away entirely empty handed. When you leave in the morning I will give you the small sum I had saved for your future. But my advice to you is to find the father of your child. He is responsible for your condition. Let him look after you now.'

Her stepfather left the room. She flung herself onto her bed and wept.

On the following morning Amy was pleased that there was a thick mist and she was the only passenger waiting for the carrier to take her over Long Hill to Churchtown, where she would board the train back to the nearby city. She hugged her winter cloak about her and did not look up at the carter. Thank goodness he was a stranger, and he seemed to be as wrapped up in his thoughts as she was in hers.

She could hardly believe what had happened. To be turned out of her own home and told never to return. She had read of such scenes in the cheap novels that were popular among her fellow students, but she had thought her own parents far too modern and enlightened to behave in that way. Of course her predicament would have caused a scandal in the village and it would indeed have reflected badly on her family but such things pass. After all she was Ella's daughter and John had treated her as his daughter for so many years, and now, when she desperately needed their help…

But as the journey continued her determined personality began to shine through. She would manage. She was not destitute. She had hidden the sovereigns that John had given in a very secure place. If she found some cheap lodgings that sum would last for quite a while. Surely her parents would soon come round; especially her mother. Meanwhile she would write to Huw again and wait for his reply. Of course he would invite her to Tynygraig and when he saw her situation he would do the right thing. It was not the future she had planned but at least her baby would have a proper home. And it would be wonderful to see dear Nan again.

Amy found cheap but decent lodgings near the river, with a woman who owned a millinery shop, and her spoiled son. She informed the college that she would not be continuing her studies, telling them that she had been offered a post abroad. She did not immediately write to her mother. It seemed best to give her time, but she did write to Huw and waited eagerly for his reply.

She was now five months pregnant and just beginning to show, but with looser clothing and her winter coat she was able to disguise her situation. Her health was good and her appetite keen: she found herself craving for the strangest things, including fish paste and coal. Another symptom was a weariness that would suddenly overwhelm her, even in the middle of the day, so that she would slump on a bench in the park and close her eyes.

Life began to pass in a haze. Each day she would walk around the city, or by the river, or out into the nearest villages. She avoided those places where she was most likely to meet any of her former fellow students. The main point of every day was the arrival of the post but no letter came. She wrote again, this time to Nan, who would surely reply.

Amy had told her landlady that she only needed the room for a few weeks, until she went to join her husband in Wales. She had purchased a small gold ring, which she wore on the appropriate finger and called herself Mrs Morris. Her room was quite comfortable and her rent included fuel for her fire which Alan, her son, brought up to the room each day. There was something about Alan which made Amy squirm. She thought he may be slow witted. He did not go out to work. His mother never denied him anything, so he was overweight and went out each evening to drink at a local hostelry. When he brought up the coals for the fire he did not speak, though his jaw kept working as if he was about to and his lips glistened with spittle, but sometimes Amy caught him looking at her with a sort of leer.

A few weeks later she returned from her daily walk to find Alan in her room, looking through her underclothing in the chest of drawers. When he saw her his face turned scarlet and he scuttled downstairs. Amy checked that the little purse, where she kept the money that John had given her, was still in the drawer and sighed with relief when it was. But later when she looked inside she found that some of the coins had gone, which meant that were only four left and some small change she had in her coat pocket. When she confronted her landlady the woman became very angry, telling Amy that her son would never steal and giving her immediate notice to quit. Alan had left as usual for his evening drinking session.

Now there was only one thing that Amy could do. There was no point in trying to get her money back. Who would believe her? And she was left with so little money that there was no point in looking for more lodgings, so she packed what she could into a single suitcase, made her way to the railway station, enquired about the route to Dolgellau, and bought a single ticket. There was no train until next day so she settled down to sleep in the waiting room.

The rail journey was long and tedious, with several changes, and when she finally reached Dolgellau it was if the seasons had gone into reverse. During the last few weeks in the city the weather had been mild, almost spring-like but as she left that Welsh station a biting wind from the north blew flurries of snow into her face. She did not waste her dwindling money on a cab but set out on foot up the steep hill out of the town. It was very hard work. Her weariness, the extra weight of the growing child, the suitcase she carried and the slippery road all made the journey seem much further than she remembered, but the thought of that little house with a warm fire, a smile from Nan and some of her broth, and Huw taking her in his arms when he returned from the quarry sustained her.

At last the road began to descend and although Amy was worried about falling on the icy road and injuring the child inside her she hurried downhill. It had taken most of the day to reach this point of her journey and the light was already beginning to fade. The snow flurries had turned to a blinding white blizzard and she could only see a few yards of the road ahead, but at last she recognised the beginning of the driveway to Tynygraig.

As she hurried towards the house she was surprised that no light shone from its windows, but she reasoned that the family would all be huddled round the fire in the kitchen at the back. There were no animals in the little fields but again they would surely all be comfortably housed on this winter evening. At last she reached the door and knocked. There was no reply. She knocked again as loudly as her frozen hands would allow. No one came to open the door. Then she noticed that someone had fixed a padlock onto the outside of the door. Obviously this could only be unlocked from the outside so surely there would be no-one inside. What could have happened?

There was just enough light left for Amy to look around the farm. The wind had dropped and the snow stopped falling. There was not a sound. Amy walked wearily along the front of the house and tried the windows but they were firmly shut. She looked into the cow shed but it was empty. There was no pony in the little stable. She crossed to the chicken house but that was empty too. She listened for the sound of sheep, huddled in the fields but they too had gone. It was obvious that the farm and the house had been abandoned. Where had everyone gone? By now she was very cold and utterly exhausted. She returned to the stable, lay down on the pile of hay, pulled some more of it on top of her and, in spite of her fears that she might be sharing that hay with fleas or rats, soon fell asleep.

Next morning she was woken early by the songs of birds enjoying the sunlight filling the valley, though it had not yet reached the house at the bottom of the hill. The straw had kept her warm and she lay contentedly for a while imagining that when she returned to the door the Morris family would have returned. Suddenly she felt the child inside her give a gentle kick, making her momentarily queasy, followed by a moment of joy, then misery overwhelmed her again. What was she to do? It was no good dreaming. It was obvious that the Morris family no longer lived at Tynygraig. She had no idea how she might find out where they had gone. But her most immediate need was for food and drink.

Tynygraig was still in shadow and as Amy left the stable she shuddered in the frosty air. She walked around to the back of the house, used the privy, where several pages of newspaper hung unused, then peered through the kitchen window. She found a piece of slate, smashed the window, lifted the latch and climbed carefully inside. It was typical of Nan that the place had been left clean and tidy, as if she was expecting to come back or perhaps she just wanted the next occupants to see how well she had managed. There was a pile of logs next to the stove and some kindling in the grate. It may be damp but if Amy could find a match she might well get a fire going. The kettle hanging above the fireplace was half filled with water. She searched the whole room, but saw no means of lighting the fire, until she saw a man's jacket hanging behind the door. She recognised it at once as Gwyn's working jacket and when she felt in the pocket there indeed was a pipe stuffed with tobacco and a box of safety matches. Here was another mystery: why had he gone out without his working jacket and his beloved tobacco?

The only positive legacy of her stay at the milliner's house was the many times she had watched that horrid Alan laying a fire and setting it alight. Now she removed the kindling, found an old magazine on a chair, scrunched it up in the grate and replaced the kindling. Soon she had a fine blaze going and placed a couple of logs on top. Next Amy looked around her for something to cover the broken window. She was shocked to find that almost all the furniture remained in the other rooms. On one wall hung a framed sampler, its finely embroidered letters suggesting that the meek would inherit the earth. It was just the right size to fill the window space.

When she had looked around the rest of the house, increasingly puzzled by the fact that everything had been left as it was, Amy returned to the kitchen and heard the kettle burbling away. She opened the kitchen cupboard expecting to be disappointed but was overjoyed to find a caddy half filled with tea and a tin of biscuits, which had stayed remarkably fresh under the tight fitting lid. She shouted out loud, 'Oh, thank you Nan. Thank you. Thank you.'

As Amy dunked the biscuits in the milkless tea and greedily swallowed them she considered her situation. It was now March. The baby had been conceived in mid-August so she was now seven months gone. She felt reasonably healthy and the child had just proved that it was healthy too. She must have this child, she wanted this child, but where on earth could she go? Perhaps she should stay here at Tynygraig; after all it was Huw's child, but how would she live? And if she did somehow manage to stay until the baby was born she could not possibly cope with its birth on her own.

Perhaps she should find the nearest workhouse and ask to be admitted. At least then the baby would be born indoors and a midwife or some other capable person would attend the birth. But she had heard dreadful things about the workhouses. She had heard, especially, that after the birth of an illegitimate child it was often taken away from the mother for adoption. Who had told her that? Of course, it was Joseph, when he had been telling her about the Liverpool poor. Joseph! Why hadn't she thought of him before? Good kind, Joseph. If she could get to Liverpool and find his house, he would surely take her in. Of course it would mean facing Philip again but surely Joseph would take her side. She knew that Liverpool was somewhere to the north, but she was not too sure how to get there. The added problem was that she would have to find people to ask who spoke English.

Amy checked her purse. She had three sovereigns left and a few pennies. She could not spend all that on railway fares and find herself in Liverpool with nothing. After all it may take her some time to find Joseph's house. No she must walk or beg lifts as far as she could. But she could not continue to lug that suitcase with her. She would leave it here and take only the minimum of clothes, but she needed some sort of bag that she could carry more easily. She began to look around the house and there it was, hanging in the hallway, Huw's bag. But why was it here? Surely he needed it at the quarry or wherever he worked now? As she took the bag from its hook she could almost smell Huw and the memories came flooding back: that wonderful day on Cadair Idris; hurrying after him next morning with those sandwiches he had forgotten on purpose and running into his arms. Now she hugged the empty bag and wept.

'Mama, can we walk again. I'm getting cold.'

Gradually her daughter's voice cut through her reverie and Amy realised that she had been standing, gazing at the straining tower for ages. She took the little girl's hands, felt how cold they were, rubbed them between her own and walked on again.

'Poor Nan. You should have said something earlier. I've just been day dreaming.'

'Yes, Mama. Your face was very sad.'

There was a long way to go, and the pains that had returned throughout her body made each step an effort, but they must get to Bala and catch that train. It was not so far, and perhaps some kind person would come along and offer them a lift.

Soon they got into their stride, the pain eased a little and Amy began to remember that other much, much longer walk, from Tynygraig to Liverpool, when that baby – now her dear little Nan - was just beginning to make its presence felt inside her.

3

To Liverpool

It had taken almost two weeks for Amy to walk from Tynygraig, via Dolgellau, Bala, Ruthin, Mold, Queensferry, where she crossed the River Dee back into England, before trudging across the Wirall until at last she reached Birkenhead. Now she stood looking over the Mersey at the vast waterfront of Liverpool looming out of the mist on the other side. She could hardly believe the size of those buildings, or the mass of ships docked in front of them.

Amy was hungry and exhausted; her clothes were filthy rags, her boots worn through. When she began her journey she had hoped that by walking rather than travelling by train she would have some money left for food and lodgings when she reached Liverpool but on the very last night of her journey, she had lain exhausted in a doorway and while she was asleep her purse had been stolen. Now she had only enough money in her coat pocket to pay for the ferry, but her spirits lifted as she saw it coming towards her across the river, its paddle wheels churning and its funnel sending great gouts of black smoke up into the grey sky. At last her long journey was nearly over and soon she would find Joseph and all would be well.

During that long journey she had often gone without proper food, she had been soaked to the skin by driving rain, and because she had only the vaguest idea of her route she often got lost. It was on one of those occasions, when she had been crossing some bleak moorland, frequently lashed by showers, that she had accepted a lift from a man with a pony and cart. It was getting dark and she knew that she must find shelter soon or spend the night on the moor and perhaps perish in the cold and wet.

The Stolen Valley

The man seemed pleasant enough; he was middle aged and quite respectably dressed. She was reassured when he explained that he was the caretaker of a chapel just a few miles ahead and lived in an adjoining cottage. He spoke English but with a strong Welsh accent.

'I'm sure my wife won't mind you staying for a while.'

Amy was delighted. The thought of a night spent in a warm dry cottage and in the company of a generous woman gave her renewed hope that she would get to Liverpool and find Joseph. By now it was very dark. They passed no other dwellings but at last a black structure loomed ahead and as they grew closer she saw the dim outline of a chapel, surrounded by a graveyard, shrouded by yews and when the cart came to a halt there was the cottage, but there was no light in the windows and something unnerved Amy again.

'Isn't your wife here?' she asked.

'Oh yes. She's nearby.' The man asked, lighting a lantern left in the porch. 'Do come inside'

She followed the man into the cottage, where he lit a candle. The room they were in, the living room she supposed, was very untidy, with unwashed crockery on the table and clothes strewn everywhere. The man cleared a chair and offered Amy a seat. When she sat he stood nearby and in the candle light she saw how his long lank hair fell over his face which held a strange smile. The room was very cold as if a fire had not been lit in it for a long time.

'Do you have something I might drink?' asked Amy. She began to tremble slightly as the man hovered nearby.

'I must go and stable my pony and tell my wife you are here,' he said, taking the lantern, as he went back outside. As he closed the door the draught blew out the candle. Amy suppressed a scream and hurried to the door, but it was locked. Now she knew that she was in real danger.

Suddenly the moon came out from behind a cloud. Amy hurried to the uncurtained window and saw a strange sight. She was looking out over the graveyard and the man was kneeling in front of a grave. In the light of the lamp which he had rested on top of the gravestone she could see his lips moving as if he was talking to someone. Then he stood up again and seemed to see her watching. He picked up the lantern and made his way back to the door. Amy saw the big brass candle stick glinting in the moonlight. She picked it up and hurried to the door, and just as it opened she brought the candlestick down on the man's head. He groaned and fell. Amy picked up her bag which had been left near the door, stepped outside and ran.

She did not run down the road, because when the man recovered he would surely follow her in his cart. Instead she set off across the moors and soon entered a wood. He would never find her here. She walked among the trees, but the moon went back behind the clouds and she could not see her way. Unseen branches whipped across her face and she stumbled over hidden roots. But at last the trees ended and she heard a strange lapping sound. She was about to step forward again, when the moon re-emerged and she saw that her next step would have taken her down a small cliff into a large lake. She stepped back among the trees, lay down on the fallen leaves and cried herself to sleep.

When she woke again the sun was shining. The trees had sheltered her from further rain in the night. She stayed prone on her bed of leaves for a while feeling the baby moving about inside her. Then she took a piece of stale bread and an ounce or so of cheese from her bag and chewed both slowly, before scrambling down the bank and drinking from the lake.

She brushed the crumbs from her skirt and set off again, following the edge of the lake, and then the side of the wood until she reached the road. She could just make out the chapel in the distance but there was no sign of that man, so she stepped out onto the road and hurried forward, but glancing back frequently, ready to run and hide in the bracken if the man appeared. When she had covered several miles she began to relax. She wondered briefly if she might have killed him, but then decided that she did not really care.

On her journey she had slept in barns, cattle byres, sheep folds and even a chicken house. She had seen the best and worst of mankind.

Once she had almost been arrested as a vagrant but had quickly learned to lie convincingly; telling a huge, beetroot-faced policeman that she had a sister in the next town - was it Ruthin or Mold? - and that her husband was meeting her there. On another occasion a market woman accused her of stealing an apple, which had rolled off her stall. The woman came round belligerently from behind her stall and was about to call for help, when she saw Amy's circumstances and bid her go on her way after pressing another piece of fruit into her hand.

When she thought of the kindness she had received at one point on her journey tears of gratitude filled her eyes. She was approaching a small village when it began to sleet, the strong wind pushing icy needles straight into her face. On the edge of the village there was a small church, the door was open, so she took shelter inside. The vicar's wife had found her, taken her back to the vicarage, let her bathe, given her a change of clothes and a good meal, before sending her on her way with a few extra pennies in her purse, saying, 'You must go now. My husband would be angry if he found you here.'

All the time the child inside her grew and seemed to thrive, moving around within her as if it was on a journey of its own.

When she stepped off the ferry at the Pier Head Amy's spirits sank again. She had never seen or even imagined a city of this size. The offices and warehouses towered above her. The streets were packed with people scurrying dangerously between laden wagons, handsome cabs and horse-drawn trams. Amy knew that she must find a quieter spot where she could rest for a while and consider her next move. She walked toward the city centre and at last found some quiet gardens behind a large stone building. She sank gratefully onto a bench that was quickly evacuated by a well- dressed couple when they saw, and smelt, the new arrival. She tried to think what she should do next, but it was more than two days since she had eaten anything substantial and she began to feel faint. She lay down on the bench and passed out.

When she came to, a woman was leaning over her, holding some smelling salts under her nose. Amy gradually focussed on the woman's face and saw that it was florid, flabby but with the kindest gaze.

'You're all right now dear. Agnes Warboys is with you.'

The woman offered Amy a drink of something from a flask, which immediately revived her. She sat up and looked at the large woman sitting at her side. The woman's clothes were very fine, and her hair beautifully coiffured but the voice did not match.

'I can see under all them rags and dirt you'm a pretty little thing. And it's obvious what your trouble is. Best get you back to my place as soon as possible. 'Ave you cleaned up, get some good grub into you and let you rest. Then you can tell me your story.'

Mrs Warboy's 'place' was in a smart, cobbled street, not far from the city centre. It was a tall narrow house, with several rooms on each floor. Mrs Warboys lived on the ground floor, which was luxuriously furnished. The servants, and there were several, lived in the basement. Amy was installed in a large attic room, simply furnished, but warm and comfortable. One of the servants filled a bath and took away her filthy clothes. When she rose from her bath Amy found some fine bedclothes laid out on the eiderdown. A large meal was delivered on a tray. For a while she ate greedily, but soon pushed the tray aside, lay down and slept. She did not know it but she slept for almost two days. When she woke again Mrs Warboys was sitting beside the bed.

'I knew I was right. You've got fine features. Look at that lovely hair and them green eyes. And I bet you've a good figure when it aint all swelled up.'

Amy could not imagine why this woman should be so interested in how she looked, but she felt so grateful for her kindness that she simply smiled. Mrs Warboys asked her name and what had happened to her but Amy did not know where to begin.

'Well, Amy dear, best you start by telling me which fella got you in that state. That's if you knows.'

So Amy told her briefly about Huw and about her parents turning her out and what had happened since. Mrs Warboys nodded and tut-tutted as the tale was told. Towards the end Amy began to sob.

'Now you can pack that in, dearie. It's all over now. There's thousands of girls got stories like yours. But you'm one of the lucky ones 'cause Mrs Warboys found you. Now I'll tell you a bit about myself.'

Amy wiped away her tears and listened.

'See, it's hard to imagine now but I was once a pretty young thing like yourself.'

Amy looked at the plump, sagging woman with her crumpled face and did find it hard to imagine her as a 'pretty young thing'.

'I was serving in my parent's tavern, down London way, when I caught the eye of this old gent. Well dressed and well-spoken he was. To cut the story short he ups and marries me and brought me 'ere. Couple of years later he pops off. Too much of several good things, p'raps? So there I was, a young widder, living in this place, and with a very substantial inheritance. But I knew life wasn't like that for lots of young girls. I'd seen 'em in the tavern, I seen 'em in the streets around 'ere, poor little wretches, worn out by twenty, living in back alleys, treated cruel by the men who kept them, so I made a vow, I'd use my luck to make their lives better.'

Amy thought for a moment.

'So you're saying there are others like me staying in your house.'

'Oh yes, nine of them- ten with you- at present. All young and pretty like yourself – well perhaps not all so young or quite so pretty- and it just happened that one of them had moved on recently and this room was available, so when I saw you in that sad state on that bench in St. John's Gardens...'

'And you mean you let them all live here and support them out of your own pocket.'

'Well, no, it's not quite like that. You see, when they're back to 'ealth and strength, they 'elps me out. But you don't need to worry about that 'till your baby's born and you're bright and bonny again.'

Two months later Amy gave birth to a daughter. She had thought of calling her May, because that was the month of her birth, but as soon as she saw the baby's black curly hair and berry bright eyes she was reminded of Huw. Of course she could not call her that, so it had to be Nan. Her birth weight had been low, perhaps because of the struggles Amy had gone through for a while, but she was a strong, lively baby. Mrs Warboy's thought her the most beautiful baby she had ever seen and was always willing to look after her if Amy needed to go out for a while. A little box room next to Amy was cleared and became a nursery and the next few months were some of the happiest in Amy's life.

As the weeks passed Amy's figure began to return. Apparently the woman who had vacated the attic room must have been quite similar in size and shape. There was a wardrobe full of fine dresses, which Mrs Warboy's encouraged Amy to wear.

'She won't be needing 'em no more, where she's gone.'

Gradually Amy met most of the other women in the house. Most of them looked well, wore good clothes and were happy and friendly. One did not look so well, kept herself to herself and was suddenly not there anymore. When Amy asked Mrs Worboys about her she said,

'Moved on, dear. Got herself a man.'

Strangely all the women rose late each day and spend most of their time in the house, but in the evening they all dressed up and went out so the house became very quiet. When Amy asked one of them where they went each evening she replied, 'Oh, we all does our bit for dear Mrs W.'

Almost a year had passed when one day Mrs Warboys came to Amy's room and sat down heavily, panting from her climb up the stairs.

'You're looking very well my dear. A good colour in your cheeks, your hair all glossy and your figure trim again.'

'All thanks to you,' said Amy, putting Nan down on the floor where she crawled about rapidly like a four legged animal.

'Well, my dear, the time has come for you to repay me a little.'

'Gladly,' replied Amy, but as Mrs Warboys explained how that repayment would be made Amy's face lost its colour and she thought she might be sick.

'I won't be sending you out just yet. And then only with my very best clients. You're a bit special and I needs to talk more to you first. See there's tricks of the trade as in any other business.'

When Mrs Warboys left the room Amy sat stunned for a while. At last she stood up, flung off her fine dress, found that old bag and began to pack, but then she saw Nan, sitting on the thick rug, playing with a beautiful doll that Mrs Warboys had given her. Amy picked up her little daughter, hugged her so tight that she squealed and carried her across to the window. It was raining hard and the street was filled with people scurrying home from work across the greasy cobbles, and there were several who remained on the street because they had no job to hurry from and no home to go to. Amy knew what it was like to be penniless and at the mercy of the elements. She could not face that again. Not for herself and definitely not for little Nan. She put her healthy, happy daughter back down on the floor, unpacked that bag and put on her dress again.

4

Old Acquaintances

'You're looking a bit peaky, Amy dear,' said Mrs Warboys. 'Reckon you could do with some sea air. It's a grand day. Take the ferry to New Brighton. I'll look after young Nan while you're gone.'

It was true that Amy had been feeling slightly unwell of late. She had wondered briefly whether she was pregnant again, in spite of all the precautions she had taken, but then her flow came only slightly later than usual. Sometimes these days she felt a dull ache in her lower body and her work had become a painful chore.

She had been with Mrs Warboys for more than four years now. She was still the old woman's special and was only ever asked to serve the best clients. They would take her to the theatre or one of the best restaurants and afterwards she would accompany them to a hotel or a little flat they rented, but occasionally they would simply drive round in a cab. Many of the men were quite elderly and by the time the moment came they were too sleepy or drunk to make much use of her, and all had been vetted by Mrs Warboys when they paid her so were usually quite gentlemanly with her until their passions were roused. Even then Amy had learned ways of pleasing them without actually giving her all. Of course she knew that what she was doing was wrong, in the eyes of the world, but how else could she provide little Nan with such a good life.

At nearly four years old, Nan had her namesake's looks but none of her problems with speech. She chattered away to everyone she met and watched them all with her bright dark eyes. Mrs Warboys thought the world of her. It would be impossible for Amy to change things now.

It was a 'grand day' as her employer had said: a lovely August morning. Amy would be glad to get out the city with its dusty streets and the awful smells that became ever more pungent as the spell of warm weather continued.

'And put on that new dress,' continued Mrs Warboys. Wear it in. That green satin really suits you. You'll have the lads of New Brighton foaming at the mouth. Of course you can lead them on a bit –get yourself a free lunch- but no more than that. I don't want you mixing business with pleasure.'

Amy's smile in reply was forced and she thought to herself that there was very little pleasure in her business anymore.

At the Pier Head the landing stages were crowded. A large passenger ship was about to leave for America. As she boarded the ferry Amy watched the poor emigrant families shuffling along towards that ship's gangway; the men carrying pathetic bits of luggage, flimsy suitcases or brown paper parcels, and the women trying to comfort their fractious babies, while other youngsters tugged at their skirts. Amy felt that what she had to do for her clients was a small price to pay for the comfortable life she and Nan now shared.

Soon the ferry left the landing stage and made its way across the choppy Mersey, busy with steam tugs and sailing ships of all shapes and sizes. Amy leant against the rail on the top deck feeling the fresh air on her face. She had never gone this way down the Mersey before. It would only be a short trip but it lifted her spirits to be heading towards the open sea. She remembered how she had once wanted to travel, to see other parts of the world, like her stepfather, but there was little hope of that now.

Amy thought for a moment of her mother and stepfather and her little brother – he would be quite grown up by now. How horrified they would be if they knew how she made her living these days. But it was partly their fault, for turning her away when she was pregnant. Now she could not really imagine any other sort of life. She had that comfortable room at the top of Mrs Warboy's house, with a pretty little bedroom for Nan. She had fine clothes to wear, good food to eat. Until quite recently she had felt well most of the time and her health had shown in her looks. Her fine figure was enhanced by the latest fashion in corsetry and her hair tinted professionally to bring out those golden tones. Her skin did not perhaps have its old rural glow, but skilful makeup created a competent simulation. She knew that she turned men's heads wherever she went. She felt a certain pride in that and she knew she gave her clients some satisfaction. But today she would forget all about the way she earned her living and be simply a young lady out for the day in her best dress, enjoying the sun and the sea.

As the ferry approached the landing stage next to New Brighton pier Amy could see the red sandstone fort and the lighthouse. When she disembarked and moved on to the pier she lingered for a while among the crowds, watching the children playing with the penny slot machines while their mothers queued outside the fortune teller's booth and their fathers took a furtive peep at 'What the Butler Saw'. She bought a couple of postcards to show Nan when she got home, then made her way along the King's Parade where she strolled between the pretty gardens and the gently tumbling waves. The tide was going out and several families sat below her on the beach, while their children paddled or dug in the sand. Perhaps she should have brought Nan, but no, it was good for them both to spend some time apart, and Mrs Warboys would spoil her rotten.

When she reached the end of the promenade she gazed out to sea, where vessels of all types were making slow progress towards or away from the mouth of the Mersey. And beyond them she thought she could just make out the purple smudge of another coastline but perhaps it was simply a trick of the light on such a sunny day. After a while she glanced back along the promenade, thinking perhaps she might make for a tea room in the town, when she saw a young man gazing at her in a quizzical way. She was used to this of course, but at that moment the sea breeze rose a little and disturbed her hat, so she took it off and adjusted her hair. The young man came towards her. She felt annoyed. Was she never to be free of men and their appetites? She wondered whether to turn and walk quickly away but the man seemed determined to approach her and as he drew closer and lifted his hat in greeting she knew exactly who he was and her annoyance turned to anger.

'You!'

If she had been carrying an umbrella she would have struck him, hard.

'Amy!'

'Philip! Get away from me! Now!'

'Amy, please...'

'There is no-one in the world I want less to see.'

'I only want to talk to you. Please Amy, I am much changed.'

Yes, she thought, as he faced her, he was much changed, physically at least. His fair hair had been cut short so that his face stood out with a new strength, especially the mouth which now had a determined firmness and his eyes which at that moment were bright with tears. He seemed to have aged since she had last seen him; grown up perhaps. For a moment the shock of seeing the change in him filled her with curiosity and weakened her resolve. But she tried not to betray that in her voice.

'Well..?'

'I am not here to court you. I would not be such a fool. '

'I am glad of that. So what...?'

'I just want to tell you how sorry I am. And ask you to forgive me. Then I will go away out of your life for ever. And perhaps I too can begin to live properly again.'

'So why have you waited so long?'

'I did not have the courage to contact you. And when at last I wrote to you via John he said that you had gone away and would not want to be reminded of your time in Wales.'

'Well, what has given you the courage to speak to me now?'

'I hadn't planned any of this. It is purely by coincidence that I am here. But you looked so fine, standing there. Just as I remembered but perhaps even more...It is obvious that you are happy now.'

Even his voice had changed. The haughty drawl had gone and a note of sincerity, even humility had taken its place. She knew that she had to hear him out.

'What have I to forgive? Except your unwelcome attentions and your sneaking to my stepfather.'

Philip looked about him for a moment. There was a bench just behind them. He led her to it. She was surprised at her obedience as she sat down. He turned away from her and looked across the water.

'About Huw. I never meant that to happen.'

'What? What happened?'

Astonishment showed in Philips's voice, 'You don't know?'

'He went away. That is what I was told.'

'Oh, yes, he went away all right. He was arrested that night and taken to prison in Liverpool. He was accused of blowing up the tunnel and sentenced to seven years hard labour.'

'Seven years! But why did no-one ask me? I could have told them that he was innocent. He was with me.'

'Your stepfather would not allow you to be called as a witness. He said that you were far too ill. And he said that he had no intention of helping the man who had seduced his innocent daughter.'

'But you knew that Huw would not have helped those hot heads. He told us on the mountain that he did not agree with those methods. He did not have the courage, though he sometimes felt they might be justified. Why didn't you tell them?'

'Because at the time I was glad to see him taken away. I was filled with jealousy. I still hoped that with Huw out of the way...'

'Never!'

'I know that now.'

'Seven years! So he is still there? In prison?'

'No. He was released a few months ago.'

'How did that happen? Where is he now?'

'Oh, Amy. There is so much to tell you. But let me begin at the beginning.'

'Very well.'

Phillip sat down beside her, but made sure that there was a comfortable distance between them. She no longer feared that he would make advances. He seemed too far away in his own thoughts.

'I suppose the day after Huw was arrested I began to have my first feelings of guilt. I went to see Gwyn but he had gone, presumably in the cart because it and the pony were nowhere to be seen.'

'Poor Gwyn. And Nan. Whatever would they do?'

'First things first. Joseph and I returned to Liverpool. I completed my studies. He took up his practice again. The exhibition of my photographs was arranged.'

'Was it a success?'

'I suppose it was. But I no longer cared. I had completely lost interest in photography. I have not taken a single picture since that time.'

He paused, almost as if he had just become aware of this fact and was trying to assimilate it. Amy thought it was a pity he had not given up photography a little sooner. If her step-father had not seen those particular photographs things might have turned out differently.

'And it was not just photography. I seemed to have lost interest in everything. You probably don't remember but that was a particularly gloomy autumn. Liverpool seemed to be permanently covered in a pall of smoky fog. But perhaps that was just my mood.'

He paused again and shook his head.

'My guilt about Huw began to gnaw at me daily. And I thought more and more about Gwyn and Nan and how they were coping without him. At last I had to find out. So in the following January I set off for Tynygraig.'

Amy decided not to tell him that she had gone there as well and just a few weeks after his visit.

'I will never forget the little farm at the foot of the mountain,' she said.

'You would not have recognised it. That winter was a hard one. There was a thin covering of snow, even as I left Dolgellau, and the flakes continued to fall so that by the time I reached Tynygraig I could hardly distinguish the road ahead. The first thing I noticed as I rode up the drive was the silence and stillness. There were no animals at all, but it was winter so I assumed they had all been taken into shelter.'

As Philip paused Amy remembered her own arrival at the abandoned farm.

'When I knocked there was no answer. I looked around the farm but there was no sign of life, either human or animal, so I decided to go on to the quarry and see if I could find out what had happened.

'It had stopped snowing but the roads were deep in drifts and I had to leave my horse in the stable at Tynygraig and continue on foot. It was hard going but at last I reached the top of the pass and looked down on the quarry. At first I was simply astounded by its ugliness. A great gash had been made in the side of a mountain and vast piles of waste slate were strewn everywhere. All that broken blue-grey rock mirrored the sky, heavy with snow and filled with smoke and steam from the machinery. The whole scene was utterly depressing. My next shock was that even on such a day there were men crawling across that shattered landscape, going about their work, without regard to the weather or their safety.

'At last I found the Manager's Office and was about to enter, when two workmen appeared, carrying a third, who had a nasty head wound, which was leaking blood. One of the men called out, and though I did not understand the words, which were in Welsh it was obvious that he was asking for help. A man appeared from within, short, fat and immaculately dressed, with a newly cut flower in the buttonhole of his expensive suit, and told the men, in English, that the doctor had given notice and gone away. They must deal with the injury as best and as quickly as they could.

'I explained that I was a doctor and if he could find me some basic medical equipment I could deal with the injury, so he showed me into a dingy hut where the men laid their injured colleague on a filthy table. Then they were told to leave me to it and get about their work.

'The man had a deep cut just above the eye. A fraction of an inch lower and the eye would have been lost. I found some antiseptic liquid among the scanty medical supplies on a shelf, cleaned the cut and bandaged it. The man, manager or overseer, or whoever he was, watched me as I worked and kept up a constant moaning about the workmen under his charge: how they would use any petty injury as an excuse to down tools; how lazy and stupid they all were; how hard it was for him to keep up the level of production expected of him by the owners of the quarry. I became so angry that I was about to turn on this little, portly tyrant, when he said something that temporarily stunned me.

"I can see you know what you're at, in the medical line. We need a new medical officer. They never stay long up 'ere. Too dam cold and lonely. You can 'ave the job, if you like."

'I stared at the man in astonishment and began to make objections, but strangely I already knew that I would accept.

"But I have no experience. I have only just completed my studies. I am not even sure that I have passed all my examinations."

"You'll do. I've seen you at it."

'The man on the table moaned a little. He sat up and felt his head. Then he shook my hand, muttered something in Welsh and struggled out of the room.

"See what I mean," said my companion. "Right as rain"

The manager explained that accommodation was available for the Medical Officer and we agreed a salary which though not over generous, was several times more than the wages of the men who worked with the slate. My future employer introduced himself as Thomas Reynolds, manager of the quarry, and asked, "So when can you start?"

"I must return briefly to Liverpool and tell my father what I have done. I will be here again in a couple of days."

Philip paused again, looking across the water, before turning back to Amy.

'I have been there ever since.'

'So you do not see much of Joseph these days?'

'On the rare occasions that we meet we could be strangers. Whenever I go back to Liverpool I am appalled by the luxury in which I once lived, and the useless lives most of father's friends lead. I have seen such suffering at the quarry, not just the terrible accidents but the poverty of the quarrymen's lives, their poor health due to the dust in the air, the cold and the damp, the pittance they are paid and the risks they must take to satisfy the owner's needs for greater profit. I have the greatest respect for them now. I have even learned their language as best I can.'

Amy was shocked by the changes in Philip but also fascinated by the man he had become. She laid her hand gently on his and heard him sigh. She asked, 'And what had happened to Gwyn and Nan?'

'Gwyn was dead. He had never got over Huw's imprisonment. And he felt useless not being able to work at the quarry. He spent more and more time up there, just wandering about, trying to talk to old friends, asking for work, but they would not have him back. So with no Huw to help them and no work for himself they could not afford the rent for the farm and were given notice to quit. Gwyn began to drink heavily. His old workmates felt sorry for him. They bought him drinks. He usually finished each evening in a drunken stupor. One night he fell asleep on the line of the little railway that takes the slate down to the boats at the quay near Machynlleth. There was a thick mist next morning. He was cut in half by the first train of the day.'

Amy took Philip's hands in hers. They sat like that in silence for quite a while. When he spoke again it was at first merely a whisper.

'Of Nan the news is better. Apparently she went to live with an older sister in South Wales. She looks after their children. One of the quarrymen's wives had heard from her. They were friends from school days.'

'And Huw? You say he was released.'

'Yes, I began to work on that as soon as I had settled at the quarry. I wrote to men of influence. I acquired character references for Huw. Then I had a piece of luck. One day at the quarry this young man was brought to me with a splinter of slate in his leg. He had taken on Huw's old job as a rockman, but something had gone wrong with the blasting. While I dealt with his injury he began to talk about Huw and the other men who were killed in the tunnel.

"They were a mad lot, you know. Real hotheads. Especially Daffydd. But at the time I was one of them. Angry at the English and at what they had done to us. Ready to take revenge. Determined that the bloody English weren't going to steal our valleys and our water as well. I know you're English. But we think of you as one of us now. Anyway, that time, I went with them to the Vyrnwy valley. We found the camp that Huw and his father had set up and asked him to show us how to set off the explosive. He refused. He would have nothing to do with it. He told us it was a stupid idea. Dangerous too. And a waste of time. He tried to dissuade us. He convinced me. We were to go our separate ways and meet up later that night. Well, I thought about what Huw had said and I decided he was right. I didn't join the others. I came back here instead."

"So why didn't you tell someone what you have told me?"

"Because I was afraid. I knew that if I said I had been involved I would lose my job and the house that went with it. I was about to marry. I would probably lose my dear Myfanwy as well."

Philip explained how he had convinced the man to come with him to Liverpool and make a statement. And at last, after much legal wrangling, Huw was released.

'So where is he now?' asked Amy. 'Did he go back to the quarry?'

'No. Prison had changed him. He came out a very bitter man. He did not want anything to do with his old life. They would not have him back at the quarry anyway, because of his involvement with the saboteurs. And all the other quarries had blacklisted him as well. So as soon as he could he arranged to travel to America. I paid his fare. I have not heard from him since.'

Amy studied Philip again and saw what a handsome man he had become. He had always been tall but all that walking about the hills and scrambling about the quarry to help after an accident had much improved his physique so that now he filled out his simple, hard wearing clothes. His face was tanned with being out of doors and his eyes blazed with commitment to the causes he had taken on.

Amy remained silent for a while, digesting all the information Philip had given her. Suddenly he asked, 'What about you, Amy? What are you doing here?'

'I have been given a day off by my employers'

'I see. What do you do?'

Oh, Philip, she thought. You have changed. You are now a fine man, but how shocked you would be if I told you the truth.

'I am a governess. I look after a boy and girl. He is nine and she is six. My employers are quite well off and have a fine house in another part of the town.'

For almost the first time since they had met Philip looked directly into her face and smiled, 'I must say, Amy, you don't look like a dowdy governess. You are more beautiful than ever.'

Amy blushed.

'My employer is very kind. This is one of her old dresses, which she has passed on to me.' She got up from the bench. 'But you promised that you would not court me, Philip.'

Philip stood as well.

'I'm sorry. But it is so good to see you again. This is the first time I have been away from the quarry for almost a year. Surely, as an old acquaintance, I can spend some of that time with you.'

'I suppose...'

Amy was filled with conflicting feelings. She admired this new Philip. She would be happy to spend time in his company, but on her side it was all a fraud. He knew nothing about the person she had become and if he did he would want to get away from her as quickly as he could. The more time they spent together the more she must lie to him. Nevertheless she linked arms with him as they walked back towards the centre of the town. Suddenly he stopped and turned to her.

'Look, I earn far more money at the quarry than I can possibly spend up there. Let me at least buy you a lunch.'

'Very well, but after that I must return to my position. The children have gone out for the day, but they will be returning in the late afternoon.'

Amy found that her lies came so easily that she almost convinced herself.

As they strolled along the promenade and back into the town Amy noticed that sometimes other people turned to look at them and occasionally smiled. She realised what a fine couple they made. 'Oh, if only...'she thought. Then she began to worry that they might meet someone who knew her from that other life. How dreadful that would be.

They found a pleasant restaurant away from the front, more discreet and less crowded, and lingered over a splendid meal. Philip apologized again for the boorish man he had been and for the underhand way he had behaved. She told him that he was forgiven and gave him more fraudulent details of her new life. She explained that she and her stepfather had become increasingly at odds -that at least was true- and that she found her studies at college much less interesting than she had expected, so when she saw her present post advertised she decided to move up here and start a new life.

Towards the end of the meal Philip tentatively enquired, 'I know I shouldn't ask, Amy, but is there anyone...has there been any one special in your life, since Huw?'

Amy looked away to hide her tears as she thought of all the men she had made to feel special since her brief introduction to physical intimacy in that tower so long ago. She pretended that it was the memory of Huw which had caused her tears, wiped them away and said that, no, there was no-one special in her life. She waited for Philip's next inevitable words. But first he looked at his watch.

'I have to leave soon, Amy. My train leaves in one hour and if I am to make the connection at Chester... But this has been the pleasantest day I have spent for a long, long time. I wondered if you might give me permission to write to you and perhaps we can arrange to meet again.'

So she made up an address for him to write to and they walked together towards the station. He kissed her hand and walked away, and she thought what a fine man he had become and how much she wished they might have a future together. Then she returned to the pier and took the ferry back to Liverpool and her real life.

It was on the ferry that Amy first experienced a searing pain in her lower body. She doubled up and sat heavily on a bench left empty when its previous occupants stood up to watch the ferry's arrival at the Pier Head. She began to sweat but her face looked pale. An older woman sitting nearby asked her if she was feeling all right.

'Just a little sea sickness I think.'

The woman laughed, 'Sea sick on the Mersey! 'Ere, take a nip o' this.'

The woman handed Amy a hip flask and soon she felt the spirits flowing through her body and easing the pain. She was reminded of the first time she drank brandy, on that hillside when the wheel had come off the cart and she, John, Philip and Gwyn lay sheltering from the storm. Now Gwyn was dead, John had disowned her and Philip...Well, she would never see him again.

As the months went by Amy learned to deal with the pain, though she found her work more and more difficult and complaints began to be made. She developed sores around her mouth and other intimate places and that led to more complaints from the clients. At last Mrs Warboys sent her to bed and called a doctor. After examining her he explained to Amy that she had caught a disease often associated with her profession, but that with rest and care she would in time recover. However, in a private chat with Mrs Warboys he was much less optimistic. He knew very well how the woman afforded such a luxurious lifestyle.

'It's not just the usual, Mrs W. There's some complications inside. I'm afraid that unless the girl gives up the business she will not live long.'

Mrs Warboys was not a bad person and she was prepared to be patient, so for a while Amy was given tasks about the house, light cleaning and needlework, but eventually her lack of earnings, which had been high, began to tell and in addition she was occupying that room, which was needed for another, more lucrative employee.

'The truth is, my dear, you're no longer a commercial proposition. I'm going to have to ask you to leave. I'll give you a bit of cash for some cheap lodgings and perhaps you can find work with less discerning gentlemen.'

Amy thought of Nan who at four years old had never known anything but a pleasant life and a comfortable home.

'Tell you what. I'll let the kid stay on. I'm very fond of her as you know. And it won't be too long before she can help me out. There's gentlemen who like them really young and are prepared to pay a good deal extra.'

Amy was horrified. She had no intention of letting that happen. But she could not take Nan to some terrible room in the slums where she was likely to catch some dreadful disease (she remembered Joseph telling her about such things) or simply fade away from misery in a dark, damp Liverpool court.

For the moment it would be best to let her stay here, with Mrs Warboys, but as soon as Amy found some work, preferably not what she had been doing, and a decent place to live she would collect Nan, and they would be together again.

So Amy moved out. She was allowed to visit Nan once a week. After a couple of months the money that Mrs Warboys had given her was all used up and she no longer had the strength or inclination to make her living in the old way. She found employment for a while as a cleaner in some offices by the docks, but she didn't have the strength to move the heavy furniture and was given the sack. A neighbour in the court asked her to help out on a market stall, and she managed that for a few months, then her health began to fail and sometimes she simply could not get out of bed.

These days when Amy visited Nan she was only allowed into the kitchen, where at least she was given something to eat and drink. She noticed the shock in her daughter's eyes when she observed how her mother had changed: her clothes were growing more ragged week by week; the bones of her face and wrists were outlined clearly; her hair clung greasily to her pale skin. On one visit Nan wrinkled her nose and pulled away when her mother tried to embrace her. From that moment Amy made every effort to keep clean, however difficult it was in her present circumstances. But still Nan always seemed glad to see her mother and on each brief visit they managed to grow close again before they had to part. It was probably those visits and the food and drink she received in the warm kitchen that got her through that terrible winter.

When spring came Amy felt a little better and decided that she had to do something to escape her situation. She thought of writing to her parents, letting go of all her pride in desperation. Several times she began a letter but could not go on. Next she thought of trying to contact Philip, but that would mean admitting all her lies, and she was sure that when he learned the truth he would turn her away. There was Megan but she was an old woman now and it would not be fair to ask for her help. At last she thought again of Joseph, but when she enquired about Doctor Lever she was told that he had ceased to practice and no one seemed to know where he lived.

As spring turned to summer Amy found employment again, selling flowers outside Lime Street Station. The warm sun and more regular eating improved her health, her good looks returned slightly and she was able to smile so that men, in particular, were happy to buy her flowers. She had learned to live with that pain, which was now a constant dull ache, which caused frequent vomiting. But as September passed into October, then early November and the wind turned chill Amy began to dread the coming winter. Soon there would be no flowers to sell.

On the morning of the first frost that season Amy took up her position outside the grand entrance to the station. She had only a few flowers left. As the early trains disgorged their passengers, who streamed out onto the streets, Amy thought she recognised one young man, but by the time she had recovered from the shock he had disappeared into the crowd. She dropped her meagre bunch of flowers and went to find him. Suddenly she saw him again, getting onto a tram, and yes, it was definitely George.

Amy ran across the street, almost being knocked down by a cab, but just managed to board the tram, which was headed for the docks. She could not see George, who had been at the front of the queue and was therefore hidden by the passengers in between. Each time the tram stopped she carefully checked the passengers and at last she saw him get off in Derby Square and walk along James Street, but by the time she had forced her own way off the tram, he was a good way ahead and would not hear her even if she called out. At last he turned into a side street but when she reached it he had disappeared. However there was only one building which had an entrance in that street and above the imposing doorway was the name of a famous shipbuilding company. Amy stood outside the door for a while wondering what to do. She did not have the courage to go inside but at last she approached the doorman and asked, 'Could you tell me what time the people who work here finish in the evening?'

'Depends,' said the dour doorman. 'The big wigs start to leave round about four o'clock, but the small fry usually goes about six.'

Amy decided that George, for all his proud look and smart suit, was probably still 'small fry' but she decided to come back soon after four and wait.

When she returned to Lime Street she discovered that her few remaining flowers had been trampled underfoot, so she went back to the waterfront and walked along beneath the overhead railway, which had recently opened. This sheltered her from the chill drizzle, the walking kept her warm and there was always something going on in these busy streets to keep her distracted. She checked her purse and found that she had just enough money left to buy food for a couple of days.

The light was already fading on that damp November evening when Amy returned to look out for George. She was moved on once by a policeman who thought she was back on the game. The hours passed and well-dressed men began to leave, at first in ones or two's, often met by cabs which had been called for the purpose. At six o'clock there was a sudden surge of men, and a few women, who hurried towards the tram stops in James Street or the nearest station on the overhead railway. At last this exodus petered out but there was still no sign of George.

The wind had begun to blow in from the river, driving the drizzle down the gas-lit streets and Amy could not remain in the open for much longer. Twice she was propositioned. A woman alone waiting in the street was an obvious target. After she had got rid of the second man she crossed to the doorway. Luckily there was a different doorman on duty, who called her in out of the rain and asked her what her business was.

'I was waiting for someone I know. I believe he works here. Mr Owen. George Owen.'

The man's face lit up. 'Young George. Oh, we all knows 'im. A grand lad. Always got a smile and a cheery word. He'll go far, that'n will.'

Amy was pleased to discover that George actually worked here and that he was well thought of, but now she was puzzled. She asked, 'Why hasn't he left the office yet?'

'Oh, he has. He left at lunchtime. He's gone back home to be at his grandmother's funeral – tomorrer. Did you know the old lady?'

Amy nodded.

'Then you'll know how fond of her he was. Apparently she brought him up. He'd been there a week or so to be with her. Only just got back to Liverpool when the telegram came. I delivered it to him.'

Amy thanked the man for his kindness and hurried back to her room. She had already decided that she too must make her way to Llanwddyn by the earliest train in the morning and that she must take Nan with her.

It was the scullery maid who answered the kitchen door at Mrs Warboy's house next day. Amy asked to see Nan and was told that she was still in bed. She rarely rose before nine o'clock. When the maid went down to the coal cellar Amy hurried up the stairs, panting with the effort and grasping the bannister as that pain returned. She managed to reach her daughter's room without being seen. In such a house, where the inhabitants worked late into the night, no-one rose early. Luckily Nan was awake and playing with her dolls. Amy put a finger to her lips and Nan understood at once. Her mother whispered to her that they were to go on a special journey and that she must wear her oldest clothes in case the roads were muddy. The little girl obeyed, enjoying the idea of a secret. She was just about to add a warm coat when a voice in the next room called sleepily, 'Nan. Nan... Come in here will you.'

Amy grabbed her daughter's hand and they ran together down the stairs, through the kitchen and out into the street. As she ran Amy felt that pain nagging at her, like a stitch in a lower place. At first Nan shivered in the cold air but soon warmed up as they hurried to the station.

5

An Ending and a Beginning

Amy and her daughter continued their journey beside the lake but with Nan's little legs quickly tiring and that pain inside Amy throbbing ever more insistently they had not managed more than a mile or so. They came to a bridge over a stream which, filled by the recent rain, tumbled noisily down towards the lake. As the stream entered the lake a little estuary had formed where the wind-stirred water lapped gently onto a gravel beach.

Something about the view across the lake suggested to Amy that they were near the place where the old village had once stood. She thought this might be that stream, now she remembered that Huw had called it the Afon Cedig, which once wound across the meadows and through old Llanwddyn, before joining the Vyrnwy lower down the valley. Of course there was no sign of the old village now, just the silvery rippling surface of the lake.

'Mama, I'm tired, and hungry. Can we rest for a while?'

Amy knew that she herself could go no further at present. They must rest and hope that someone would come by and offer them a lift. Unless that happened they would never make the train from Bala that day, but perhaps it didn't matter anyway. She helped her daughter down to the little beach where they sat on a fallen tree trunk. From her little bag Amy took the last of the bread she had bought in Bala that morning. It was rather stale by now. She took a small cup from that same bag and filled it with water from the stream. Surely if the water was clean enough for all those people in Liverpool it would do them no harm. The water was clear and cold and helped them to swallow the bread.

The Stolen Valley

Amy sat her daughter on her lap and began to tell her about the old village, and about meeting her father, but when she glanced down she saw that Nan had fallen asleep.

Just above the little beach a rocky outcrop had formed a miniature cliff, topped with stiff grass and heather. Gasping with pain Amy carried her daughter up onto the rise, took off her shawl, wrapped it round Nan and laid her gently down on the heather. Without her shawl she shivered in the November air as she walked back to the water's edge. At that moment the clouds in the west parted and the last rays of the setting sun laid a pathway of light across the lake. She was about to take the first step along that pathway when that pain swept through her again, stronger than ever and she doubled up. When at last the pain eased she returned to the place where Nan was sleeping, lay down beside her and also fell asleep.

She dreamt that she was walking beside the Afon Cedig as it meandered through the meadows towards the village. In the distance she saw the August sun glinting on the tumbled stones of a recently demolished house. Huw was sitting on one of those stones waiting for her. She sat beside him in the warm sun and felt completely at peace. The terrible pain had gone. She felt no hunger or weariness, no guilt or responsibility. She had reclaimed the valley that had been stolen from her so long ago. She would never leave it again.

The last of the guests had left and Ella was helping Mrs Evans to clear the tables and wash up in the back kitchen. George was saying goodbye to the last lingerers and John was slumped in an armchair near the fire, gradually slipping into sleep. Little John lay on the hearth rug flicking through some books that George had lent him. They were mainly about inventions and the boy smiled as he saw how old-fashioned many of these already appeared.

Mrs Evans looked up from the suds and whispered to Ella.

'Course, the lad will be well set up now. He's got good prospects I do hear. And I believe that benefactor of his is very generous.'

'Joseph? Oh yes.'

'I'm sure young George won't want to come back here to live. There's nothing for him here now his grandmother's gone.'

Ella took another plate from the garrulous widow and dried it carefully, her mind filled with confused feelings. Mrs Evans went on.

'I was surprised that pretty daughter of yours didn't come today. She and George were once very close.'

'She's living abroad now. She could not have returned in time.'

Ella flushed with her lie- which she and John had agreed beforehand - and turned away to add the dry plate to a pile on the table. It was thoughts of her daughter that were causing the turmoil in her head. 'Oh Amy! My Amy! Where are you now?'

She had begun to feel guilty almost as soon as John had sent his stepdaughter away. But she dared not oppose him. And surely he was right to say that Amy was now a grown woman and could manage her own affairs. But lately she had thought more and more about her daughter and today, in this place, she had seen her face everywhere. She had seen it at the church reflected in the polished brass of the lectern and behind the flickering candles on the altar. It was among the flowers laid beside the grave and it had appeared on the surface of the lake, distorted by the ripples, as they crossed back over the dam. Now here it was again on the next wet plate that Mrs Evans handed to her, and each time she saw that face she thought she heard a voice crying, 'Mother, I need your help!'

At last the washing up was finished. Mrs Evans left by the back door and Ella returned to the living room. Her husband was asleep. George was sitting by the window, deep in thought.

'Would you like to walk with me, George? I have hardly had a chance to talk to you all day.'

George turned slowly and took a moment to grasp her words.

'Why, yes. I would be glad to get out of the house for a while.'

'What about you?' Ella asked her son.

'No thank you, Mama. I've walked enough today. And I'm enjoying these books George has given me.'

So Ella and George dressed warmly and set off. The wind had dropped and a pale sun lingered in the afternoon sky, casting a lemon glow across the lake. There would probably be a frost that night. They set a brisk pace at first, until their limbs were warm, then, as they crossed the dam, Ella grasped George's arm and brought him to a halt. They gazed together at the huge expanse of water.

'Do you ever think about your old life in the village under there?' asked Ella.

'Not much. My life is so different now. It is almost as if that village...the old valley, never existed. This...' He pointed across the lake. '...is the reality now.'

As they set off again Ella said, 'I know that Amy was happy here, at that time, until...'

George laughed, 'And I was a lovesick schoolboy. I don't know how she put up with me.'

'Amy always spoke kindly of you.'

George smiled and walked on briskly. He told Ella about his engineering training in Liverpool and his present employment with that shipbuilding company.

'All the shipping companies are trying to outdo one another. Cunard have the edge at the moment. But I hope to be involved when we plan our next fleet.'

Soon the straining tower came in view. George described the night he had followed Amy when she went to meet Huw.

'That was the night I began to grow up. When I saw Amy rush into Huw's arms I realised that in her eyes I was just a child. I was angry with her for a while, but soon after that my life became so full that I almost forgot her.'

They reached the tower. Ella shuddered with the memory of her daughter collapsing into her stepfather's arms.

'So where is Amy now?' asked George.

Ella did not answer at once and when she did it was with tears in her eyes.

'I don't know?'

'But surely...'

'I have not seen or heard from my daughter for almost five years. She did something that caused us to disown her. I don't suppose I will ever see her again.'

George was curious.

'She must have done something very bad indeed for you and John to disown her.'

'We thought so at the time.'

George waited for her to go on, but instead she set off walking again at a faster pace. The sun was setting and the November twilight was gathering among the trees. He caught up and they walked on without speaking. At last George said, 'I don't think we should walk much further. It will be dark soon.'

They had reached the place where the Afon Cedig flowed down into the lake. Ella suggested that they walk down to the little beach before turning back. George agreed.

They stood together on the gravel beach gazing across the darkening lake. George explained that the old village was out there under the water. Ella sighed. 'Now you would never know.'

Suddenly they heard the voice of a child nearby.

'Wake up Mama! Wake up!'

They climbed up the little bluff and saw a child sitting next to a woman, lying on the ground, apparently asleep. The child, a little girl, was shaking the woman's arm. When George and Ella arrived the little girl pleaded, 'Please wake my Mama. She's getting so cold.'

Ella leant over the woman and touched her face. She recognised her daughter at once and knew that she would never wake again. She wanted to scream but forced herself to speak quietly to

George, leaning over her daughter in case he should recognise her. She needed him to be strong.

'Go back to the village and fetch help. Quickly!'

He ran off at once. Ella unbuttoned her coat and laid it over Amy's body and spoke to the little girl, 'I think we should let your mama sleep a little longer.' Then to distract the child she asked, 'What's your name?'

The little girl seemed to find comfort in Ella's voice. She wriggled closer and said, 'Nan. My name is Nan.'

'That's a splendid name. Well Nan, I have a big surprise for you.'

The little girl came close to Ella who gathered her in her arms.

'You see, Nan. I am your grandmother.'

The little girl snuggled into Ella's lap. After a pause she asked, 'Are you really my grandmother?'

'Oh yes,' Ella replied and knew at once that she would have to be much more than that, just as dear Megan, whom they had buried today, had been to her grandson, George, for all those years.

THE END

Printed in Great Britain
by Amazon